THE AMERICAN COLLECTION 3: GRACE

Dixie Lynn Dwyer

MENAGE EVERLASTING

Siren Publishing, Inc.
www.SirenPublishing.com

A SIREN PUBLISHING BOOK
IMPRINT: Ménage Everlasting

THE AMERICAN SOLDIER COLLECTION 3: AMAZING GRACE
Copyright © 2013 by Dixie Lynn Dwyer

ISBN: 978-1-62740-552-2

First E-Printing: October 2013

Cover design by Les Byerley
All art and logo copyright © 2013 by Siren Publishing, Inc.

Printed in the U.S.A.

PUBLISHER
Siren Publishing, Inc.
www.SirenPublishing.com

DEDICATION

Dear Readers,

I hope that you will enjoy another addition to my new American Soldier Collection. *Amazing Grace* is dear to my heart. We all have experienced the sadness and pain of losing someone we love. Sometimes, a loss so great changes a person's personality, lifestyle, and ability to open up their heart again.

That is not an easy task.

But with love and empathy, anything is possible.

Enjoy the story.

~Dixie~

THE AMERICAN SOLDIER COLLECTION 3: AMAZING GRACE

DIXIE LYNN DWYER

Prologue

"Help me, Grace! Help me please!" Clara called out to her sister who just stood there watching. Grace couldn't move or speak. Instead she stood frozen as the tears rolled down her cheeks. The faceless monster stole Clara's last breath and cast his shadow over her body. Grace stood still and stiff. Her body, just a shell around her as she fought with all her might to break through and save her sister, before the monster got her. But it was as if imaginary binds kept her in place and forced her to witness the tragedy. Grace watched the scene unfold. She couldn't close her eyes and block out the images. She couldn't cover her ears and diminish the sounds of pain and death. All Grace could do was scream and yell and attempt to break the shell of iron surrounding her.

Suddenly in one quick and angry bang of her fists against the blockade, it shattered, sending her body freefalling toward the darkness and what could only be described as hell.

Grace Thompson jolted awake, stunned at the fact that it was only a dream and hadn't been real. She looked around her, embarrassed at her actions, but relieved that the male passenger next to her lay undisturbed, snoring away. She felt her body shaking. After all this time, after hundreds of nightmares and waking up in a cold sweat, why was she being hit with this now? It had been months.

She lifted her hands and stared at the perfect manicured fingernails as her fingers trembled. Calming her breathing, Grace couldn't help but wonder if she made the right decision in taking this trip.

The stale, recycled air filled her senses. She hated airplanes, she hated to fly, and she wished she never left Europe.

Grace knew that she needed to refocus, take her mind off the bad memories, and focus on something positive. Work always made her feel better and always took her mind off of those unwanted memories. She reached down toward the brown leather Pineider laptop carrying case that her boss bought her as a gift. Even making the money she did, she would never think of purchasing the three-thousand-dollar briefcase, no matter who the designer was. She opened up her laptop computer and finished reading her e-mail messages.

She was not the least bit surprised that her brother Peter had sent her another message. The wedding was tomorrow and he wanted to be sure Grace had not changed her mind about attending. Peter knew how difficult coming back home would be for her. She sighed, amazed that nearly two whole years of her life had passed. Two years spent away from the family, the pain.

Her family knew why she left, why she had not returned and seemed to empathize with her, especially Grace's cousin and closest friend, Jamie. Grace smiled to herself. *My best friend is getting married.*

Grace thought about seeing Jamie and the rest of her family. They had kept in touch through e-mails and letters, but that wasn't the same as seeing them in person. Everyone would be there to celebrate. She instantly thought of her mom, Peter, and her two older brothers, John and Frank. Then of course there was her stepfather Eric. Mom was blessed to have Eric around.

God, how I missed them all.

Looking out the window, she reminisced about her flight away from home two years ago and the long way to Europe. Initially the thoughts had consumed her mind. It was tough, having to leave home at twenty-two years old, after all that happened to her and her poor sister. The memories of their wonderful times together should have overpowered the tragic way her sister Clara died. However, Grace still felt that leaving home was the best decision she had ever made. That tight, insecure feeling crept up into her chest. She hadn't felt that sensation in months, but considering that she was headed home and about to face her family, she knew why that insecure feeling resurfaced.

She was going to face her mom. As grown-up and mature as Grace was now, there was still that young, college-aged girl who looked for her mom's approval and encouragement.

Her mother Sarah had been angry with her back then. She had told her repeatedly that running away wasn't the answer. That no one was making her take her sister Clara's place. But they were. Everything Grace did was compared to her older sister Clara.

The way Grace dressed, the way she spoke, and the way she did her hair was always compared to her dead sister. It was as if they were twins instead of fourteen months apart. *Goddamn it, I can remember it like it was yesterday.*

Sighing, Grace reached down under the seat in front of her and pulled out her camera bag. Photography had been her means of escape. Losing herself in the scenes before her and the people and places she shot was her therapy. She took hold of the picture she kept in her camera case, the one from three years ago.

Her sister was gorgeous and her smile at the time, brilliant. She remembered that day at the fair and would cherish the memories. Those were the days when she still believed that the world was a safe place filled with opportunities and good people. Until then she rarely worried about the dangers of the darkness, the evildoers that lurked in the shadows waiting to strike. Until her sister was taken and murdered.

Glancing back at the photograph just as she had done over a million times in the past few years, Grace tried to understand and accept the fact that they looked so much alike and that Clara was really gone. If Clara were alive, she was certain that they would be just as close as they were back then. They would take lots of pictures together. They would probably even go on dates together and hang out in the same crowds. She ran her fingertip gently across the picture. In her mind she wished so very hard that Clara was still alive. *Why? Why did this have to happen to Clara?*

Whenever she thought about returning home, the anxiety would start. There were so many negatives and so many fears in returning there. She recalled the other reasons for her leaving her home and her family. It was obvious to Grace that her family was comparing her to Clara. Every time they looked at her, their eyes saddened and she couldn't help but feel uncomfortable. Although they denied it, Grace could see the sadness, the pain they felt. It was this insecurity and fear that kept her afar. It was also what made her so damn nervous about returning home. She could only hope that the comparison days were over.

Grace couldn't deal with the memories of that dreadful day she found her sister's body. No one could understand how that destroyed her. There was something huge taken from her heart, her soul. Something until this day she could feel continuously. Her family tried to console her but they couldn't comprehend her feelings, her mind, the visions and nightmares she continued to have, not so frequently, but they were there. Being the one to find her sister's body hardened her heart. She no longer felt that instant connection to anyone. It was a guard, a shield of some sort that kept her from truly opening up her heart and loving again. Which explained the two ex-boyfriends and noncommittal relationships she had. She was scarred for life, so what did it matter anyway?

Grace shook the thoughts from her head then smoothed out her red dress as she looked out the window toward the clear sky. "Almost home," she whispered, feeling the shaky breath. She was a completely different person now. A mature, sophisticated, worldly woman who probably no longer fit in the small country setting in the suburbs of

Houston, Texas. Not that she was stuck up or snobby. No way.

She grabbed the fashion magazine and stared at the gorgeous sunset and equally attractive model posing on the cover. Pride filled her soul.

She remembered the scene, the warmth of the air, the feel of the sand from the Italian beaches as she focused and refocused the lens of the camera to capture the moment perfectly.

In the two years she spent away from home she continued her exciting career as a professional fashion model photographer. Recalling her conversation with the owner of the magazine, she was certain she would win an award for the brilliant photograph.

"Grace…you are amazing, absolutely amazing. There isn't a soul out there who could have pulled this photo shoot off, never mind capture such a breathtaking scene. Get ready to add another award to your shelf and a nice fat bonus when the issue is released."

Grace smiled to herself.

"How long are you planning on staying in the States? I want you in Milan in three weeks. We have a tight schedule approaching."

At the moment three weeks seemed like a lifetime away from Europe and work. There was no reason for her to stay that long. No reason at all.

Besides, she would be lucky if she lasted a few days. As excited as she felt about seeing Jamie, she was dreading the awkward moments among her family when she arrived. Two weeks from today would be the three-year anniversary of the death of her sister Clara. A homecoming visit that could be misconstrued as bad timing.

Grace sensed the plane's descent and felt her belly drop at the sensation, which added to her anxiety as the wheels touched down and the rush of warm Texas air surrounded her. She was home. She hoped she was ready for this and prayed for her sister's guidance.

As she walked through the terminal, she saw her brother Peter standing there waiting. The anxiety of seeing her brothers and her family was now overtaken with deep emotion and need. She missed them all so terribly.

Peter was handsome and looked older, more sophisticated, than she recalled. He was only thirty-eight, still as good looking as ever, her oldest brother and her best e-mail friend.

* * * *

Peter stood in the terminal waiting for his baby sister to arrive. He wondered how she would look. His baby sister was now twenty-five years old, a professional photographer, and world traveler. He was going to be so supportive to her. He wanted her to stay here in Texas back home where she was supposed to be. The worry about her being abroad, all alone, and on dangerous photo shoots bothered him. He was always protective of Grace, but now that she was back home, he intended on her visit turning into a complete return. He and his brothers and family missed her way too much.

He was pacing now and his heart was racing as he heard the announcement come across the intercom confirming once again that Grace's flight had arrived on time. He was excited, he was nervous, and he didn't know what to expect. Many times he had thought of traveling to London or Paris to visit her and make her come back with him but he knew that would cause a wedge between them. He lost one sister and he didn't want to lose another. His brothers and mother had discussed the idea plenty of times but their mother just kept saying "She'll come back when she's ready."

Peter wondered how his mother dealt with Grace leaving. She was so understanding and accepting, yet he knew how she would cry herself to sleep at night worrying about Grace's safety. They all worried about Grace.

Peter knew everyone would be shocked and surprised at the sight of Grace at the wedding. They all missed her so much and wanted her to be home. Their cousin Jamie was sad that her best friend and cousin couldn't attend her wedding. She wanted her to be her maid of honor but Grace declined. She told her she just wasn't ready to come home yet. That was when Peter bombarded Grace with e-mails and phone calls insisting that she attend the wedding. Then he would work on keeping her here, in the States.

He smiled, filled with the feelings of success.

Peter looked across the terminal, glanced at his watch, then looked again and saw the most attractive brunette. He watched as others in the airport turned their heads to take a look. Peter thought she was a model, standing at about five foot six, with long legs and a very thin figure. She had on a short one-piece, fitted, floral red dress and matching red heels. It took him a moment. Then his mouth dropped when he realized the beautiful model was his baby sister Grace.

Moments later he was pulling her into his arms, hugging her, and nearly causing her to lose her breath.

Grace was crying, and Pete was just glad that she was home again and wondered how the hell he was going to keep her here with the family forever.

"Oh my God, Grace, you look gorgeous. You shouldn't be the photographer. You should be the model," Peter told her as he stepped back to look at her some more.

She didn't look like Clara so much anymore. She was much thinner and her facial features were different. He would never say what he thought out loud. He knew that would upset Grace to still be compared to Clara after all these years. But he wasn't comparing his two sisters. He was admiring his one and only baby sister.

Peter hugged her again and she responded by hugging him tightly in return. "I missed you, Peter."

"And I missed you, baby sister." He stepped back and looked at her again. He gave his head a shake. "Damn, woman, I am definitely going to have to keep my eye on you." He grabbed her suitcase and then took her free hand and led her out of the airport. She looked at him as if not understanding his comment. Could she be oblivious to her beauty? His baby sister was stunning.

They traveled to the hotel where Grace insisted she would stay for a while until other plans were made. He cringed when his sister said she wouldn't be staying in the States too long.

Peter of course got her the master suite at the best four-star hotel in the area. He could afford it and he only wanted the best for his sister. He wanted to spoil her and to love her. After all they had some time to make up.

They talked in the hotel room for a while and Peter informed her that no one knew she was coming to the wedding. Not even his wife Lindsey.

"She's going to kill me when she finds out I've been hiding this from her." Peter laughed.

"Hopefully she'll forgive you quickly. How's Mom doing?"

"Mom's been keeping busy with Eric's social circle and feeling pretty good. That guy's always trying to make friends. Life as a politician I guess," Peter said with a smile and they laughed.

Eric was a nice, quiet man who owned a local hardware store in the area. He was just beginning to get his feet wet in the local political ring when Grace left for Europe.

Everyone knew of the family's tragedy and Eric was a big supporter of the local law enforcement and their need for programs to better train them in homicide investigation. They lived in a small town and things were handled differently.

"Everyone is going to be so happy to see you tonight. Jamie's going to go crazy, Mom's going to be shocked, never mind John and Frank. I'm going to have a lot of people angry at me."

"I hope they really are happy to see me. I know I've missed everyone so much. So how is her fiancé, Tod? Is he still a really nice guy? "

"He's a great guy and a great detective. He has an awesome reputation. He's a lot like dad, Donald."

Peter proceeded to tell Grace a little bit about Tod. He was enjoying how easy it was to speak with her. It was as if she'd never left and he loved every second they shared one another's company.

"Donald is going to be so thrilled to see you there tonight as well. You know every time I've seen him at the office or courthouse he asks about you. This is going to be great. Now let's go over the plan. "

* * * *

They sat down to prepare their surprise, and with each detail Grace couldn't help the nervous feeling she had.

Her brother had every detail covered thoroughly, and she watched him closely, admiring his strong features and uncanny resemblance to their father.

There was no doubt in Grace's mind that her brother Peter was amazing at his job as a prosecuting attorney who worked in the district attorney's office. He was very smart and very well known in the area.

Grace's whole family was involved in some public service job or another.

Her oldest brother Frank had been promoted to detective last year. Her brother John became a SWAT team member a year before Clara was killed. Now he was a SWAT team trainer of some kind.

Her mother's husband Eric was a local business owner and politician, and Sarah fell right into the position of politician's wife. She was a charity worker and the main reason why Eric was so successful.

Grace, however, chose a different path. She had enough of police officers, detectives, politics, the media, and everyone knowing her business. She didn't want to walk down the street and be known as the girl who found her sister's body.

She left the state and the country to be alone and unique. She was her own person and it was her own motivation, determination, and hard work that got her to where she was today.

As a professional and established photographer, people waited and held off major photo shoots until she was available.

It was all positive attention. Being in the spotlight with such a strong, immediate reputation for being one of the best was what kept her away from home and away from the negative spotlight that surrounded her. Always being known as the sister who was alive, the one who found the body, the sister of the victim of a serial killer. God, she hated that one, she hated all the quirky little headlines that ran every day for a year, and each one more shocking and emotionally heart wrenching than the next.

Grace knew she had to leave. Everywhere she went reminded her of Clara. She missed her sister so much. She just couldn't bear to remain in the town where they grew up together and enjoyed life. It was too sad.

She had no choice or she, too, would die.

That was the way she felt then and she knew she had made the right decision in leaving.

Her soul, her spirit was evaporating. She was depressed, weak, and losing confidence in herself daily.

If she was to survive, be her own person, and succeed in life, she had no other choice but to leave her family and friends before it was too late.

Peter left the hotel room an hour later and Grace decided to indulge in a long, hot Jacuzzi bath. The hotel provided a wide range of bath oils and after-bath fragrances to enhance the experience.

Grace noticed the large ivory pillar candles scattered about the room. They were those cool battery-operated ones, so she turned the switches on each one.

Once the room was glowing with soft candlelight, the aroma of jasmine filled the air, and the last bit of hot water rose to the precise level in the tub, Grace turned off the faucets.

She finished putting the last couple of bobby pins in her hair to help keep it above her head then removed the thick, warm, complimentary hotel robe.

As she entered the water, she could feel her muscles relaxing then her eyes close as she leaned back, lost in the solitude of pleasure. But in the back of her mind, that uneasy, worrisome feeling ate at her gut.

Chapter 1

Cheryl Perez couldn't stand the pain any longer. She knew this was it and that she was going to die. She didn't want to die but he continued to touch her, cut her with some kind of long, sharp object. She couldn't see what it was or his next move, which was driving her crazy. Just kill me already. Just stop the pain. *She was shaking profusely as he continued to talk to her, repeating himself, saying sick, mean things to her. She wanted him to stop. She prayed for him to stop.*

"Stop talking to me! Stop talking to me!" she screamed as she shook her head.

The tape laid flat against her eyes and they stung with every move she made. The sick bastard did it on purpose, he knew the pain it would cause and it gave him such deep satisfaction to do it.

He laughed at her and continued to terrorize her with his slow, deep, chill-inflicting voice.

* * * *

"You're not as lovely as you appear to be in your pictures. You don't even come close to her, but you've been close to her, you know her. You've spoken to her and for this I needed you," he told Cheryl as he grabbed hold of her throat, laughing as his latest victim gasped for air.

"One breath, two breaths, dead." He released her then took the picture and laid it on top of the lifeless body.

* * * *

Detective Jim Warner stood in the main office with Detective Masterson and FBI Agent Sully "Sandman" Sandstone. He was a good friend of Jim's and he was doing him a favor by looking over these files. They had worked on a few cases over the years, including his cousin Gia's abduction two years ago. He was good at his job and now it seemed as if they were being hit with a doozy of a case. Jim figured that the situation was getting worse and perhaps they did need some assistance from the government agents. Sandman was the best at what he did. He worked a lot of special cases and he usually worked alone or with his two brothers, Duke and Big Jay. At six feet four, Sandman made his presence known the moment he stepped into a room. He had a fierce look about him and an intense personality. His time as a Marine taught him well.

Jim stared at the piece of paper, a sick poem left at the latest crime scene. His stomach churned.

Heaven is crying tonight,
Filled with sadness and fright.
She cries for help, she yells, she pleads,
She is punished for both our deeds.
I take her now, do what I will
To hell with her, my latest kill.

"This sick bastard had the nerve to leave this note for the detectives. They don't have any idea who this guy could be or what his motivation is. All they know is that there have been five murders in the last three months and the press is all over them," Detective Jim Warner stated.

"Well that's just the beginning of their problems. Looks like these detectives, who really aren't trained for this type of thing, were a little too quick to wrap up some of their earlier crime scenes. There's a lot of mismatched information, lack of concrete evidence, things just don't add up. But the evidence points to the same killer, the same MO," Sandman told Jim and Detective Masterson.

"We're making these connections. The media knows we're involved. I think we should keep looking at the Thompson case. There's something there. I just can't put my finger on it. The evidence that was found in the perpetrator's home was laid out in plain view. This is not the work of the same killer. I think the killer was feeling the pressure of possibly being caught and planted the evidence," Sandman said.

"Until you have the test results from the lab as concrete evidence, it's only your gut that you're going on, Sandman. We need more than that even though your gut has never been wrong. Question those involved in the Thompson case then head to New York and talk to the detectives about their latest victim," Detective Masterson said then left the room.

"Well get your suitcase ready, partner. It looks like we're headed to New York and then back here to Houston," Jim stated.

"Shit, Jim...I haven't unpacked from the last trip."

Jim shook his head. Sandman had just finished wrapping up a case in Pennsylvania two days ago.

"I need you on this one."

"I wouldn't let you down, Jim. I'll meet you at the airport."

* * * *

Grace looked at herself in the mirror one last time. She wore a stunning, long red Vera Wang dress. There was a high slit up one side, which revealed her long tan leg. The pedicure she'd received in the downstairs salon was showing through her high-heeled, strappy red sandals. The red fitted dress lay snugly against her perfect figure, causing just the slightest bit of cleavage. Her hair was all pulled up in a fancy style one of the models had shown her to create so simply. A few tiny curls scattered here and there along the bottom of her neck. She looked spectacular as she headed downstairs to the limo Peter had waiting for her.

She arrived at the wedding venue and was escorted by Peter to a side door. She wished she could have watched the wedding in the church, but she didn't want to take the spotlight away from Jamie. As she walked down a side hallway, she saw through the widows on the terrace family members and friends arriving from the church. Everyone was laughing and enjoying the celebration. Grace told Peter that she would wait until after the couple arrived, so that she wouldn't take away any special moments for them.

The bright golden sun shined down over the gazebo as a warm May breeze gently traveled through the crowd of wedding guests. Jamie and Tod stood kissing one another for the first time as husband and wife.

The large crowd of family and friends stood clapping and smiling with joy at the sight. It was a day of celebration, rejoicing, and it was so uplifting.

The band began to play the couple's wedding song as Tod led his lovely bride to the dance floor. They danced with one another as if they were in another place, lost in each other's eyes, caught up in the moment. Tod kissed Jamie again and the guys in the crowd hooted and hollered and the women smiled in envy.

Grace peeked through the door with tears in her eyes as she saw the happiness on Jamie's face and the glow that surrounded her.

* * * *

"The ceremony was beautiful, Jamie. You look gorgeous today," Sarah stated then kissed Jamie softly on the cheek.

Sarah couldn't help but wonder if her daughter Grace would ever come home or get married some day. She wondered if they would all be a family once again. It saddened her still, to not have Grace here, being part of this celebration. As she looked around at the family and friends, she spotted Donald. She felt that little flutter of excitement she always got whenever she saw him. He looked especially handsome today. He was a good man, a great friend. At the thought, her heart sank and her belly quivered with regret.

Looking up, she caught Donald watching her. He winked and she smiled. If only her own marriage to Eric was better. Instead, he focused on his political ties, his investment deals and the value of the land around their community, instead of on her.

Sighing, she tried to push those thoughts from her mind as well as her feelings toward Donald. Nothing could ever come of that.

There were nearly three hundred people attending the wedding. All family and friends who had not seen one another for such a happy occasion in years. It was a magnificent day outside, perfect for an outdoor wedding. Everyone was enjoying the party, dancing and talking. The band was playing wonderful music—country, classic, and old rock and roll—and the best man finished giving his toast.

Sarah sighed. *Oh how I wish you were here, Grace. I miss you so much.*

* * * *

Grace was inside waiting for Peter to come get her. He had told the band announcer to introduce a special guest and the time was coming for her to appear. It was well past the couple's first dance together as husband and wife and Grace knew that her surprise appearance wouldn't take away any spotlight on the bride. Perhaps most people wouldn't be so happy to see her, because she may remind them of a time of sadness and loss.

The band stopped playing and the crowd became silent as the announcer began to speak.

"Ladies and gentlemen, may I have your attention please. Tod and Jamie, can you please come up here by the stage. Your cousin Peter has a very special surprise for you."

The announcer had everyone's attention and they all watched Jamie and Tod walk toward the front of the dance floor. The crowd gathered around waiting for the surprise.

"I'd like to draw everyone's attention toward the main patio entrance as your surprise emerges." The announcer directed his hand toward the curtain.

As the doors opened, Peter and Grace stood arm in arm and Jamie began to cry. The crowd roared in excitement, some gasping with joy as Peter and Grace walked toward everyone.

Instantly Jamie was in Grace's arms, hugging her and crying hysterically.

"You made it. I can't believe you're here. Oh God, Grace, I've missed you so much. "

Grace's brothers, John and Frank, made their way through the crowd escorting their mother Sarah.

"Grace, it's really you, baby?"

Grace turned to see her mother, tears in her eyes, and her arms opened wide.

Grace thought her mom was the most amazing sight. She was five foot four, with light-auburn-colored hair. She was striking, and instantly Grace hugged her, overwhelmed with emotion.

"I'm home, Mama. I'm home."

Grace's brothers joined in the hugging and celebrating.

* * * *

Grace made her way toward the table where her mom and brothers were seated.

Donald Friedman came over to Grace next.

"You look wonderful, Grace. You've grown into a stunning woman. I'm so glad you decided to come back home. We've missed you."

Grace smiled.

Donald looked at John who was pulling his sister toward him to hug her again. Grace squeezed her brother back. It was such a beautiful sight to witness.

Donald knew Grace's family so well now. They had missed her something terrible and wanted her to be home with them.

Donald had become part of the family while investigating Clara's death. The family welcomed him and continued to keep him part of their lives. He grew to love each of them like family as well.

He looked toward Sarah and the huge smile on her face as well as the tears of joy in her eyes. It made his heart soar. She was a beautiful woman, but had been so sad over the years since Clara's death and Grace's move to Europe. He wished he could do more for Sarah, but that was Eric's job. As Donald looked toward Eric, to see why he wasn't here with Sarah, he saw the man talking to one of the real estate agents that was a friend of the family. Donald couldn't help the angry feeling that consumed him.

Eric should be beside his wife and welcoming his stepdaughter back home.

"Back home where you belong. Safe and with your family," John added, hugging his sister again and bringing Donald's thoughts back to Grace. She sure did look gorgeous and he couldn't wait to get to know her again.

* * * *

"Grace, you'll be here when I return from my honeymoon, right?" Jamie asked, her arm wrapped around her cousin's.

"You bet I'll be here. Don't worry, I know we have a lot of catching up to do. Plus I want to get to know your husband Tod better."

They walked together along the beautifully landscaped gardens outside the reception area.

"This is a perfect day for a wedding, Jamie. I'm so glad I didn't miss it."

"I'm so glad you didn't miss it either. I guess I owe Peter big-time. Everyone does."

"He was quite persistent that I make the trip. I'm happy that I did. I would have regretted missing this special day."

"We have a lot to catch up on, so while I'm gone you should make some plans for us, some quality alone time. I'm sure you are going to get booked up real fast. Everyone's going to want a piece of you." Jamie added with a wink.

"I can't wait to hear about what everyone's been up to. Peter only told me bits and pieces here and there. I suppose he didn't want to ruin things for me." Grace smiled, glancing back toward the dance floor and all her family.

Her brother practically pulled off a miracle, and she was so happy he did.

"I have to tell you, Grace, you look so different. Absolutely stunning and sophisticated. Is this what Europe does to young American girls? "

Jamie seemed impressed and a bit envious. Jamie had chosen to stay local and close by the family. Grace couldn't seem to get far enough away from the family.

"I suppose I have been exposed to a bit more than the average American girl. After all I'm around gorgeous models all day long. I've picked up a few pointers."

"Well I'd love for you to show me some of those pointers you picked up. I could use them," Jamie added and the girls laughed.

"I think you're gorgeous and your new husband is very lucky he was able to snatch you up."

Jamie smiled then glanced back toward the party. Tod and Jamie locked eyes and the two newlyweds smiled simultaneously.

Grace watched and giggled.

"See what I mean. He's keeping an eye on you."

Jamie giggled then smiled and linked her arm over Grace's again.

"It must have been so exciting seeing all those beautiful places. Paris, Rome, Venice. How many places have you traveled to? Do you remember all of them?"

"I wouldn't have if I didn't take along my camera. I'll show you the scrapbook I kept on my travels. Now how about we go out on that dance floor and show them how to really do the twist?" Grace took Jamie's hand, pulling her along with her.

The celebrating continued and Grace was introduced to many of her brothers' single friends. When everyone found out she was single, they all turned into matchmakers and started introducing her to every bachelor at the wedding. It was quite embarrassing. She also had the feeling that her family expected her to stay for good. That just wasn't an option for her.

Her aunt Grace, who she was named after, even introduced her to one of the waiters working the party.

Grace couldn't help but laugh to herself. It was as if she never left or at least had not been gone for as long as she had.

"Honey, come sit down with me a moment. I want to look at you."

Grace smiled at her great-aunt Betsy.

She took a seat next to the older gray-haired lady who always reminded her of blackberry preserves. That was what Aunt Betsy was known for.

"You wouldn't happen to still be making your famous blackberry preserves, would you?" Grace asked.

Her aunt knew how much Grace loved them, and she smiled wide that Grace asked.

"Yes, I do and you better be sure you stop by my place tomorrow to have some with me. Your mom and Aunt Grace will be there, too," Aunt Betsy added then she smiled at Grace.

The day brought more plans and invitations than Grace felt she could possibly be part of or attend but she would try her hardest starting first thing in the morning. She needed to find a place to stay until she could figure out what she would be doing.

As the wedding festivities drew to an end, Grace's family would continue the celebration back at her mom's house. It was a night to remember and cherish forever.

* * * *

The following morning Grace's phone at the hotel wouldn't stop ringing. By late morning everyone knew she was back home and they were organizing party after party. She had a few moments of silence and opted to watch TV while she touched up her manicure.

She stopped immediately when she heard the news. She could hardly breathe. Did she imagine it? There was no way it could be true. No one said a word to her at the wedding, neither did Peter.

She turned up the volume and listened to the reporter.

"The Houston Police Department has no comment at this time. When we feel we have information we can release to the public there will be a press conference, and Special Investigator Sandstone will announce his progress. Thank you." The news representative from the Houston Police Department interrupted her thoughts. Grace just stared at the television screen.

Grace was still uncertain she heard the words "serial killer" correctly. Then she changed the channel and they made the announcement.

Apparently these killings had some similarities and they felt that they could possibly be connected to other crimes from the past.

Grace didn't like the sensation she had in her gut and was startled when the phone rang as she jumped up to answer it.

"Hi, honey, it's Peter. Have you turned on the television?" Grace could hear the concern in her brother's voice.

"Yes, I just heard the reports. It's terrible. What's going on? I hope they can find the one who's doing this." Grace was rambling.

And she sensed Peter's hesitation before answering her.

"It's a little worse than the media knows. John just called me, Grace, and they think the killer could be the same person who killed Clara."

Grace was speechless. She was shocked by her brother's words and she began to shake. That panicky feeling filled her instantly. Her ears buzzed and she couldn't even hear what her brother was saying now. It couldn't be true.

"Honey, are you okay? Talk to me. Say something." He raised his voice to her.

"Talk to me, Grace. It's okay. John's on his way. He should be there any second. He's bringing his friends."

* * * *

Peter knew his sister was scared and he feared her reaction to the news.

He couldn't help to think that she would just pack up and go. She left because of Clara's murder and now she finally returned and this happened.

He had just heard from Donald and they were sending two special agents over to his mother's house to ask some questions. Of course they wanted Grace there as well.

"It can't be. They caught the guy who killed Clara. He's in prison. They found the evidence in his house."

Someone knocking on the hotel room door interrupted her thoughts.

"Hold on, Peter, someone's at the door. It must be John."

"Stay on the line and use the peephole," he directed her.

"Oh God, this is really happening."

* * * *

Grace put down the phone and answered the door. It was her brother John along with two other guys she didn't recognize.

"Are you all right?" John asked, pulling his sister into an embrace. Over her shoulder he could see the phone off the hook.

Grace didn't answer.

"Is someone on the phone?"

Grace nodded. "It's Peter."

John picked it up, speaking to his brother before hanging it back up.

"Johnny, this can't be happening. It just can't be happening. Peter's wrong. He has to be." John took Grace's hands into his own and stared down into her eyes. She knew that serious look. He was in police mode.

He was concerned.

"It is happening, Grace. The word is out. We have friends who are working the case. They got the wrong guy three years ago. The investigators feel that the real killer planted the evidence in Stew Parker's house. The detectives know that there have been nine other homicides in the past three years with similar patterns and evidence left behind. These killings have been occurring around the surrounding states as well as Florida. The federal government is involved now." John led Grace to the couch.

"Nine murders? Jesus, John. How come the detectives can't catch this guy?"

"It's a work in progress. As they get close, they lose their lead or something else happens elsewhere and throws them off. Two men have been arrested, and then the charges were dropped after lack of evidence. Whoever is responsible is resourceful."

She was silent a few minutes

Grace looked up at the other two men who accompanied her brother.

"I'm sorry for being so rude. My name is Grace." She reached out her hand to greet the men.

"This is Charlie and Mark. They work with me. We were on our way to the shooting range when Peter called. Frank went directly to Mom's house. That's why we're here. We're going to help you get your things together and check you out of here. You'll be staying with Mom and Eric where we can keep an eye on our family," John stated then headed toward the bedroom.

"What are you talking about, John? What do you mean keep an eye on me? What's really going on?" she insisted, not moving to help her brother but instead holding her ground.

Grace knew there was more to this and she wouldn't leave the hotel room until John gave an explanation.

Charlie and Mark laughed.

"If you think one of us won't throw you over our shoulder and carry you out of here kicking and screaming, you're kidding yourself. Even my two buddies here would be up for the job," John said then continued toward the bedroom to pack Grace's clothes.

Grace was shocked. Her brother had changed over the years. He was more dominant and demanding. He hadn't even given her an explanation for this decision to leave under their protection. It aggravated her and obviously challenged her individuality and independent nature.

"You wouldn't dare do that." Grace looked toward Charlie and Mark.

"Yes, ma'am, we would. I think I'd actually enjoy it," Charlie stated with a smile and a wink.

Grace felt herself blush.

Her brother's friends were very good-looking men, and she knew the rigorous training the SWAT team officers had to go through on a daily basis. They were in excellent physical condition.

"Johnny, come on and tell me what's going on," Grace called out, calling him Johnny as she used to do when they were little.

Her brother stopped a moment to look at his little sister. "I think it would be better if Peter explains it to you, sis. You saw how they're reacting on television already. If the media gets wind of this new information and finds out you're back in town, it could lead to some unwanted attention and dig up some unhappy memories for the family." John didn't finish his thought. She got the message, and they continued to pack Grace's things.

Chapter 2

Grace was worried as a thousand possibilities scattered through her mind.

She looked out the truck window as John drove the car in the direction of their mother's house. The long dirt driveway and her mom's house was nearly a half mile deep into the woods. They had plenty of privacy and owned about twenty acres of land.

The house was now painted a light cream color with burgundy shutters and a large dark wood wraparound porch. Very different from the old white-and-black house she grew up in. She stared toward the woods and instead of seeing the beauty of the forest, she saw the darkness of what possibly lurked within.

There were a few other cars and trucks parked outside the front and Grace knew one of them was an unmarked police car.

Near the side detached garage sat a BMW and Frank and Peter were standing next to one another. She could see Frank's revolver sitting in its brown leather gun holster on his waist.

They started walking toward the car as Grace got out. "Okay, we're all here, now tell me what's going on."

Her brothers knew she was still as independent and stubborn as always. Before they could respond, their attention was drawn toward the front porch.

The screen door opened and a tall, large figure emerged.

Grace's heart jumped and the temperature in her body rose to an instant uncomfortable temperature as she felt her face become flushed. She prayed she didn't look as red as she felt. The man before her was a god, handsome like some young heartthrob movie star yet rugged like the cowboys one might see in some old Western. He was huge, too. At least six and a half feet tall and filled with muscles. Who in the world was that guy?

He was dressed nicely in his white button-down dress shirt and black jeans. She noticed he wore dark cowboy boots and laughed to herself at her ability to instantly and correctly label the man before her. She quickly gathered her body's emotions and attraction to the man and hoped that no one noticed it.

The stranger stepped out onto the porch along with Grace's mother who appeared dwarfish next to the big guy.

Then another man emerged from the house as well. She wasn't sure who he was, but he was definitely law enforcement. The gun and badge gave it away. Grace didn't like the fact that so many law enforcement officers stood around her mother's home. It brought back unhappy memories and made her feel fearful again. She swallowed hard as she tried to calm her breathing.

The good-looking guy spoke first.

"Miss Thompson, I'm Investigator Sandstone and this is Detective Jim Warner."

He spoke with such a deep, strong voice Grace's belly filled with butterflies. She had a hard time trying to seem unaffected by his looks. The man was very attractive.

She shook both men's hands and was more affected by the investigator's touch. She shyly looked away and straightened back her shoulders. *Boy, he sure has big hands.*

* * * *

Sandman was surprised to see such an attractive young woman in front of the house. The pictures that decorated the fireplace mantel inside the mother's home were old pictures of a young girl from four years ago.

This woman before him was a knockout, with a perfect body and long, wavy brown hair. Her eyes were magnificent, nearly a hazel-green color that drew him right to her. He thought she was stunning as he introduced himself and Jim.

"I'd say it's nice to meet you but I have a feeling I'm not going to like this," Grace said then walked up the stairs. She brushed right by him and kissed her mom on the cheek.

"Mom, are you okay? What's going on? No one seems to be willing to tell me anything. It's making me very nervous." Sandman continued watching her.

"Miss Thompson, it seems that some information and evidence has come to our attention during one of our investigations," Detective Jim Warner began to explain. "First of all, it seems that the man who was arrested and charged with your sister's murder was not the one responsible. The evidence found in his home was planted there by the same person we feel is responsible for other killings we've been investigating."

"Okay, so the investigators who were involved in Clara's case made some mistakes and you're here to ask us a few questions?" Grace let out a premature breath of relief. The poor woman hadn't a clue what this could mean for her.

"No, ma'am. Unfortunately it's more complicated than that. You see some evidence was found at the last crime scene. This one took place in Pennsylvania. A picture was found at the scene and that picture was of you. The woman who was found murdered was a model for the company you worked for in Europe."

The detective spoke so quickly, Sandman wondered if she got the information correct.

Grace appeared confused.

"My picture? Who was the model?"

"Cheryl Perez. Were you two friendly enough for her to have your photograph at her place?" Detective Jim Warner asked.

She covered her face with her hands and attempted to hold back the tears that were forming in her eyes.

She turned her back toward them.

Instantly, her brother Frank was at her side, putting his arms around his sister and directing questions at the detective.

"What the hell, man, you just tell my sister a friend of hers was murdered and that Grace's picture was there and before she can recover from the news, you're asking her other questions. Give her a minute, will you!"

Frank raised his voice then softly spoke to Grace.

Sandman's friend, Detective Jim Warner, was caught off guard at her brother's anger. He probably should have waited a moment before asking other questions but it seemed that patience and empathy were not his strong points when Jim was after a serial killer. They were all on edge and uncertain where this investigation was headed. Sandman figured he'd better try to calm the situation down a bit.

"I'm sorry, Miss Thompson. It's just that we are trying to find a killer and—"

"Miss Thompson, we're sorry for your loss and for bringing up bad memories about your sister," Investigator Sandman Sandstone interrupted. "We were hoping you might be able to answer a few questions for us. You see there have been some other murders that we feel are connected. What we need to do is go over some of the other cases. Maybe there's a clue or some evidence that wasn't picked up the first time around. They'll be short and direct questions, ma'am, and we would really appreciate your cooperation. Your brothers are more than welcome to be present during the questioning." He stood in front of Frank, towering over her brother and appearing dominant. Grace seemed to notice that as well.

Grace was looking up now, trying to catch her breath and gather her thoughts as she held his gaze. Her eyes were stunning, but the fact that they were welled up with tears bothered him.

"It's all right, Frank. Investigator Sandstone, Cheryl would have my picture at her place. We had become friends during the photo shoots over the past year and had exchanged pictures for the scrapbooks we kept. I can't believe she's dead. Murdered." She corrected herself then took a tissue her brother Frank offered. She used it to blot the tears from her eyes.

Sandman took the seat next to her.

"What can you tell me about her? Do you know whom she hung out with, any friends, boyfriends, or perhaps anyone who may have been bothering her?"

"She never mentioned anyone and she didn't have a boyfriend that I know of, Investigator Sandstone."

"Please call me Sandman. It's what everyone calls me," he replied as he held her gaze.

"Are you sure about that?" He challenged her knowledge of Cheryl's personal life.

"Like I said, Sandman, I can only tell you what she told me. She never mentioned a boyfriend."

* * * *

Grace had to admit that even the man's nickname was mysterious and sexy. Sandman, as he liked to be called, had incredibly dark blue eyes that gave him an appearance of seriousness and intrigue. He was experienced in all aspects of the word. She just knew it.

She tried to remain focused, but this guy was really hot. Every ounce of her body knew it and when he spoke to her, he held her gaze. He was giving her his complete attention. What woman wouldn't love that from a man like Sandman? Grace tried to answer the questions and felt she wasn't quite giving them the answers they were looking for. Peter and John took their mother into the house leaving the detective and the investigator alone with her on the front porch. Frank stood close by and remained supportive. She loved him for it.

"I get the feeling there's something you're not telling me. There's obviously more to this questioning. Two agents, well, a detective and investigator, would not come out here just to ask me some simple questions that Cheryl's family could have answered or I could have answered over the phone. What's the real deal?" Grace stood up.

"Grace, this is a very serious case we're working on and right now it's our job to investigate every possible lead. We appreciate your..."

Just then there was a large bang and the shot nearly took off Grace's head, missing her and hitting the glass window behind her instead.

Investigator Sandstone tackled Grace to the ground, pulling her behind some wooden table he kicked over instantly, barricading her from further shots.

He and his partner had their guns drawn along with Frank, John, and the others, who now joined them on the porch.

Grace was shaking and her elbow was bleeding from hitting the wooden porch floor so hard.

Sandman hit her like a rock and still covered her as he looked out toward the woods and the direction the bullet came from.

Charlie, Mark, and Jim cautiously walked toward the woods in search of the shooter or some evidence.

"Are you okay? Are you hurt?" Sandman asked Grace in a very serious and loud tone. He was practically straddling her and she dared not move.

She was in shock and wanted to get up and when she attempted to, Sandman placed a large hand on her shoulder and kept her down.

"Wait. Not yet. Where's the blood coming from?" he asked all concerned. The dark blue eyes she admired earlier now looked so dark and filled with concern she felt guilty for being the culprit. That was such an odd feeling to have.

"My elbow." She tried again to push herself up.

He insisted she wait as he held her down by her shoulder, and then gently caressed his fingers against her cheek so she would focus on him. The touch aroused her. She wasn't accustomed to that or to being this close to a man, to anyone.

"Get off of me. It's obvious the shooter's gone. Why would he stay around when the others are headed out after him or her?" Grace snapped at him, trying to remove the Sandman's hand. She wanted to get up and run inside the house.

Sandman stood up then took her hand to pull her up. The blood was dripping down her arm through her white blouse and onto her dress pants.

She felt like a truck had hit her as she rose from the floor, trying not to moan from the pain. The man was gigantic.

* * * *

Sandman knew he had hurt her but at least she wasn't dead. Who the hell was taking pot shots at this woman and why?

"I'm sorry if I hurt you. I was trying to protect you," he told her in an angry voice.

She wasn't annoyed with him. Why would she be? No, she was scared and rightfully so. This investigation just got a bit more intense. A fucking shooter? What the hell?

"I know that, Sandman. Thanks for saving my life. Now maybe you can tell me everything that's going on instead of the minimal?" she asked. But before he could answer, her brother Peter was by her side asking if she was all right.

Grace said "yes" then began to unbutton her blouse, and used it to wrap around her elbow.

Sandman felt his gut clench and his cock harden instantly. The woman had a great body and the fact that she used her designer blouse to cover her bleeding wound showed a lot. He was even more impressed with the lacy white tank top that was once hidden underneath the white blouse. She was built well up top, which only added to his attraction to her. Grace was one sexy, sophisticated woman. The fact that someone seemed ready to kill her pissed him off big-time.

Grace looked up at him and they locked gazes. He glanced at Jim who appeared frazzled. Then the mother came outside crying.

"I'm okay, Mama. Everything is going to be all right." Grace consoled her mom, immediately hiding the fear he saw in Grace's eyes when the shot missed her head. She had been shaking but now seemed as cool as a cucumber. She was hiding her emotions from her mother and he wondered why.

"Let's get you inside. It's safer," Jim said and opened the door for Grace and her mother.

* * * *

Grace went upstairs to her old bedroom. She needed a little time alone to gather her thoughts about what was going on.

Downstairs was filled with police officers and forensics teams trying to dislodge the bullet from the siding on the house and look for clues in and around the perimeter of the property.

Grace looked around the room. Her mom kept a lot of her things and she made a scrapbook of all the pictures Grace sent her from overseas.

Why would someone want to kill me?

And Cheryl was such a nice girl. Who would kill her and leave my picture by her body?

The agents said another woman was murdered. She was the wife of some hotshot attorney in New York. The agents had little to go by but felt that Grace's safety may be in jeopardy. *No shit.* That was obvious to her considering only minutes ago her head was nearly shot off her shoulders.

The agents and other detectives, including her brothers, were bombarding her with questions. She couldn't think straight and her head was spinning.

She didn't have any answers for them.

Grace heard a horn honk and a car pull quickly up the dirt driveway. She peeked out the window and saw Eric emerge. Instantly Peter and Frank were at the driver's side door.

To the right of the driveway she saw Investigator Sandstone and he saw her.

The stern look told her to get away from the window and she did.

Grace recalled her mother saying that Eric was on his way home from the store. He had waited for his main worker Richie to get back from some delivery before heading home. Sarah said Eric was so upset that this was happening. He felt that Grace coming back home was such a blessing and was definitely what his wife Sarah needed and was missing in her life. He looked scared and frantic in the driveway but maybe Eric would be able to calm Sarah down.

Grace was trying to figure out how Clara's murder could be connected to the others.

How could the investigators have put away the wrong guy? Could Clara's killer still be out there? *Could he have been the one who just tried to kill me?* She asked herself a thousand questions.

She looked at her elbow, which was now covered with a bandage. She couldn't help but think how close she came to dying. Investigator Sandstone, Sandman, had saved her life and the thought of his body against hers sent a tingling feeling through her. He was so sexy and rugged. Talk about bad timing and bad circumstances. She never had much luck with relationships. Not that she really had any at all. Her inexperience and inability to commit always got in the way.

Deep down Grace felt that her fear of losing someone so close to her again kept her from falling in love and taking chances. She wanted little to do with dating and feared commitment. She had survived living away from home, away from her family, but she was lonely, frequently experiencing nightmares, flashbacks and fainting episodes. She knew they stemmed from her sister's death, from leaving home, moving on alone. That was when she met Pierre Joudeou and her life had begun. He was exactly what she needed and he was her cure.

She had met him at one of the after-parties the magazine editors and producers would throw at the completion of a photo shoot. Everyone would dress up in his or her most expensive designer evening wear and party until the following day. Grace and Pierre hit it off immediately, getting caught up in the music, the atmosphere, and the celebrities around them. He was handsome, wealthy, and charming. When he spoke to her in French, she felt weak, hypnotized, drunk.

Grace was a virgin. She was inexperienced and he knew it. She was nervous about doing it but she knew the time was right, she was ready and when he kissed her, touched her, she didn't want to stop, she wanted more. Did she regret it? Absolutely not.

Now here she was in the middle of a huge mess. She would have been safer in Europe. Paris was enchanting and so romantic. Her troubled past and the traumatic memories were just that, memories. But here, in this current situation, she was facing the pain and the past head-on.

She was lucky she didn't get shot downstairs. She might just have to fly back to Paris and hunt down that hunk of a French man and become very experienced. Grace laughed at the thought. A fear of death made her suddenly wish she had taken more chances in life. But the truth was, she feared a lot of things. She feared the pounding in her chest as the reality that a bullet nearly grazed her skull as she stood on her front porch. She also feared the pounding in her chest as Sandman tackled her to the ground and covered her with his exceptionally fit body.

People were dying, emotions she had buried were resurfacing and this entire situation had the ingredients for disaster.

It was just like her to take an incredibly dangerous, depressing, and life-threatening situation and make light of it. That was how she dealt with leaving home and her sister's murder behind her.

Grace looked around the bedroom and began thinking about Clara and even Cheryl. She didn't want to allow herself to cry or give in to the fear. That would be a sign of weakness, a characteristic of the old Grace she had left behind years ago.

She had done so much crying in the past. There was just too much sadness in her life, in her soul, but now layers of professional success and the fact that she constantly kept busy either working or exercising had covered all that sadness.

She didn't want it all to resurface, emerge again, and destroy everything she had worked so hard for the past two and a half years. She wouldn't allow it. No way.

Just then there was a knock at the door. Her brothers John and Frank entered.

"How are you doing, hun?" Frank asked then sat down on the bed next to her.

John joined them as well.

She turned her head sideways, not knowing quite what to say. Her brothers were worried and Grace knew her mom must still be hysterical downstairs.

Peter called the doctor, and he was sending over something to help her to relax. Grace couldn't even imagine what all this was doing to her mother. She was sure her mom was thinking about Clara.

"This doesn't make sense, guys. I was fine in Europe and then I come home and all this stuff happens in less than twenty-four hours."

"Don't even think about leaving. You're not going anywhere without that Special Investigator Sandstone or one of us at your side," Frank replied.

Grace gave her brother a sideways look.

"Don't look at Frank like that. This is bad, Grace, really bad. For God's sake, you just nearly had your head shot off. Being with one of us, the agents, or Charlie and Mark are your only choices." John raised his voice then tried giving her his toughest stare.

Grace stood up and saluted him.

"Yes, sir, SWAT Team Commander, sir." She giggled.

Frank and John both laughed a little.

"You haven't changed that much in three years, sis," John added with a small smile. He was concerned. That was obvious as he squeezed her hand.

"Yeah, she's still an immature prankster," Frank added, giving his sister a light punch in the arm as he looked at her. She giggled again. He stared at her as if her were memorizing her laugh.

It was unbelievable how just sitting in her room with her brothers brought back such great childhood memories.

* * * *

Frank was glad she was home but he couldn't help but be concerned about her welfare and safety. Frank had heard a little bit about the murder of Cheryl Perez as well as the few recent others. The individual responsible was ruthless and violent. Grace and his family had good reason to worry.

"That Sandstone guy seems okay. It was pretty cool the way he turned himself into your own personal body armor. You'd be very safe with him." Frank winked at his sister.

"I think she's better off with her family. Between our friends and us, she should be safe and protected at all times," John added.

"Where is she going to stay tonight?" Frank asked his brother.

"Excuse me but may I be part of this conversation please? This is my life you're talking about here and I am not going to stop making a living. Those investigators don't even know if someone's after me or if I'm involved in any way."

"This investigator thinks it's a good bet that if someone just tried to shoot your pretty little head off, then to them you're better off dead." Investigator Sandstone pushed the bedroom door opened.

John and Frank just looked at Grace who seemed annoyed.

"Haven't you ever heard of knocking?" Grace asked as she gave him a dirty look.

"You save someone's life and how quickly they forget," Sandstone replied sarcastically, and both Frank and John laughed.

"I'm sorry. I appreciate you saving my life but I'm trying to have a private conversation with my brothers. They think I've just entered their own personal protective custody program."

The guys laughed.

"Hey that has a nice ring to it," John stated and Frank agreed.

They were trying to make light of the situation but both of them were very concerned. Frank looked at the investigator. He had friends in the Marines, and he'd looked up some info on this guy Sandstone. He was legit and then some. So was Detective Jim Warner as far as Frank could find out. Sandstone also had files connected to his name that were coded and top secret.

"Well we discussed it downstairs. They have you in their program for the next couple of days while I'm in New York. I'm going to see what I can find out there. Then I'll be coming back this way. The agency is setting up our main base in the Houston Police Department. A few of my guys will be helping the detectives deal with the media coverage and go over all the evidence there is so far. When I get back, I might have a few more questions for you. Keeping you and your family safe and alive is important to me. Hopefully you won't need my protection, Miss Thompson."

"No offense, Investigator, but I hope I won't either," Grace replied and Frank felt his gut clench. *Why is this happening to my family? Why?*

Chapter 3

"So what's up with this new case, Sandman? We haven't seen you in days," his brother Big Jay asked.

"It's complicated. I may need you and Duke. Can you let Duke notify his commander so he can take off if needed?" Sandman said.

"Shit, it's that bad? You haven't needed both of us in a while. What's the deal?"

"You been watching the news, Big Jay? You heard about the serial killer and the eleven murdered women?"

"Oh shit, that's the case you're working on? That's some pretty brutal shit, bro. What the hell kind of monster cuts up gorgeous women, tortures them, and then kills them?"

"Exactly what I'm trying to find out. Jim Warner had called me. There was this latest case."

"A model right?" Big Jay asked, and Sandman knew that his brother had been paying attention to the news.

"Exactly. The killer left a picture of a woman there. His next victim possibly. Anyway, it turns out that this woman has been out of the country for nearly three years. Gorgeous photographer who left Texas and headed to Europe at twenty-two years old. She had found her missing dead sister."

"Shit, I heard about that. Are you in charge of protecting the woman?"

"If things get worse before they get better, I just may need you and Duke to help me out."

"Hey, are you into this chick or something?"

"What?" Sandman asked, surprised that his brother would ask

something like that. They weren't even face-to-face. They were conversing over the phone, with a bad connection before Sandman boarded another plane home.

"You heard me. You sounded differently when you described her. You sound like you care."

"Oh, fuck you if you don't think I care about potential victims or victims' families. It's my fucking job."

"You do care. But you're also a hard-ass, a quiet, keep-to-yourself ex-Marine. Don't give me any of your bullshit. What's the deal?"

"No deal. She's in danger right now and I'll know how deeply once I return to Houston. Just be prepared."

"I'm always prepared. Later, bro."

"Thanks, Big Jay. See you in twelve hours."

* * * *

Grace insisted that she leave her mom's house. She didn't want to put her through any more upset or danger. Her brothers agreed but decided that Grace should stay with one of them.

They wanted to be sure she was with someone most of the time, so John decided that Grace should stay with him and his roommates in a house they rented down by the local marina.

She wasn't too happy about living with the four bachelors but the marina was beautiful and drew in a lot of tourists with its little boutiques and specialty shops.

Grace had been there for two days and she already loved the little place on the corner that made funnel cakes and fried zeppoles as well as the coffee hut next door to it.

Charlie had gone with her for a jog this morning and they sat together on a bench down by the water.

"It's going to be hot today. It's only 6:30 a.m. and that thermometer over there is reading eighty-eight degrees," Grace pointed out and Charlie checked it for himself.

"Damn I'm glad I'm working inside the office today. John and I have some new rookies we have to break in," Charlie told Grace.

"Well with it being so hot today you may want to break them in outdoors if you two can handle the heat," she teased him and he smiled.

"You're too much, Grace. I like your thinking though. I guess we'll see how cocky they act first."

"I'm sure you guys were just as cocky when you were accepted into the SWAT team unit. I have a couple of pictures of John posing in the mirror in his bedroom. Of course he had no idea I was snapping pictures." Grace laughed at the memory.

"Oh man. I'd love to see those. He'd go crazy if he knew that. I love it. Were you like one of those real annoying little sisters who kept nagging their older brothers and wanting to hang out with them and their friends?"

"Kind of. I was mostly the prankster. Clara was the one who wanted to follow Frank and Peter around. She thought their friends were cute." Grace looked toward the water again, thinking about her sister. The memory was vivid.

The five of them had so much fun together. She wondered if her sister would be the same way today if she were alive.

"I'm sorry, Grace. Does it still hurt a lot to talk about her?"

"I'm sure it's always going to hurt a little but I'm glad I decided to come home in spite of the current situation. I've missed my brothers and my mom so much. I've been away nearly two years and my brothers act as if it's been only two weeks." She smiled at Charlie.

He was a real nice guy and very good looking. She had met his girlfriend last night when she accidentally walked in on them making out in the kitchen.

"Are you ready to go back? Maybe we should bring coffee with us." Grace smiled at Charlie. He knew how much she liked the coffee hut. The guys liked it, too.

"Yeah let's bring back coffee. Your brother John is going to need it. He was out until 3:00 a.m. with Maggie."

Grace smiled.

"I don't think we're supposed to know about her." Grace giggled.

"I think you're right. He has been hiding their relationship. I guess he figures she works in the department and it could cause some problems."

"Well you would think that if we know about her, then I'm sure half the department knows about them. Why hide it?"

They ordered five coffees to go.

"Maybe he's afraid you'll sneak up on them with a camera snapping pictures," Charlie added jokingly.

"Hey, I'm sorry about walking in on you and your girlfriend. I'm sure it has been kind of an inconvenience having a woman living in your bachelor pad. I've invaded your privacy."

They headed back to the house carrying the cardboard holders filled with steaming coffee cups.

"Are you kidding? That dinner you cooked last night alone is worth you staying with us as long as you need to." Charlie rubbed his belly. "I made a pig out of myself," he added as they laughed.

They turned the corner and headed up the street to the house. It was an older home with a nice large backyard the guys often had barbecues in and a nice wraparound front porch to sit on and look out toward the water. They were laughing together as she and Charlie headed up the steps.

Leaning against the front door was a large yellow envelope addressed to Grace.

"Who delivers this early in the morning?" Grace asked and Charlie followed her inside. They brought the envelope and the coffee into the kitchen.

John and Mark were in there as well as Jerry, their other roommate.

They said good morning and handed out the coffees as Grace set the envelope down on the kitchen counter.

"Late night there, brother?" Grace teased John as he yawned and added sugar to his coffee cup. The other guys began to laugh.

John gave his sister a light punch in the arm and she giggled then drank down a bottle of water. She didn't even feel sweaty anymore because the guys had the air-conditioning on sixty-six degrees. It was like walking into a refrigerator.

She took a seat between John and Charlie then began to open the envelope.

She reached inside and found two other envelopes.

The first one showed pictures of a young woman with long brown hair standing in front of the coffee hut down by the marina. Grace recognized it immediately.

"I don't know who this is," Grace said as she handed the picture to her brother and the others looked at it.

"Where did you get the envelope?" John asked, still tired from his late night as he rubbed the sand out of his eyes and took another rejuvenating sip of hot caffeine

Grace then opened the other envelope.

She let in a large gasp of air and took a step back. When she saw the contents of the envelope, she dropped everything.

The guys looked. The picture that fell on the floor was that of the once-stunning brunette, now beaten and murdered.

The killer had enclosed a lock of her hair, which was covered in blood as well.

Grace had touched it.

She never even looked at the note that came along with it.

Time stood still in Grace's mind. She was speechless and unaware of the chaos that went on around her in the kitchen.

It felt more like minutes that the police were at the house and detectives arrived.

Grace couldn't speak. She couldn't breathe. She wasn't even sure this was happening as her brother and Charlie kneeled down on the floor near her chair and tried to comfort her.

John was so angry. He never even thought to open the envelope first. This was serious and his sister was in grave danger.

"It's all right, Grace, everything is going to be okay." John squeezed her shoulders and became angrier and angrier as he looked at the way she stared at her fingers. She held the locks of a dead woman's hair in her hands.

"She's dead, John. Oh my God, that poor, beautiful, young woman is dead and she was right down the street. He knows I'm here. Whoever this is found me."

The detectives arrived, packaged the evidence preparing to deliver it all to the crime lab. Grace went upstairs to the bathroom to try and remove the sensation of touching the hair from her hands. It was disgusting.

She closed the door, and the instant she was alone, she began crying.

She was scrubbing her hands so hard. She thought it was still on her hands as she kept scrubbing and scrubbing, shaking her head in disbelief.

She closed her eyes and saw the pictures first of the pretty brunette, then of her beaten, and murdered.

In her mind she saw images of Clara's body in the woods and the dirty fingers with pink nail polish on them, one horrible vision after the next.

The killer was still out there and now he was taunting her. Grace wondered why he wanted to cause her so much pain. She cried for the woman in the picture. She cried for her sister. How would she get through this? No one would be safe around her. She needed to go away. She thought to herself as she dried her hands then covered her face with them. She wiped the tears away, wanting to stay strong, but her whole body practically shook in defeat.

Suddenly the bathroom door opened and she jumped. She was edgy and so scared as she reached back behind her, bracing the cold, white, porcelain sink.

Sandman appeared in the doorway and she instantly turned, trying to hide her face, her tears, and the fear she had as she held her hands in place, trying not to fall to her knees.

* * * *

Sandman closed the door. He knew Grace was trying to stay strong but she was pale and shaking as he made his way swiftly toward her, turning her around, and pulling her into his arms. She held back the tears, not wanting to need anyone or show her fears and emotions

He hugged her, holding her tightly, rubbing her head and her hair.

He could feel her shaking, trying not to cry. She was trying so hard to be strong.

The events of the last week were weighing on her. First receiving the news that one of her friends had been killed, then being shot at, and now holding evidence of a murdered young woman in her hands. She was amazingly strong and if this killer got more intense and was determined to kill Grace, then she would need all that strength, then some.

"I'm so sorry. I'm so sorry this happened," he whispered, truly wishing that it hadn't.

He'd heard the news and raced his car to the house ignoring every traffic light and stop sign along the way. He had to get to her. He should have listened to his gut, his instinct when it told him to place Grace in protective custody. Her brothers were adamant about being involved and he didn't want to cause any unnecessary friction between the departments. But he was a specialist, only called in for cases like this one.

Grace had been on his mind constantly in New York. He was worried about her safety. The killer was after her and she needed protection. She was not going to stay with her brother and his friends anymore. He was taking her with him. Where he could protect her.

Sandman was a highly trained professional killer and whoever was responsible for these murders meant business. It should be obvious to everyone now.

He was a classic psychopath. He had no fear, no concern about being caught. He just walked up the steps of the house, right to the front door, and left that disgusting envelope for Grace.

A house where four trained officers lived and believed they were protecting this delicate woman in his arms.

He was angry and disgusted at the thought of what just happened.

He knew he had to protect her and he told himself it had nothing to do with the physical attraction. She needed his professional training.

Grace looked up at him, her beautiful hazel eyes full of fear and sadness. She was scared and so upset. Now she pulled away, embarrassed.

He reached up and touched her face.

She turned away and lowered her eyes. The attraction wasn't there for her like it was for him. What did he know? He never had a serious relationship in his life. Just like his two brothers, Duke and Big Jay, they waited for that special someone to love and share together. As others around them found it, they remained alone. This situation shouldn't be misconstrued by him to mean anything other than his professional responsibility. *Snap out of it, Sandman. You're a man made of stone.*

Sandman's hand fell back to his side. "It's going to be all right, Grace. I'm not going to let anything happen to you."

Chapter 4

Sandman was talking to Roger and Donald. They now had a copy of the letter that was sent to Grace. As Sandman absorbed the words, he had a combination of a reaction. Initially, he was angry that something like this was happening to such a beautiful woman who had experienced personal tragedy in her life. Then came his professional response. Every part of his instincts told him that the person responsible knew Grace and her family and what happened to her sister. He had a suspicion that this same person was the one who killed Clara. It was as if this individual wanted to punish her and put fear into Grace. As far as he was concerned, it was working.

Sandman checked out the letter. He read it line for line and wondered what it all meant. Was there a clue in here somewhere?

My treasure has returned to me,
Thousands and thousands of miles across the sea.
I've yearned for you so very long,
Through every lover, through every love song.
I'm watching every move you make, every place you go and see,
Knowing when the time to take and capture you, make love to thee.
Grace, my love, you cannot hide,
I take her now, thoughts of you inside.

Sandman finished reading the letter and handed it back to Donald. He felt that the detective was sincere in his concern over Grace and her family. From what Jim had explained earlier, Donald was the lead investigator in Grace's sister's disappearance and murder almost three years ago. He felt responsible and was personally affected by this. He looked at him.

"So this guy has been leaving these letters only after the recent killings? How do you know he's connected to the others?" Donald asked. He was angry. Sandman could tell.

"He does the same things to each of his victims. He uses the same equipment and restraints. Even though the letters only recently started, we feel it's the same person. The killer is trying to spice things up now. He needs more excitement. Grace's picture and name have only recently entered the crime scenes," Detective Jim Warner stated.

"Why Grace? She's been away for nearly three years. This letter sounds like he's known that and has been waiting for her. Why didn't he follow her to Europe?" Donald asked.

"There could be many reasons for that. It's a whole different ball game to commit a crime in another country, out of his familiar surroundings. It would be more likely for him to get caught. Or he could have liked the idea of waiting for her like an award, a goal to achieve. You have to remember, Donald, we're talking about a real psycho here. He's ruthless, daring, and violent and believes no one is capable of stopping him. He's gotten away with so much for so long," Sandman stated.

"Grace needs your protection, Investigator Sandstone. She needs to be kept hidden and safe. She won't be able to handle the emotional effects of this. She needs to be safe or he could catch her and kill her at any time." Donald stood up from the chair, a look of concern evident on his face.

"I know, Donald, that's what I want to talk to you about. She's already feeling responsible for these women getting murdered. That's this guy's sick plan. He'll break her down, make Grace feel powerless. We need to take her out of the equation while Jim and my other investigators track this piece of shit down."

"Other investigators?"

"Yes, I'll explain it to you and also my idea," Sandman said as they walked out of the house and onto the driveway.

* * * *

An hour later Grace sat in Lieutenant Donald Friedman's office at the Houston Police Department.

"Grace, honey, I don't know what to say. I'm sorry this happened to you. I'm going to do my best to protect you and your family," he said as he sat across from Grace.

"I just don't understand who would want to do something like this? I've been over this a thousand times in my mind. I didn't know any of the other women who were murdered. I only knew Cheryl and of course my sister. Everything was fine in Europe. I should have stayed there. My poor mother must be going through hell right now."

"Personally, I think that you're better off here in the United States, at home where we can protect you. Eric is with Sarah and I've stationed an officer at her house at all times," Donald replied but Grace still felt so unsure and on edge.

"I appreciate that, Donald. I want to help in this investigation as much as I can. Can you tell me more about the other murders this person has committed? I mean, Sandman and Jim haven't really filled me in on anything."

"I've been kept out of the loop since the shooting at your mom's house. This is their investigation. I kind of feel responsible for not catching this asshole, and I have the feeling that these investigators and detectives don't think I'm seasoned enough to handle it."

"That's not right. You were there when Clara went missing and you did your best to solve the crime. Nothing like that had ever occurred in our town. Sure you don't have the same training as an investigator in the city but you did what you could."

"Yeah, and got the wrong man placed behind bars." Donald ran his fingers through his hair. Grace couldn't help but feel bad for him. Donald was a good man and a good family friend.

"The only other information I know, Grace, is that all the women killed so far have similar resemblances. Other than that there's nothing to go by. The murders are at number eleven. Once they find the young woman in those pictures the killer sent to you—"

The knock on the door interrupted his sentence but Donald didn't need to finish. She got it. The number would be at twelve.

"I knocked this time. Are you happy?" Sandman teased Grace, and she gave a small smile.

* * * *

Sandman hadn't liked leaving her out of his sight, even while he made plans and organized the detectives. He watched her closely as she gave him a small smile. She looked sad. Her eyes were still red and she appeared drained and tired. He wanted to hold her again and keep her safe in his arms. He was so attracted to her and instantly felt the need to protect her. No matter where he was or what he was doing, she was on his mind. He never had a reaction like this to a woman before. He actually thought that his heart had grown solid as a rock. Nothing really got to him or bothered him. In his profession he focused on the goal of capturing the criminal, solving the crime, and then heading home to his ranch to recoup before the next job. His brothers noticed the change in him yesterday, and when he told them about Grace, they were intrigued by her.

As Grace watched him, hesitating to respond to his teasing statement, he approached and placed his hand on her shoulder.

"What's going on? Any news yet about the woman in the picture?" she asked him, and he was impressed with her strength.

He squeezed her shoulder lightly before removing his hand.

"I don't want you to worry about that. You look like you could use some rest," he told her and Donald agreed.

"Can we go back to the house now or are the detectives still there?" she asked.

"You're not going back to the house, Grace. You're going to come stay with me."

Her eyes widened. "With you? Why? Won't the house be safest with my brother and the other SWAT team guys around? It's not their fault the envelope was delivered to the house. They were asleep and Charlie and I were out jogging. You can't hold them responsible, just like you shouldn't keep Donald out of this investigation because you feel that he messed up."

"Whoooa...hold on there. I'm not blaming anyone for what happened. I never said that Donald messed up or couldn't be involved in this investigation. I'm just saying that whoever is responsible for those pictures and the eleven women who have been brutally murdered is after you. I'm here to protect you, and I'm better qualified and trained to do so. I've already discussed this with your brothers John and Frank. They've agreed, and the detectives working the other cases feel that you need the best protection right now."

"They've agreed? You all have discussed this? What about me? What about what I think? Doesn't anyone give a shit about what I might have to say here? My whole world is being turned upside down and everyone's talking behind my back and keeping information from me. Don't I have a say in all this? How do I know you're more capable of protecting me?"

"He is more than capable, Grace. He's a special investigator, and from what was not deemed classified in his file that I was able to read, I'd say he's definitely the most qualified," Donald said. Sandman knew the lieutenant had checked him out.

Grace looked at Donald.

* * * *

She wasn't sure what was happening here. Why was a specialist called in anyway? Who was Sandman? Looking at him, she felt intimidated, yet protected. She didn't want to admit that she would definitely feel uneasy staying with her brother and his friends back at the house they shared. That would be a lie. Right now, it probably didn't matter where she stayed or with whom. She would be a nervous wreck.

She knew for sure that Donald would not put her in harm's way. He was like family and he had shown nothing but kindness and love for her mother and her brothers. She looked back at Sandman. He stood at complete attention, perfect posture, like a soldier waiting to strike. It was sexy, it was nerve wracking, and it showed his confidence and a hit of potential abilities. She had to admit, she was curious about what exactly Sandman would be capable of.

Her pussy clenched at the thought, nearly shocking her with a verbal reaction.

She bit her tongue as Donald watched with curiosity.

"Well?" Donald asked.

"Give me a minute," she whispered while watching Sandman.

He was definitely quick on his toes the way he tackled her and covered her entire body with his. Then the way he came through the bathroom door and pulled her into his arms. A place she liked and truly felt safe.

But she didn't want to see anyone get hurt. He was willing to protect her and take her into his own home, knowing that he could be shot or killed because of her.

"Why are you willing to do this? You don't know me? It couldn't possibly be part of your job requirement. I hate to repeat myself but there has got to be more to this situation."

Donald seemed to be enjoying the interrogation.

"Grace, there's an evil person out there killing innocent, beautiful young woman like yourself. Eleven victims so far and after the attempt on your life and the envelope that was delivered to you I'd say you're somehow a connection to all of it. I don't want you to be a victim and you're the closest clue we have to catching this guy. Worse could have happened at the house or when you were out jogging with Charlie. This guy is good. Really good. He's been able to evade capture for more than three years. That's why I and the other agents are involved now. I'm here to protect you. You're now in my protective custody program."

She swallowed hard at that statement. She didn't want to come off as some damsel in distress though. She needed to feel somewhat in control here.

"Why not have some of the local detectives and their protective custody program watch over me? Why you, an outsider and independent investigator? Do you think something fishy is going on around here and perhaps this is an inside job with other agendas?"

Sandman squinted his eyes at her. Donald cleared his throat.

"Grace, some of the same ideas were tossed around between myself, Jim, and Sandman only yesterday. We just don't know and we're being extra cautious. He'll take care of you. Jim and Pete agreed. Pete's known Sandman's brothers for years," Donald told her and she knew he was trying to ease her concerns.

"We're discussing and investigating many possibilities. The truth of the matter is, Grace, as we keep digging, we keep finding similar connections and murders that have taken place around the country. By the end of this week we could be looking at over twenty-five connected homicides. Not all of them have been women, but they show similarities that myself and the other detectives are not willing to dismiss as a connection of some sort," Sandman told her.

She was shocked and so was Donald as he leaned forward in his chair.

"When did this come about?" Donald asked.

"We started making the connections before visiting Grace at her mom's house. Then more information came available in New York and Pennsylvania. It looks like this individual has been killing in various ways for more than a decade. Unfortunately it's taken this long to link all of the murders. There also seems to be some sort of connection to illegal business dealings but I'd rather not divulge unproven information at this time. We're looking into it."

"How come the government can't come up with some kind of profile for this killer? Don't you have an idea of his type of personality, possible lifestyle, an age or profession he may be in? I thought that was part of a government agent's job. Investigate personalities by putting information in your complicated, hi-tech computers that spit out lists of suspects or potential criminals. How could someone get away with this for so long?" she asked in annoyance.

"First, Grace, I'm not a government agent. I'm what local authorities and the government call in when there's an investigation with this magnitude and no exact leads in a case. It's my specialty. So you understand, Grace, it doesn't matter what type of profile we come up with or what information is spit out of our computers. The fact of the matter is, you're our only clue and I'm not letting you out of my sight," Sandman told her as someone else knocked on the door.

Detective Jim Warner came to the door just as Grace's cell phone rang. She answered it and began speaking to her mother.

Grace told her what was going on and about staying in a safe location. Sandman stopped her from telling her mother exactly where they would be. Grace was annoyed with him but respected his advice, not telling her mom too much. The investigator seemed like he didn't want to take any chances at all.

She tried to focus on her mom's questions as she stared at the cabinet behind Donald's desk. It appeared that he had gained some awards in the community over the years and was involved in politics now, too. Some sort of new building and affordable housing award was displayed in the center of the other awards. Donald had always had a big heart and enjoyed volunteering at community centers and fundraising for the poor. She figured that he must have helped raise money for the new affordable housing neighborhood being constructed about a half mile from Grace's mom's house.

"What do you mean a safe place? Can't I see you? Where are you going to be?" her mom asked her, bringing her back to the conversation.

"I can't say, Mom. They want me to be protected and I suppose I won't be able to see you. I'm sure I can call you or something." Grace glanced at Sandman, who nodded then continued his conversation with Jim. The man was somehow able to converse with Donald and Jim while also eavesdropping on her phone call with her mother. Geesh, the man was good at his job.

"I can't believe this is happening. I finally have you home again where you belong and this happens. I'm so scared and so worried about you. Oh God," her mom said as she began to cry.

"Oh, Mom, don't cry…please…it will be okay," Grace said and she noticed that Donald appeared upset and Sandman looked at her, too. She turned away.

"It will be all right, Mom. Investigator Sandstone is very special. The departments and the government know that this is a unique situation and so they sent in the best. I think he's a trained killer, you know. Most of his file is classified, spy-like stuff. It will be like being with 007 and the Terminator at the same time." She joked around with her mom, trying to make her laugh, and hoped that the investigator couldn't hear her. She didn't want him to think that she was impressed with him. When she heard her mom sniffle then giggle, Grace felt a bit of relief.

"Oh, Grace. I love you honey. Please be safe."

"I will, Mom, I love you, too," Grace said and hung up the phone.

Grace paused for a moment, closing her eyes, picturing her mom inside her head. Why was this happening to her family? Why did she come back to America? Right now she should be making plans with her family to celebrate, spend time together, and get to know everyone again. She needed to contact her boss, set up some small jobs, and prepare for the big photo shoot she had in a few weeks. There was so much going on in her life right now. This was supposed to be a positive time and someone was out to destroy her and her family.

Just then her cell phone rang again. She looked at Sandman and Donald who seemed concerned from her previous conversation and she answered.

"Hello."

"Miss Thompson, this is Brian Watson with People of Houston

Eyewitness News. I'd like to set up an interview with you and perhaps your family in regards to some information we received from one of our sources. We were told that the serial killer has tried to contact you and even sent physical evidence to your brother's house where you have been staying. Is this true, Miss Thompson? And if so do you know who the serial killer is? And what does he want with you?"

Grace didn't know how to respond. He was speaking so quickly. She looked toward Sandman and Donald as she asked the caller, "Who is this?"

"Give me the phone, Grace," Sandman told her as he took the phone from her hand.

"Miss Thompson has no comment at this time. Please don't call this number again," Sandman said then hung up the phone. He asked what the reporter had said and she told him. She asked how the reporter was able to get her unlisted number.

"I don't know how he got the number, but I'm going to have to hold onto this for now." Sandman took the phone and placed it into his back pocket.

"What? Now you're going to screen my calls, too?" she asked, all annoyed.

"It would be the best thing, Grace. I'm sorry," he told her as she abruptly walked away from him and headed over toward the window in Donald's office.

She was looking out toward the police cars and could see reporters and camera crews everywhere. Instantly she turned back toward the men in the room.

Jim was explaining that what happened to Grace this morning was leaked to the press. They were carrying on about interviewing her and about her being the only connection to the murders. They were showing pictures from three years ago, when all the press surrounded Clara's murder and of Grace at her sister Clara's crime scene. The media was playing the tapes over and over again on the television sets.

Donald, Jim, and Sandman looked at the main TV in the office outside Donald's room.

The detectives gathered around listening to the reports, watching a scared, crying twenty-two-year-old woman shaking with fear as police officers and friends tried to comfort her. Then they showed the funeral and the same young sad Grace crying, mourning her sister's death.

The news reporter spoke as the pictures covered the screen.

"Grace Thompson has returned home after nearly three years away. She has returned to her loving family and friends and with her return comes the news that a serial killer is loose in the area. The serial killer could possibly be the same person who killed her sister Clara Thompson nearly three years ago. The anniversary of Clara's death will be next Wednesday. We hope to share an interview with the Thompson family and perhaps Grace herself as new information surfaces on this killer who remains on the loose and unidentified," a reporter stated.

Grace stood in the doorway. She remembered it like it was only yesterday. The media had little respect for what her family was going through. Then they showed her mother and Eric holding her, comforting his grieving wife.

Grace recalled Eric's ability to control the reporters, give them just enough information to make them leave the family alone. She was thankful to him for that.

A tear escaped her eye as she leaned against the doorway. Sandman and the others looked at her with sadness in their eyes. They probably remembered the incident as if it were only yesterday. As she glanced around at their faces, she recognized many of them. The way they offered support, searched day and night for Clara. The community came together pooling their hopes and prayers for a miracle that never happened.

Then her brothers John and Frank were at her side, pulling her attention away from the television set trying to once again console her as they brought her back into the office.

"I shouldn't be here. I should be back in Europe. I should have never returned." Grace pulled away from Frank and walked toward the corner of Donald's office. She ran her fingers through her hair then placed her hands on her hips. The sadness that the scenes on the television set had caused her was now turning into anger and frustration.

"Don't say that, honey. You belong here with us, your family, not in Europe," said Frank as he stood behind his sister.

"We're stronger than this asshole, sis. We're Thompsons and we don't give up without a fight," said John.

Grace gave a small smile at her brother's attempt to lighten things up. "I know that and I'm just getting frustrated. You should call Mom and make sure Eric is there with her and she's not alone. This is going to upset her badly. Seeing those scenes on the television and remembering that time in her life." Grace sat down on one of the office folding chairs.

John and Frank were so angry about the leaked information.

"I'll call Mom. You call Peter," said Frank as they took out their cell phones.

* * * *

Sandman knew that Grace found her sister's body. She had gone through so much, that was obvious. He wondered why she left home for Europe. The family seemed so close, so loving. A lot of questions went through his mind.

He watched her on the TV and then standing there by the door so hurt, so sad, and scared all he wanted to do was take her away from all this.

He needed to get her away from here. Her life depended on it.

"Sandman." Grace softly said his name as he turned and walked to her. She sat on a cushioned folding chair looking drained and exhausted but wanting to talk.

He squatted down next to the chair, still towering over her petite size, reminding him how feminine and delicate she was. She needed protection. He took Grace's hand into his. He spoke to her softly, quietly, and she was thankful for his kindness.

"I can't leave my family, Sandman. I can't run away from this…From them again. I don't know why this is happening. I just don't understand it. My mom….Oh God, my mom needs me. I need her, too. I've been away for so long. This isn't fair. I'm not going and you can't make me." She wiped an escaping tear from her eyelash.

Sandman felt terrible and this was definitely a bad situation. He knew his main priority would be to protect her and he wasn't confident that he or his men would be able to accomplish that if she stayed here.

"Grace, honey, I know this is terribly difficult for you and for your family but…" He couldn't continue his sentence as Grace began to speak.

"No buts. I'm not leaving my family." She looked away from him, determined to fight him every step of the way. Sandman needed to come up with something fast or Grace could refuse his protection completely and that would be suicide.

"How about a compromise? If things stay the same for a while, if this killer doesn't try to contact you, try to hurt you in any way, and as long as I feel your life is not in danger, then we can stick around here. How does that sound?" he asked her.

Grace looked at him and smiled as she squeezed his hand.

"It's a deal. Thank you."

He smiled then walked out of the office to join the other agents.

* * * *

"Donald, when did you get into all the political stuff and building the low-income housing?" Grace asked Donald as he leaned against his desk.

"Oh about two years ago. Actually, it was after everything that happened with your family. As we were searching and investigating, I came across a family living in the back of their minivan. It upset me. Then I found out there were others out there, too. I couldn't believe that this town, this suburb, had people living on the streets. Anyway, one thing led to another and I found out about a government-funded program for the poor. Your mom actually helped me find some jobs for the people so they could qualify to be part of the program."

"That is fantastic. So was that the affordable housing project that is still being constructed right now?"

"Yes. We received approval for an extended set of seven units. As you probably saw the other day when you visited your mom's place, it's a great location. Despite some negative remarks and feedback, the program has been working for the last year. I can't foresee it causing any other issues."

"What kind of negative feedback?" she asked, wondering how anyone could find anything wrong with such a program that helped those in need.

"Just some complaints, a bit of freak accidents during the construction, but nothing too crazy."

"Freak accidents?"

"Yeah, some things went wrong during construction, then there were lumber deliveries that were set on fire, things like that. It shocked most of the citizens of the area."

"That's terrible. Well, I'm glad that it all worked out. There haven't been any problems since?"

"No, and I'm planning on helping with another project over in Colton, two towns over. They've been approved for the same program and set up."

"Excellent. Well good luck with that. Let me know if there's anything I can assist with while I'm here. Well, if I can," she added and he smiled as they walked out of the room.

* * * *

The mail had been delivered to the offices, and a stack of envelopes as well as a box were placed on Donald's desk. Grace was standing by the window looking out at the chaos the killer was causing. She hadn't even looked at the person who delivered the mail. She didn't want anyone identifying her as the woman who found her dead sister and the one a killer was after. People might believe she was at fault or somehow responsible.

Everyone had cleared out of the room to give her a few minutes alone. That alone time made her feel more insecure than anything.

Just as she had noticed the box, Donald walked back in.

"Are you doing okay, hun?" he asked her as Grace walked toward the door. She peeked outside and saw Sandman talking to her brothers. She was sure they were discussing her new living arrangements as well as the compromise she and Sandman had already discussed.

"I'm okay. I can't believe this is going on. I wish I knew more or could do more. I don't know, maybe there's something I can help with to stop this person. I don't know," she told him as he stood next to his desk.

"What more could you do? I think it's a good idea that you stay with Sandman. This killer is bad news and I don't think you're safe. Sandman is highly qualified and seems very alert and confident." Donald picked up his mail, then saw the brown box. She noticed his expression changed and he appeared annoyed.

"What is it?" she asked him.

Simultaneously Sandman came through the door as Donald looked at the return address on the box he held in his hands.

"Where did that come from?" Sandman asked.

In the same instant there was a large bang and once again Sandman was tackling Grace to the floor just as she covered her head with her arms.

There was a lot of smoke and everything she heard echoed. She was having trouble breathing as she gasped for air but with each inhale the pain in her chest became worse. Her arms and her neck ached. She saw some blood and little black tacks were sticking in her arms, her neck and her hair.

Sandman was asking her if she was all right and she could tell he was panicking as he looked at her arms.

Officers were rushing in wearing gas masks and offering one to Sandman, which he gave to her first.

Jim was by the desk next to Donald who lay on the floor.

She was breathing into the mask as she heard the fire alarms going off inside the building. Everyone was in a panic around them.

She tried to pull the mask off. She wanted to make sure Donald was okay as she pushed herself into a sitting position. Each move, each motion causing tiny pinches of pain around her body. She realized she was covered with little black tacks. She felt that they were meant to cause her pain but not to kill her. She knew that, she felt it was what the killer wanted…to cause her pain. The way her mind instantly thought that the killer was responsible shocked her.

"Stay still, Grace, you're covered with this stuff. Keep the mask on until the room clears." Sandman told her as he held her close to him.

She noticed he had only a few of the same black tacks stuck in his arm and he had begun to pull them out.

She could tell he was angry and knew he felt responsible.

Maybe he felt like he should have noticed the box being delivered sooner. But who would have thought the same person who was killing women would also send a bomb to Donald? Could this be something different? A coincidence?

* * * *

Grace could have been killed and I was supposed to be protecting her. I promised her she would be all right. He said to himself as John and Frank entered the room.

The air was clearing up and the paramedics were making their way to the office.

Donald had hit his head on the desk and was just regaining consciousness. He didn't have any of the black tacks on him and they assumed the initial explosion scared him and as he jumped and dropped the box, the bottom of his desk took the hit.

Grace looked at the desk. He was sure that she could see the wood of the desk had hundreds of little indentations in it. The carpeting on the floor was covered with a bunch of black tacks that hit the desk, and then fell to the brown rug below.

Sandman and her brothers were kneeling in front of Grace looking over her injuries.

"Get these things off of me," she said in a panic as she started pulling out the tacks.

"Be careful, baby, some of those are in there pretty good," Sandman whispered, consoling her as he took her shaking hand to stop her from pulling out more tacks as her neck and arms continued to bleed. Her whole body was shaking, her lips were quivering and when she spoke her speech sounded shaky.

"Oh my God, Grace, what the hell happened?" John asked, filled with concern. Sandman couldn't even imagine how he and Frank were feeling. This was their baby sister.

"We heard a large bang and then the place filled up with smoke. I couldn't hear or see and then Sandman tackled me again," she said in a quivering voice. He felt bad for hurting her, but he didn't know what the explosion was or what would happen next. He went into protection mode instantly.

"There was a package on the desk. Donald was holding it, looking it over. I asked where it came from and as he looked up at me, it exploded," Sandman explained to Frank and John.

"You saved my sister's life again. We owe you man," John stated very seriously.

"That bomb was just a message," Sandman stated. "It wasn't meant to kill anyone. He just wants us to know how vulnerable we are. He's telling us he can get to Grace or whomever, whenever he wants to. He's resourceful and I don't like it one bit." He got up off the floor and began giving orders to the crowd of officers and detectives.

The search was on for the person who delivered the package.

* * * *

The paramedics entered the room and Grace sent them to treat Donald first.

He was acting funny and she was certain that he had a concussion.

Grace on the other hand felt dizzy and light-headed. The paramedic told her it was a combination of the gas in the explosion and the trauma she was exposed to. *No shit trauma.*

He had no idea what trauma the past few days had brought her. She wondered why the killer did this. What could he want from her? Who could he be? Her head was pounding as two paramedics removed the little black tacks from her arms and neck.

"You were lucky that one of these things didn't hit you in the eye," said one of the paramedics as he carefully removed each tack from her body then finally the last tack from her neck.

When they were all done, both Grace and Donald refused to go to the hospital to be checked out thoroughly.

"You should go, Donald. You might have a concussion."

He appeared so serious and scared. He was looking for something in his desk files, and when she asked him what he was doing he told her "nothing." She didn't think it was nothing, but she wouldn't push the issue. He was in a state right now and was trying to maintain his professionalism. She got that.

Grace was relieved that Donald was safe. She didn't want to see anyone else get hurt.

"I'm so glad you're okay, Donald. I'm so sorry about this. You could have been killed."

He stopped what he was doing and stared at her. He dropped the folder onto his desk, walked around the front of it, and stood before her.

"I'm a tough old bastard, don't you worry about me." She gave him a hug and he hugged her in return.

Grace sat down on a small brown-and-green-checkered couch. After being treated by the paramedics, both Donald and Grace moved to another office down the hall. Grace waited, knowing that at any moment Sandman would arrive and she would be going off somewhere with him instead of her family.

The room they were sitting in was a kind of resting area with no windows, a small love seat, and a few other single reclining chairs. In between the furniture were different magazines. Grace took notice of one in particular called *Guns and Ammo*.

Donald was filling a blue-and-white paper cup with water from a water jug that stood in the corner of the small room.

The door to the room opened and both Donald and Grace turned to see who was there.

Sandman entered looking tired and still rather annoyed. He was a huge man, intimidating, powerful looking and somewhat mysterious, like one shouldn't underestimate his capabilities. She sure as hell was intimidated.

He smiled at Grace then got himself a cup of water. She followed him with her eyes, absorbing the way his dark jeans clung to his long, thick thighs. She could practically make out the muscles beneath the material. *Hell, I felt his muscles when he tackled me.*

"Well we found out that a delivery person brought the box to the front desk. From there on it went from officer to officer until finally reaching your desk, Donald. I'm sure in about an hour we'll find out everyone who touched it when it entered the building. As far as before the delivery person, we still don't know. The bomb squad is gathering evidence still but believe this bomb was homemade. There was a timer, and activator, and, therefore, a person with knowledge of its contents had to have delivered it here." Sandman tossed the paper cup into the recycling bin.

Grace was looking at him as he stood there so strong and serious. He was not a man to trifle with. She could see that in his eyes and in his body language, which only made her more attracted to him. She was feeling battered and emotionally drained but she needed to fight those feelings and she needed to be strong. She had learned to depend on herself and that was what she needed to do right now. It was her only defense, her only protection she had as she once again had to leave her family and her home behind her. Poor Donald could have died.

"Explosive devices, handmade bombs, what the hell is going on?" Donald asked then ran a hand through his hair

Sandman promised to protect her and she felt he could do it. He would try his hardest and he was determined to keep her safe. He was strong, so compassionate about his work and her safety. She had watched him as he gave orders to the men standing around him, calmed everyone down after the explosion, took control, and got organized. He had so many great qualities that she found attractive and likeable. How could she not? He was handsome and fit, standing before her with his rather large gun sticking out of its holster by his rib cage. She knew he had another one, smaller and hidden on his ankle because she felt it against her leg when he covered her body with his.

"I have a plan to sneak you out of here. It involves you putting on a uniform. I'm going to leave in a separate car and make sure I'm not followed. You're going to leave with one of my associates, who will also be dressed in a police uniform. We'll meet up at a private hangar near the airport. No one can know where we are going, Grace. That means no phone calls." She was about to object but Sandman stopped her.

"We're doing this my way from here on. This is the only way it's going down. I'll set up some secure lines when we get to our destination. You and I have a lot of information to go over. You may not know it but you could be holding the answers and the clues we've been waiting and looking for."

Sandman placed his hand over her knee and spoke softly to her.

She stared into his dark blue eyes and swallowed hard.

"I know you must be very scared right now. I'm here to protect you. After we leave the building separately and meet up at the airport you no longer will be out of my sight, you understand me?"

She nodded yes.

Grace could tell by his eyes how serious he was and she knew he was still upset about the incident in Donald's office. He looked fierce, and as she absorbed the sight of the muscles in his jaw, she thought he was biting the inside of his cheek. *God, he smells incredible. Jesus, Grace, snap out of it. I'm leaving my family again. Someone wants to kill me.*

"Do you trust me, Grace?"

For some odd reason she did, but she was compelled to not give in so easily. After all, he was a stranger.

"What choice do I have?" she asked him as the door to the office opened.

Her brother Frank entered the room holding a police uniform.

"Here's the uniform, Sandman," Frank said as he passed it to him.

They left the room so Grace could change, and outside the door the three men spoke.

* * * *

"My family and I are putting our sister's life in your hands," Frank stated to Sandman.

"I know that, Frank. You can trust me and know that I would protect her with my own life."

"Let's hope that won't be necessary. You're going to keep in touch with us, right?" Donald asked.

"Yes, but limited phone calls are important. Jim will set up a secure line for you here at the department. I'm good at what I do, Frank. I'll take care of your sister. I promise you," Sandman stated as John came down the hallway.

"I'm going to go check on a few things and get ready to leave. You guys should take a few minutes with your sister. Have her ready at the time we discussed," Sandman said as Grace opened the door.

All four men looked at her and made similar comments simultaneously.

Grace held up her hand up to stop them from continuing.

"Stop, guys. I know. I look like some call girl stripper on her way to a bachelor party," she said and they laughed.

"I think you fill that uniform out nicely." Sandman winked at her and told the guys to have her ready to leave as they had discussed earlier.

"Keep your hair tucked in, and your hat down low, Grace. Don't make any eye contact with anyone," Frank told her as he fixed the police cap on her head and softly tucked a loose strand of hair back under it. "I love you, baby sister. Be safe." He kissed her on the cheek and hugged her.

"The guy who's driving the car is named Justin. Stay close to him and follow his lead. You'll only have to go by one or two real cops and possibly a reporter. Keep your hat down and walk like a cop not a sex symbol," John teased as he kissed her on the cheek and hugged her as well.

Grace looked at Donald.

"What are your words of advice?" she asked Donald.

"Keep asking questions and stay by Sandman's side. You can trust him. He really cares about you, Grace. You have that instant effect on people." Donald kissed her cheek.

Grace touched the bandage on his forehead and told the men to keep an eye on her mom.

Justin met them by the door and the three men watched as Grace disappeared down the stairwell.

Chapter 5

"Everything's happening right on schedule," the killer said out loud as the news reporters outside the Houston Police Department reported an explosion that occurred inside.

He listened as the fire alarms wailed and echoed through the television set and police scattered everywhere.

The package arrived on time and detonated precisely as planned.

He was feeling good as he watched the media coverage and saw Grace's face.

She looked so sad those three years ago. He remembered it so clearly. Especially the way the detectives arrested the wrong man. It was so easy to plant the evidence in the crazy guy's house. He often thought about doing the same thing in other murders he committed. It would be funny for some poor fool or enemy he wanted revenge against to be blamed for one of his killings. So easily he could set them up. He couldn't believe the media attention he was getting for the homicides. The stupid cops had no idea what this was all about. Shit, even he had changed the game plan along the way. Life was looking promising. He just needed to keep his cool. He wanted everyone to know it was the same serial killer. "Serial killer." He loved the sound of it. He was famous now. But that also served an additional purpose. One that led to getting away literally, with murder.

He was impressed with his ability to evade capture and warrant the attention of a special investigator.

He felt a little challenged by that one investigator, Sandman. Even his name was intimidating and intense. That was one huge-ass man. But as long as he kept his wits about him, then he could continue to kill and evade capture.

Sandman intrigued him, too, and the man had arrogance about him, like he was so strong and skillful. The killer would enjoy messing with him.

It was difficult to get information on the investigator. Everything kept coming up classified. Even with his small connections he was unsuccessful and he feared if he pushed too much, then he would look suspicious. Right now no one had a clue who he was. He was in complete control and would be sure to keep it that way until the time was right.

The killer was impressed with himself for getting away with his special hobby for so long. Who would have thought his ability, his talent and gift for killing, would come in handy even in his career and daily life.

"This is going to be fun." He continued to watch the media coverage.

* * * *

The police car slowly rolled into a vacant air hangar located inside a private airport.

"So far so good. Where's Sandman?" Grace asked as she got out of the patrol car.

No one had noticed who she was when she left the precinct. She fit in perfectly. She thought she was busted when a reporter bumped into her on the way out the door, but the stuck-up snob hardly acknowledged Grace as she brushed by her without saying sorry. Grace laughed to herself.

"There he is now," Justin said, and as she turned to look toward the back entrance of the building, there was Sandman. Her heart skipped a beat as she absorbed his attire. Dark blue jeans, cowboy boots, button-down blue shirt and a Stetson on his head. He removed the sunglasses and damn did her libido do a double, no triple take. *Oh my God, he's gorgeous.*

She cleared her throat as he eyed her over and then shook Justin's hand.

"Everything go well?"

"Yes, sir, no one followed us," Justin replied then smiled before looking at Grace.

She pulled the police cap off her head causing her long brown hair to fall past her shoulders. It wasn't like she was trying to look sexy, but the way Sandman stared at her then gave an intense expression made her blood pump through her veins. He reached his hand out toward her.

"Come on. Big Jay should be landing any second."

"Big Jay?" she asked as the sound of the rotors of a helicopter approaching filled the air.

Justin glanced at his watch.

"Right on time."

"No, he should have been here thirty seconds ago."

Grace wondered who Big Jay was and why Sandman was so concerned over a lousy thirty seconds. She was about to ask him when a beautiful black helicopter landed on the blacktop right outside of the hangar.

"Come on, sweetheart, your chariot awaits." She tried protesting as Justin waved good-bye and Sandman dragged her closer to the helicopter. The rotors continued to pump round and round, making that very distinct sound as her hair blew around her face.

"Sandman, I'm not going in that thing. I thought you said a plane," she protested as they stood by the edge of the helicopter door.

"Honey, this is the plan. It's safe, I promise. Big Jay is the best." Sandman stared at her with those intense blue eyes of his and she weakened.

"Oh God, I can't believe this."

He lifted her up, placing his large hand against her waist and hip. She looked at the pilot and holy shit he was just as big and attractive as Sandman. Dressed in some camouflage pants and a tight fitted black T-shirt, the pilot was filled with big muscles. He smiled.

"Get strapped in, sweetheart."

Before she could reply as she sat down and tried to figure out the seat belt situation, Sandman was moving her hands out of the way and adjusting her position in the seat. His face was inches from hers. He smiled and looked relaxed and excited. He liked this kind of stuff.

"Don't be scared," he told her and she nodded her head as he turned toward the pilot.

"Hey, brother. Long time no see. I get why now," the pilot said and they shook hands before Sandman took his seat beside the pilot and placed the headset on his head.

The pilot looked at Grace and she wondered if the two were really brothers or if it was just a friendly nickname.

"Ready, gorgeous?" the pilot asked.

"As I'll ever be," she replied and he chuckled loudly before the helicopter began to lift.

It wasn't like she had never been in a helicopter before, but she didn't know these men. She didn't know this pilot or where they were going or how long it would take. She knew nothing and that was what made her a nervous wreck.

She remembered Sandman's words. "Trust me."

God, I sure hope I can.

* * * *

The helicopter trip had only taken about a half hour. They were still in Texas, but nowhere near civilization.

As the helicopter began to land, she noticed the huge log cabin set back in a bit of wooded area. As the helicopter touched down, she noticed the pilot as he began to shut down the helicopter. It appeared that he was staying.

As the rotors continued, Sandman stood up and helped to undo her seat belt.

"We're here, Grace."

He touched her cheek and then lightly gripped her chin.

"You look exhausted. As soon as we get you settled in, you can lie down for a bit, while I go over some things with my brothers."

"Brothers?" she asked, her voice barely audible, because she felt so weak and Sandman was strikingly handsome. The feel of his fingertips below her chin sent tiny chills through her body. *I must be exhausted. He's just doing his job and protecting me.*

He took her hand then stepped down out of the helicopter first. He grabbed her by her waist and hoisted her out of the helicopter and against his chest. She was stunned as she held on to his shoulders and stared down into his eyes.

"I got you. No worries now, darling."

His bold Texas accent added a zinger of a punch to her feminine parts. He had to notice as he smiled softly, but that sweetness in his smile didn't reach his eyes. No, his eyes appeared darker and glazed over with desire.

He placed her feet down on the ground as he took her hand and led her toward the house. A quick glance over her shoulder and the pilot was preparing to leave the machine. Her thoughts were right. He was staying, too. Could the helicopter belong to Sandman and his brothers? He did say brothers. Did that mean there was another one or more lurking around? She again felt her belly tighten and anticipation skitter along her nerves.

"Duke is probably getting dinner ready. At least my brother should be doing that."

"How many brothers do you have?" she asked.

He smiled at her as they climbed the large porch steps. There was a wide wraparound deck with a dark wood front porch with scattered hunter green trimming to match the hunter green shutters that decorated the windows of the house. Large brown barrels stood on either side of the front door welcoming guests, filled with vibrant red, white, and green flowers

There were dark-stained wooden rocking chairs and a matching wooden bench swing on the front porch, inviting visitors to take a seat and relax a while.

"Two," he replied as he opened the front door. She glanced at the setting on the porch and the four rockers as well as a rocking bench. It looked relaxing. That was a feeling she didn't think she would have again anytime soon.

* * * *

Duke turned around and felt his entire body react to the gorgeous brunette his brother was protecting. She was a knockout, with an exceptional body, but why was she wearing a Houston police uniform?

"This is my brother Duke. Duke, meet Grace Thompson."

She reached her dainty hand out toward him and tilted her head way back to lock gazes with him. His cock hardened in his jeans. It was instant, and something like that never happened to him before. She was in awe of his size. He could tell as her eyes turned the size of saucers. They were a stunning green and hazel color combined.

"Pleasure to meet you, Grace."

He noticed immediately how her body swayed and she appeared as if she might faint. Quickly he wrapped an arm around her waist and she laid her head against his ribs. She sure was petite.

"Grace, are you okay?" Sandman asked as he moved her hair from her cheek.

"What's going on?" Big Jay entered the house with a scowl on his face the moment he saw Grace against Duke's chest.

"I feel so dizzy," she whispered. Duke immediately lifted her up into his arms and carried her toward the living room. He gently set her down on the sofa and she kept a hand over her belly and one over her eyes.

"I'm so sorry. This is embarrassing."

Sandman moved Duke out of the way and sat next to her on the couch. Duke watched as Sandman caressed her cheek. He had never seen his hard-ass brother react to a woman in such a way, never mind another human being. Sandman kept to himself and submerged himself in each job he did. Something was different here.

"Tell me what you're feeling, darling," Sandman whispered.

My brother is whispering? What the hell is up with you, man?

Duke walked out of the room to go grab a glass of water for Grace. When he returned, Sandman was staring down into her eyes.

"So you haven't eaten anything all day? No wonder you're so weak and pale. It's a good thing that Duke cooked up some dinner for us. How about I help you sit up and you take a sip of water."

She slowly nodded her head then locked gazes with Duke. Hot damn, the woman had the facial expressions of a natural seductress. Duke adjusted his stance as he found himself kneeling down beside her on the couch and Sandman.

"Here, try little sips."

Within a few minutes she was sitting up and some of the coloring was coming back to her cheeks.

"How about we get washed up and grab a bite to eat? Then I can help you settle down for the night in your room?" Sandman asked.

"Thank you, Sandman, Duke. Again, I'm sorry for nearly fainting. I guess with everything that has happened since this morning, I never remembered to eat anything."

Duke felt the twinge of anger hit his belly. Sandman explained a little bit about the situation, but not nearly as much as he and Big Jay needed to know. As soon as the beauty went to bed, they were going to have a sit down.

* * * *

"Is she all settled in?" Big Jay asked as Sandman returned from upstairs.

He nodded his head then leaned back against the kitchen counter. Running his hand through his hair, their brother appeared exhausted.

"What's the deal, bro? We know you're tired, but can you give us some details?" Big Jay asked as Duke looked on with a serious expression on his face.

While Sandman was assisting Grace, Duke and Big Jay talked about her and wondered why someone would want to kill her. They wanted information and considering they took off from their regular jobs to assist their brother, they knew this was serious.

"I don't know where to start. I guess at where I came involved with the investigation in a number of recent homicides," Sandman began to explain. They listened to him give great detail into the investigation and about their friend Detective Jim Warner calling him in to assist. Big Jay felt his guard come alert at knowing that Grace not only experienced finding her dead sister's body, but also being harassed by the killer and actually touching a lock of a victim's hair. The package delivered to the guys' house where she was staying was ballsy, to say the least. As Big Jay heard in detail about the explosion at the police department, his military experience went into overdrive.

"There's more to this case than just one individual getting his kicks off raping, torturing, and murdering women," Big Jay stated.

"I agree a hundred percent. The whole bomb thing doesn't even go with the killer's MO from the other cases you've described in the files you sent to me today," Duke added.

"I know. That's why I need you guys involved with this. Protecting Grace is my top priority. I need your computer hacking abilities and connections, Big Jay, to filter through these files and find a connection, different than the obvious. Duke, we need this house and perimeter of the area secured at all times. I'll need some rest in between and we'll be taking turns in shifts with her, watching her, going over the information the detectives send to me. This guy has to fuck up sometime or perhaps he has already," Sandman said then rubbed his eyes.

"You need some sleep, bro. I'll take first watch over her tonight," Big Jay said as Sandman stared at him.

"She's scared, she's tough, and she holds back a lot. Don't push her too much."

"You got it, bro."

Big Jay watched his brother walk out of the kitchen and upstairs to the bedroom. He couldn't help but feel protective of Grace now and it made him understand why his brother sounded the way he did days ago over the phone and also why his brother Sandman was in protective mode. He was worried and Sandman never looked worried.

Chapter 6

Grace awoke with a start. She wasn't sure where she was and that panicky feeling hit her all at once. She had taken a shower before going to bed and her hair was still damp. A glance by the bedside table and she saw the clock read 4:00 a.m. It was quiet. She couldn't hear a sound and that made her nervous. Too many thoughts were traveling through her head.

Were Sandman and his brothers still in the house? Had the killer gotten to them, perhaps found her somehow? Why was Sandman involving his brothers in this case? Who the hell were they?

She pulled the covers back and stood up from the bed. As comfortable as the mattress was, she wouldn't get another wink of sleep unless she knew she was safe.

Her heart pounded inside of her chest. Grace should be used to handling things alone and being alone. But someone wanted to hurt her, emotionally and physically, and he could have hurt or killed Sandman and his brothers already.

She was shocked by the thought and even more so by the fact she felt sadness, regret. *Why would I feel regret? It wasn't like I was involved intimately with him, with them. God, where the hell did that thought come from? I'm losing it. For crying out loud, get a grip, Grace.*

She was only wearing a T-shirt and a pair of cotton shorts. She looked around the room for a weapon. The bed was calling her back. It was large and delightfully decorated with an old-fashioned, country, patriotic theme.

The comforter on the bed was all white and fluffy. There were red, white, and blue solid throw pillows scattered at the top earlier and she had placed them onto the bottom of the comforter. The bed was huge and she wondered which brother normally slept there.

She tiptoed across the floor and slowly opened the door. From where the bedroom sat, there were three others and all had their doors closed. Quietly, with her heart racing, she walked toward the staircase. That was when she heard what sounded like someone typing away on a keyboard. She made her way closer to the sound in the kitchen and caught sight of Big Jay.

"Couldn't sleep, darling?" he asked without turning around, startling her.

She gasped, jumped, and covered her mouth.

Holy shit, he heard her before she even approached the front doorway.

Taking a deep breath, she entered the kitchen.

Big Jay, which was the perfect name for the man, stared at her with identical eyes to his brother's.

"I was just checking on you guys," she replied, and he gave a small chuckle.

He nodded his head as he looked her over. She suddenly wished she had grabbed a sweater or her hoodie first. But fear had a way of ruining rational thinking.

"Couldn't sleep?" he asked and she nodded her head. "How about a drink of water or a snack?"

"Water is fine."

When he stood up, she took an uneasy step backward. The man was that intimidating.

He glanced over his shoulder at her. She felt like such a twerp and was embarrassed for gawking at the fine specimen of man, so she turned away. That was when she saw the pictures on the screen.

They were of her days following finding Clara.

She stepped closer, feeling both shocked and angry.

The media had caught her facial expressions during a time of great sadness and desperation. They were private moments that lost the sanctity of that privacy and her ownership of them. She understood that the media was doing their job, just as Duke, Big Jay and Sandman were, but each time she caught sight of those images and the fear, devastation, and weakness in her eyes, it upset her. Her chest tightened and she prayed for strength to remain strong and not break down.

"I was doing some research. Trying to get an understanding of what's going on in the case," Big Jay said as he walked over with the glass of water. He handed her the glass and she took it from him. Staring up into his eyes, she wondered what his deal was.

"Researching what? What someone looks like after days of searching miles and miles of woods and finding your own sister's body? You wanted to see what I looked like then when I was going through hell?" He raised his eyebrows at her. She snapped at him for no damn reason. *God, I'm strung so tight. He's trying to do his job. Just let him do it.*

"Grace, it's not like that." She raised her hand up, took a sip from the glass then swallowed.

"I'm sorry. I'm just a bit on edge. I had no right to snap at you. I have no right to ask what you're doing or what your job is. I guess I'm used to being in control of my life all the time and now I'm out of control of it." She took another sip of water then walked toward the sink. She washed it then placed it on the drying rack. When she turned, she found Big Jay staring down at her.

"On a regular basis, I'm kind of like a private investigator, but for special assignments. My brothers and I have served in the Marine Corps as Commandoes. Duke works for Houston SWAT as a trainer and specialist. His bosses allow him flexibility when a special type of investigation arises. Same goes for Sandman. He only takes the tough ones. The cases where it seems like the bad guy might get away with the crime. But they don't. Sandman is the best."

"Then why are you working together on this case?"

"Sandman's call. He hasn't filled us in on everything but I can assume he needs more help and he wants that help to remain under the radar."

She thought about that a minute.

"He's thinking that there's more to these homicides and threats to me than just some sick bastard killing women?"

"Maybe."

She gave a sigh. "Sorry to interrupt."

She started to walk out when his deep voice stopped her immediately.

"Try to get some rest. You've been through a lot. We'll figure this out, Grace."

He turned back toward the computer and sat down. She got the feeling that Big Jay was a lot like Sandman. Quiet, observant, but detached. They really didn't show emotion. She didn't know why that bothered her. What did she expect? These men were doing a job and they weren't her family. All she could do now was sit and wait. So why was being in this huge log cabin in the middle of nowhere with three attractive, dynamic, resourceful men so unnerving?

* * * *

Sandman showered and dressed in a pair of dark blue jeans and a black T-shirt. He hoped that Big Jay made some progress into the time line of events since the first homicide and then the others Sandman felt were connected even though men were killed. He had tossed and turned most of the night and heard Grace get up and go downstairs. He followed her and listened to the conversation his brother had with her. When he knew she was safe, he headed back to bed, but not before peeking into her bedroom.

The door was open and the scent of her perfume lingered in the hallway. He saw the rumpled sheets and he was struck by the fact that there was a woman in their vacation home. Neither him, Big Jay, nor Duke ever brought any women up here. Thinking about it, they never brought any women to their home in town either. He could see himself with a woman like Grace. She had a lot of the characteristics he was attracted to in a woman, but she was out of his league in other ways.

She had lived in Europe, photographed models, went to fancy parties, and had designer everything. She was style and class, and he was vintage.

Shaking the thoughts from his head, he headed downstairs to help with breakfast. As he passed Grace's room this morning, he heard the shower running.

* * * *

Grace thought about the house the guys owned. The inside of the house was immaculate. The family room had a beautiful stone fireplace and deep large comfortable couches scattered around it.

She looked into her bag. Her brother packed practically everything she owned. She opted for a pair of jean shorts and a loose white T-shirt. She glanced around the room and saw a beautiful blue wooded armoire that contained a TV and some extra bed linens in the drawers.

There were pictures of a spinning wheel sewing an American flag on one wall, and on another wall a long, brown, wooden rod contained an antique quality quilt of the Pledge of Allegiance.

She liked the theme as she headed toward the bathroom.

The bathroom was large and contained a Jacuzzi tub and a separate glass-enclosed, mosaic-tiled shower. It was a modern touch to the whole log home idea. She actually liked it, a lot. Living in Europe and doing photo shoots, she had gotten to stay in some really amazing hotels as well as some dives. But the idea of a Jacuzzi tub was definitely positive as far as she was concerned.

She took her time and enjoyed the heat of the water. Her shoulders and neck ached and she still felt the cause was more from Sandman tackling her than the stress of the events. When she was finished, she got dressed and headed downstairs.

* * * *

The killer sat in his car as he watched Grace's brothers' house. Where had she gone? No one knew or they weren't telling.

He should have figured Sandstone would take Grace into hiding but he didn't think Sandstone could pull it off without him knowing. After all he was like part of the family.

Who was this guy Sandstone anyway? He came in out of the blue and was running the show. The killer wanted information on him and a way to get to Sandstone and get him out of this investigation. But how?

Someone in the family knew where Grace was and would open their mouth and leak the information.

Now he had to be patient. Patience was definitely not one of his strong points, especially when it came to picking a victim, relishing in the time he spent exploring them and then leaving their body to be found by the authorities. His desire, his obsession was too much to ignore. He craved another. He would have to be very cautious now that there were so many agents and police around but it actually excited him and made the thrill of killing even more pleasurable. As he put the car in drive, he headed out of town determined to satisfy his physical desires. He enjoyed the hunt almost as much as the actual acts and fantasies he envisioned in his mind. He looked at the clock on his car radio and knew he had plenty of time. He was a pro, a master at his game. He would never get caught. He would gratify his wants and needs. "Soon…Soon…"

He breathed deeply, taking his time as he passed one young woman after the next.

"Who will be the lucky one to play along today?"

Chapter 7

They finished eating breakfast and Sandman shook his head as he listened to Duke flirt with Grace. His brother was relentless but his persistence finally put a small smile on Grace's face.

"Honey, you should be the model, not the photographer," Duke stated, and Grace shook her head at him. She popped a blueberry into her mouth as she looked out the doublewide windows toward the fields and garden.

"I love being a photographer and I prefer to be behind the lens, not in front of it."

"Yeah, I know what you mean," he replied.

"Bullshit, you know what she means. You're SWAT, a commander and instructor and love being in the spotlight. Don't you get it? Grace likes to remain anonymous, and mysterious," Big Jay said as he continued to tap on the keyboard.

"All I'm saying is that she should be in the spotlight. She's gorgeous," Duke stated as he held her gaze.

"Well I agree with you there, but she's also an artist and probably likes to keep to herself as well," Big Jay added and Sandman watched as she looked toward Duke and Sandman and smiled. Duke released a sigh.

Just then, Sandman's phone rang.

"Sandstone here."

"It's Jim. We found the location of the latest victim. The one whose pictures were sent to Grace? You're not going to believe this but the murder took place only three houses down from the brother's house. The young woman worked in the records department in city hall. She often jogged by the coffee hut, too, and knew one of the girls who worked behind the counter," Jim explained.

"Holy shit only three houses away from John's place? Damn this guy is good. Grace was only at her brother's house for three days while I was in New York. He was able to scope out the neighborhood, select the victim, learn her routine, and make his move so quickly. Any evidence left behind?" Sandman asked.

"We found his usual stuff, handcuffs, whips, ropes, and of course no weapon. He did, however, leave a copy of a newspaper clipping of Grace from a few years ago."

"Did you find any prints on anything?" he asked.

"The lab still has everything we collected but I'm sure he wore gloves. "

"What about this woman who was killed? You said she worked for the records department in city hall? Could that be more than coincidence?"

"Anything is possible at this point, Sandman. I mean, we can't figure this out. We don't have any leads and even the guy who was framed for Clara Thompson's murder didn't think he had any enemies."

"I'll have Duke and Big Jay look into this a bit more," Sandman replied as he watched Grace joke around with his brothers. She wasn't going to take the latest news too well. She felt responsible even though she wasn't. He decided he would talk to his brothers first and have them find out more about the woman who was killed and about the guy the real killer framed for Grace's sister's murder.

"What was that about?" Big Jay asked as Grace began cleaning up from breakfast. Duke was bumping into her, flirting, and pretending to act nonchalant about it. They liked her. That thought hit his stomach like a ton of bricks.

"Nothing. Jim is going to send me some stuff. I want you and Duke to look into a few things for me."

Grace turned toward him.

"Is everything okay? Did something else happen?" she asked.

He felt bad for lying to her, but he wanted a little time to gather some good news.

"It's fine. Just some new details. This is why I have my brothers helping me out. So, why don't I show you the library we have and the awesome number of books. If there's nothing you like, we have an e-reader in there, too. You can download whatever you'd like," Sandman stated. Duke stared at him over Grace's head. Duke knew that Sandman was keeping something hidden from Grace.

"Hey, I'll show her the library and you can go over the things you want Big Jay and I to look into."

He stared at his brother and felt the tinge of awareness as Duke placed a hand on Grace's shoulder then ran his hand down her arm to her hand. It caught both Grace and Sandman off guard. But even more so was the way Grace immediately turned toward Sandman. "Go with Duke, honey. You're in good hands," he stated.

His words suddenly felt as if they had more meaning than he could even comprehend right now. It was instant and Grace felt it, too. Her cheeks turned a shade of red, and then to top it off Big Jay walked over to her. The sight of his brother Jay, standing over six and half feet, in front of a very gorgeous, petite woman like Grace as his other brother Duke remained holding her hand, stirred his entire body. His cock hardened, his eyes felt as if they zoned in on her face, her lips, her body, and instantly he could see them making love to her together. *Holy fuck! This is what Jim and his brother feel for Deanna. This is exactly what Gunner, Garrett, and Wes felt for Gia.*

He and his brothers thought about getting involved in a ménage relationship because of their lack of trust issues and what they felt were hardened hearts. If there were three of them to love one woman, then she would never be at a loss for attention and love. So if one of them or even two out of the three were having a hard time facing their emotions or dealing with their military pasts, then the other brother or brothers could take over providing attention to their woman. It made sense. The three of them had lost a lot of their empathy, their connection to other human beings.

"I'll come check on you in a little while, okay?" Big Jay whispered as he gently rubbed his fingers under her chin, gripping it gently. She looked like an angel as she stared up into his brother's eyes appearing timid and shy. When she licked her lower lip, Big Jay moaned then abruptly released her and stepped away. He walked over to his laptop computer and released a long sigh.

Grace locked gazes with Sandman and he stared at her, unable to say a word. It seemed the attraction between the four of them was immediately intense.

"Go ahead, darlin'," Sandman whispered and Duke led her out of the kitchen and still remained holding her hand.

* * * *

Big jay was trying to calm himself down. He nearly kissed the poor woman. *Holy shit I don't know what came over me and then she licked her lip and fuck, I almost grabbed her and kissed her. What am I thinking?*

"Hey, are you okay?" Sandman asked him and he wondered if his brother and Duke felt what he was feeling.

"No, I'm all fucked up."

"What do you mean?"

"You know damn well what I mean, Sandman. You see her, you feel it, don't you?"

Sandman ran his hands through his hair then turned his back toward Big Jay and looked out toward the sliding glass doors.

"She's a beautiful woman. It's natural to be attracted to her, Big Jay. Don't freak out."

"Fuck you, don't freak out. I saw the desire in her eyes, in Duke's eyes and yours, too," Big Jay stated as he turned his brother around by his upper arm. They were nearly toe-to-toe and even though Big Jay had a few inches on Sandman, his brother was just as big and just as strong.

"She's in danger. Jim just called and said that they found the other body. The one of the missing woman whose picture was sent to Grace."

Big Jay felt his blood pressure rising. He saw the pictures through the e-mails Jim sent along. The woman was beautiful, with long brown hair and green eyes. He also knew what Grace found in the envelope. His brother had explained everything.

"Why didn't you tell Grace?"

"And scare her, upset her even more?"

"She has to be kept abreast of the situation, Sandman. There may be some information that she could recognize as a clue. She's safe here with us. That was the point of you taking her out of the equation."

"I'll tell her. I just wanted to give her one day of no bad news. It's been nonstop for her since she returned from Europe."

"I know. I was looking up information on her last night. She came down this morning early for a drink. I think she couldn't sleep."

"There's something we all share in common," Sandman remarked.

Big Jay knew that he and his brothers had difficulty sleeping at night. The nightmares were less frequent, but now just the memories, the hint of danger on the mist of their dreams made the evening hours awful. That was why, when Sandman suggested that Big Jay remain on guard, he was more than happy to oblige.

"Listen, I want you and Duke to look into this woman who was found. She worked for the records department in city hall. Then I'm going to see if there are any leads on that bomb that was sent to Donald's office. I still think there was more to that."

"Okay, sounds like a plan. I'll let you know if I find anything."

* * * *

Grace was totally in tune to her body. Her mind, however, was hollering for her to stop acting like some inexperienced teenage girl. Yes, she was a professional woman who traveled and worked in Europe with supermodels, but she was not experienced. One lover sure didn't constitute anything remotely close to experienced. However, throw her into a house under the protection of three, sexy, hot military men, and holy shit, she'd lost her mind. It didn't matter which one of them touched her. Sandman, Big Jay, or Duke, she felt it to her nipples and her pussy. It was instant and it was incredibly strong.

"So this is the library. Not sure if you'll find something of interest, so I'll just get you the e-reader and write down the password for you. Don't worry about the cost. We have an account set up." Duke pulled open a desk drawer and handed her the reading device.

She looked around the beautiful room. There were two large windows that looked out over the backyard and some sort of pond and waterfall.

"That is gorgeous. Is that a waterfall and pond?" she asked as she moved closer to the window. It even had a sitting area around it with a swinging bench and lots of flowers.

"Yeah, we worked on that together," Duke said from behind her. She tightened up when she felt his hand on her waist and the other go to her left shoulder.

As he gave her shoulder a slow, light squeeze, she found herself leaning back against him.

"There are Koi in there, too. I'll take you outside later, once I finish helping Big Jay look over some things."

She turned to look up toward him.

"I'm sorry that you need to be involved with this. You probably wish you were working in SWAT right now and training officers."

He cupped her chin and she gripped the windowsill behind her. Every ounce of her body was aroused. She swallowed hard and nearly coughed from the difficulty.

"I don't regret being here. I sure as hell am glad that my brother called Big Jay and I in on this. We're going to keep you safe and we're going to find this guy."

She lowered her eyes from the intensity of his words.

"No one has been able to. It's been so many years. How can he still be out there and committing all these murders yet remain undetected?"

He caressed his thumb across her lower lip. The look in his eyes as she held his gaze did a number on her. The depth and emotion in his blue eyes was stunning.

"That's not for you to worry about, Grace. We're good at our jobs.

I'm looking forward to getting to know you better as well."

"It's always nice to make new friends. I just don't want you guys to miss out on important things in your life because of me and this situation."

He scrunched up his eyes and stared at her lips then locked gazes with her.

"Sweetheart, we wouldn't be here unless we wanted to be. Now, you just need to relax a little and let us take care of you. I mean that."

She gave him a small smile and as he began to move his lips closer toward her, she anticipated his kiss. But it never came as he immediately stepped back and Sandman entered the room. She hadn't even heard him coming, but Duke had.

"What's going on? Did you give her the password and the e-reader?"

"She's got it and is ready to download, right, Grace?"

"Right. Thanks, Duke."

"Later, sweetheart." He winked and she shyly looked away as Duke left the room.

When she looked up, she locked gazes with a very serious-looking Sandman.

"I'm going to get in touch with Frank and see if we can set up a call for you with your mom."

"Oh God, really? That would be great. Thank you."

She picked up the e-book reader and looked at the screen. She wasn't sure what to do.

"He didn't show you, did he?"

She looked at him and shook her head.

"Just hit this button to get online, then press add to cart, and when it states that you're at checkout, enter the password. Then the book will be downloaded instantly," Sandman said as he stood right beside her. She was shocked at the emotions she felt. She was just as attracted to Sandman as she was Duke and she was certain even Big Jay. *What in the world is happening to me?*

"I'll check on you in a little bit, just call if you need anything." He stared at her a moment before walking from the room.

Grace fell into the long lounge chair that overlooked the windows and outside setting. She stared down at the e-book reader and looked for a book to read. She was a romantic at heart but for some reason as she scanned through the synopses of the stories, she found herself submerged in an excerpt from an erotic romance novel. The ménage story interested her and before long she was hitting download and reading the amazingly sexy story.

She knew that ménage relationships existed. She knew a few models that were involved in that type of relationship and they were very happy. Grace never really saw herself in any kind of relationship. She felt she had too much baggage and too many fears to let herself go and to trust fully. She couldn't even imagine herself having a boyfriend. A lover was one thing, but believing that a man could be trusted with her every intimate thought or sexual desire scared the crap out of her. Therefore, she couldn't even imagine two or three or more men committed to her at once.

Why would a man want that anyway? Weren't men always jealous lovers? Didn't they want to keep their woman under wraps and solely committed to them? She had a lot of questions and concerns about it but as she read this particular love story, she couldn't help but wonder if it really were possible to love and be loved by more than one man. She could never let her guard down like that. Feeling the pain of a broken heart would be too much to handle again. She was so connected to her sister, her father, her mother, and brothers, but in losing Clara, she lost part of herself, too. That fear, the depth of her sadness was too much. Soon after, Grace began to build up a wall around her heart. Sure she wasn't a selfish, unfeeling bitch, but she kept her distance. She never fully gave all of herself to anyone and that was the only way she knew how to survive, how to wake up every day and continue to live without Clara in her life.

Chapter 8

Jim Warner was standing in Donald's office as the investigators clarified information on the bombs.

"It turns out that the package was delivered by courier. They were given cash in an envelope with instructions on the box. They didn't think anything of it, because similar envelopes and packages had been sent in this way before. They assumed it was from the same individual," Jim stated.

"The same individual? So this could be the guy we're looking for?" Donald asked.

"Not really sure if it is a male or female. No signature was required."

"I still don't get that, Jim. I mean, in most circumstances, the shipping companies, whether US Postal Service or a private delivery service, need to confirm the contents of the package and its sender," Teddy Warner added.

"I know. I think we should personally speak to some of the tellers down there. This is a serious situation and right now, the government has agents looking into a domestic terrorist attack as precaution. There's nothing specific that proves the same individual that did this is also the killer," Jim said.

"Something else isn't sitting right with me," Donald said.

"What's that?" Teddy asked.

"As I glanced at the return address label, I'm not certain, but it looked familiar."

"You saw the return address?" Teddy asked.

"I saw a logo. I can't be positive that it's the same, but the thought has been bothering me for days."

"Why is that?" Jim asked.

"Well, a few months back, I received an anonymous letter threatening my involvement in the affordable housing construction. I didn't think much of it, because the board and other members received a bunch of negative responses from the public. You know, people who feared that their property values would go down and crime rate would go up, just because of the affordable housing. That's why we got the approval for the land outside of town. The nearest properties are a couple of miles."

"Did you ever investigate who the people who threatened you and the board were?" Jim asked.

"No. I didn't really take it as threats and more of displeasure. Even with the new development being approved, we've gotten some unhappy responses," Donald said.

"Could you give us copies of those letters and anything else you may have from the last project?" Jim asked.

"Why? Do you think this has something to do with the case?" Donald asked.

"We leave no rock unturned, Donald. I think Sandman is going to want to know about this information, too." Jim pulled out his cell phone.

* * * *

Grace was talking to her mom on the secure line. The men had made it clear that she was not to indicate where she was staying.

"Are you sure that you're okay?" her mom asked. "That man Sandman is so big and serious."

Grace chuckled.

"He fits the image of bodyguard well, Mom. He's great and the accommodations are very nice. I just want this over with sooner than later."

"Maybe the detectives will find out something about that poor young woman they found. She worked for the town you know and was just a few houses down from John and the boys. They are really upset."

"What? When did you find this out?" Grace asked.

"This morning. Frank informed us and now the news is broadcasting the discovery. That poor girl's parents must be so distraught. I asked John to find out if I can visit them and offer any assistance."

Grace had an uneasy feeling in her gut. She wondered why Sandman hadn't told her. Was that what the call this morning was about? This was exactly why she didn't trust people. He asked for her trust, yet he wasn't keeping her up to date with the case at all.

"Who was she, Mom? Do you have a name?"

"Catherine Reyas. She was twenty-four years old. Had a great job in town and her father is Milton Reyas of Reyas Developing. They're pretty well known in the community."

She spoke to her mom for a little while longer then said good-bye. She couldn't help the uneasy feelings she had as she closed up the cell phone.

She stared at it a moment. In that second she realized that there was no one to call and she wasn't allowed anyway.

"Are you finished with the phone?" Sandman asked as he entered the room. She stared at him and knew she looked angry. She was angry.

"Here." She tossed it to him and he caught it then gave her a look.

"Is everything all right?" he asked and she stood up.

"Why don't you tell me."

"What's wrong?" he asked as Big Jay and Duke walked into the room. Both were holding papers.

"I understand that I'm under protection here and that my location cannot be jeopardized, but this is my life, my future that is at stake. I expect you to keep me abreast of the progress in this investigation," she stated with her hands on her hips.

He placed the phone back onto the clip on his hip. His narrow waist was in great contrast to his wide, muscular shoulders.

She couldn't help the skitter of goose bumps that traveled over her skin from absorbing the sight of his body.

"There's no update in the case."

"Really?" she snapped back and took a step forward.

"Catherine Reyas?"

His eyes widened then became dark and unemotional.

"What is it that you want to know, Grace?"

"I want to know everything that is happening in this investigation."

"No," he replied.

She widened her eyes in shock. "That's not the answer I want."

"Tough. This is how it is. You are on a need-to-know basis because we are the investigators. When you need to know something or we feel it's important for you to know about, then we'll discuss it."

"Go to hell, Sandman." She turned around prepared to walk away but instead abruptly turned back to find Sandman standing there with his arms crossed in front of his chest glaring at her. Duke and Big Jay looked none the better.

"Grace, you've been through a lot in the last few days. You need some recouping time. All of this stuff is too much for one woman to handle. We want you to feel safe," Big Jay said.

"Feel safe? Too much to handle? How dare you try to control my life and the information I get privy to? You do not own me. I'm the one that held her pictures in my hand. I held a lock of her hair, not you," she said, feeling herself lose her cool. She felt entirely frustrated.

When Sandman touched her arm, she pulled it away. "Who do you think you are? What gives you the right to keep me out of this?"

"We're your protectors. I'll decide what you need to know." He reached up and touched her cheek, cupping it with the palm of his hand.

He took a step closer to her and stared down into her eyes. "This is a complicated situation. My brothers and I are working with a lot of investigators to find the one responsible. We can't and we won't keep you updated about every bit of progress or failure we achieve. That is not your position or role in this. You're supposed to feel safe and protected not upset or hurt."

"Well I don't feel safe. I'll never feel safe whether he's caught or not. It's how my life is now." She heard the defeated tone of her voice.

Sandman pulled her into a hug against his chest.

"It just feels that way, Grace. Those emotions will pass when this is all done." She shook her head and began to push away from him.

She looked up into his eyes. They held no emotion and were dark and skeptical.

"You don't know. You don't understand."

He pulled her tighter, making her gasp in surprise. She instinctively wrapped her arms around his waist and absorbed the bulk and solidity of his body.

"I know better than you think."

She didn't have a clue what that comment meant but before she did something stupid like ask him or hug him, his phone rang.

* * * *

Grace had a terrible headache. Dinner was spent alone as the men were busy on the phone and computers. Something was happening, but they still didn't let her in on it. She supposed that they had a point. She wasn't law enforcement. Plus, whatever information they were discovering, they didn't feel she could assist with. She was leaning her head back against the pillow on the couch when she heard the voice.

"Maybe you should head up to bed. Get a good night's rest. In the bathroom upstairs you'll find aspirin in the medicine cabinet," Sandman told her as she stared at him a moment. She hadn't even heard him approach. It was probably due to his military training. Her belly muscles tightened. Instead of being annoyed she was aroused. She stood up from the couch.

"Thanks for everything, Sandman. I appreciate your sacrifices. I'm sure it's hard letting a stranger into your home." She saw a change in his eyes but then quickly it vanished.

"We're not strangers anymore. Remember you're in my personal protective custody program and I did act as your body armor twice."

She wondered if he was flirting or trying to make up for earlier. She wasn't certain and figured the best thing to do was go to bed and hope that tomorrow was better.

"Good night."

She turned and walked out of the room

* * * *

Sandman stayed up a little longer, wondering about Grace, her life and why the killer was so interested in her. He worked on his computer trying to still find a link or some clue he may have missed. His brothers were doing the same and trying to find the connection between the murdered women and the other murders that had been taking place in Houston. It seemed to him that those three victims were connected to the community and building corps for the affordable housing project. Right now it all seemed like coincidence. Nothing concrete linked these people.

As Sandman went over the pictures of the other female victims he could see the same resemblances. All the victims had brown hair, were tall, very beautiful, like models. They all had very good professions or at least high-paying professions and were single.

He looked over the crime scenes again, noting that the killer both strangled his victims and stabbed them with a very sharp, long tool of some kind.

He restrained them by using rope or handcuffs. It seemed like he victimized them in one location then dumped their bodies somewhere else. He had a place he liked to perform his acts and Sandman felt it needed to be nearby. Perhaps he had more than one place considering he had killed in other states.

"Going over the pictures again?" Big Jay asked as he sat down by the island in the kitchen.

Sandman ran his fingers through his hair as Duke walked in next.

"I can't look at these anymore. You know what I see?" he asked as he turned the laptop toward Duke and Big Jay. They both looked at the collage of pictures. He watched Big Jay's eyes widen then darken in anger.

"Grace?"

"Exactly. They look very similar to Grace. They're professional, too, just like she is," Sandman added.

"Shit." Big Jay stood up and paced the room. "She could be the main victim he's after, Sandman. He'll want to find her and have her."

"I still believe there is a connection to the affordable housing. That information Jim sent us from Donald has clues in it. Could this guy who harassed the builders and Donald be the same person who is killing these women?" Duke asked.

"That's what we need to find out. I asked Jim and Teddy to check out the members of the fundraising committee associated with Reyas Developing. Maybe that will give us some insight."

* * * *

Grace lay sleeping, tossing and turning as the day's events replayed in her mind. She was frantic and running for her life as the killer began chasing her.

In her dreams she saw him, without a face, but he was mocking her, calling her names as he held her sister Clara by the throat.

Grace was calling out her sister's name as she watched the killer stab Clara multiple times. She watched, unable to move a muscle as the killer plunged the knife into Clara's body. He turned to look at Grace. *"You're next."*

Grace was screaming, kicking, and punching as the killer attacked her in her dreams. She couldn't get away from him. He was too strong.

* * * *

From the other room Sandman could hear Grace's screams and

rushed into her room, gun drawn and ready.

His brothers were on his heels as they infiltrated the bedroom, too.

He was in soldier mode as he scanned the area, zeroed in on a half-dressed Grace tossing and turning on the bed. Big Jay and Duke checked the windows and the bathroom then joined Sandman by the bed. Sandman knew she was having a nightmare as Grace continued to toss and turn, kicking and fighting in her sleep while moaning. The blankets were all over the floor and Grace was wearing a tight V-neck T-shirt and short pink shorts that more closely resembled underwear.

Sandman put down his gun and sat on the bed next to her. She was hysterically crying now, calling out her sister Clara's name. His heart pounded in his chest and he felt the tightness. It shocked him to care like this and feel so much for a complete stranger. He looked at his brothers, the scowls on their faces as they stood at the edge of the bed watching.

"Grace...Grace, wake up. It's okay. It's just a dream." Sandman spoke to her softly. It took a few attempts, but then she finally opened her eyes. Startled, she sat up in bed, put her hands over her face, and continued to cry. Sandman pulled her into his arms.

She was trembling and sobbing. She had been so strong all week. Even after the reminders of Clara's murder on TV and the blast in Donald's office, she had remained strong and composed. He had taken her away from her family, her home, and didn't even tell her where she was going. He felt terrible for her as he held her tight and whispered softly against her ear and neck.

* * * *

Grace pulled away suddenly realizing she was wearing hardly any clothes and had lost it, emotionally, in front of Sandman.

She tried to get up but he held her still.

"It's okay, Grace. You've been through a great ordeal. Don't be afraid to let it out."

Grace held on to his forearms, as she stared at his bare muscular chest.

He sat there so close to her wearing only boxer shorts, with his well-toned, muscular legs showing. He was masculine and rugged looking with a light shadow of a beard.

He locked gazes with her and she shyly turned away, afraid of the arousal and the attraction she felt, only to notice the two large figures, standing at the bottom of the bed. She gasped at the sight. Big Jay and Duke were there as well. They wore only dark boxers and each held a gun in their hands.

"Are you okay, darling?" Big Jay asked while his eyes roamed over her body. She felt her nipples pebble and her pussy clench from their stares. Closing her legs tighter as she knelt on the bed, she began to move to the side and get up. Sandman stopped her.

"Don't pull away," he whispered then placed his hand over her waist to the other side of her hip. Slowly she lowered back down to the bed as he pulled her closer to his side. He was leaning over her, her head flat on the pillow, her chest heaving up and down as he stared into her eyes. When he moved his hand to her cheek and caressed the wet tears away, she closed her eyes and felt her body quiver. She had obviously been crying very hard. Even her belly quivered.

"Please, Sandman," she whispered in a shaky voice, but she didn't get a response. Not until she opened her eyes right before his lips touched hers.

She absorbed the sensations that attacked her skin, her body, and her soul. His strong hands held her face between them as his tongue explored her mouth. She returned the kisses, turned on, set aflame to the aura of his sex appeal, big muscles and heavy body that now leaned over her smaller frame. She wanted to taste more of him, accept the attraction and desire burning through her bloodstream as she reached up to run fingers through his hair.

He moved his lips off of hers and trailed kisses against the corner of her mouth, her jaw, and then her neck. When he maneuvered his hips between her thighs, she opened for him, instantly feeling the large, hard cock against her needy pussy.

"You taste and feel incredible, Grace. I don't know what the fuck I'm doing," he admitted, acknowledging to her that he was feeling just as out of control as she was. Then she felt the bed dip to her right.

Large, thick fingers caressed the hair from her cheeks as she turned from Sandman's fierce expression toward Duke. Her heart hammered inside of her chest. She knew he and Big Jay were there, too. God, how aroused and excited that made her feel. Was she so desperate for love and attention that she wanted all three men to fuck her?

"Don't be afraid, angel. We've been pussyfooting around this attraction all week. Since the moment you walked into the house I've wanted you," Duke admitted then leaned forward to kiss her cheek before he took her mouth fully.

Simultaneously Sandman caressed her left arm and moved it above her head while Duke explored her mouth. She moaned against his tongue as Sandman sat up and caressed her thighs then her belly, her ribs, until finally cupping her breasts.

She thrust her hips forward and moaned into Duke's tongue strokes while Sandman squeezed her breasts.

As Duke released her lips, she panted for breath, locked gazes with him, and lost her soul as he smiled. "Oh God, you're beautiful," she whispered and he chuckled.

"You're the beautiful one, darling," Duke said and Sandman took that moment to pinch her nipple.

"Oh," she moaned.

"Grace?" She heard Big Jay's voice and saw him standing by the side of the bed. He placed his weapon down beside his brother's and stared down at her. He was huge. His upper chest big and bulky, filled with dips like a sculpture.

"We want you, darling. All three of us," Big Jay said in such a serious tone she was instantly stimulated and a little scared.

These men were large and they represented things she feared. They had power, they were law enforcement, ex-military, resourceful, and so much more. They could truly break her heart into a million pieces that she would never be able to fix.

Sandman caressed her cheek.

"Don't look so scared. We're not going to hurt you, darling. This is completely new to us, too."

"We've been on our own, alone for years, Grace. Ain't no other women been with the three of us together. Ain't no other woman we've ever all wanted together," Duke added.

"I am scared, but I don't think I could stop these feelings I have or this need burning inside of me. This is so not typical. Three men and one woman? How can it work? What about jealousy or what if you decide you don't want me anymore. My heart isn't normal, it's broken." She felt the tear roll down her cheek. Sandman eased his body down hers.

"Shhh, baby, please don't think that way. Trust us, we're taking a chance, too," Duke said then slowly kissed her lips. She reached up and cupped his cheek with her hand. Then with her other hand she reached for Big Jay. When his large hand clasped her much smaller one, she felt the desire and the need for them to make love to her. Then Sandman kissed her bare belly.

"Let us love you, woman, the way you deserve to be loved."

Her heart soared with desire and excitement. She nodded her head and hoped that she wasn't making a huge mistake.

* * * *

Sandman smiled then made his way down her belly, taking her skimpy pajama shorts along with him.

As his eyes locked on her pretty bare pussy, his cock stood up at attention staking a claim.

"So soft and nicely trimmed. Just the way I like pussy," he whispered, allowing his warm breath to collide with her glistening folds.

"Oh God, Sandman," she said until Big Jay took her mouth and claimed his woman.

Grace lifted her torso, giving Sandman better access to her pussy. He used his fingers to spread her lips and zeroed in on her clitoris. He inhaled her scent and saw her pussy leak as his brothers explored her upper body. He needed to bring her pleasure. He wanted to hear her call his name and his brothers' names in the heat of sex. The craving was incredible as he licked her from anus to pussy. She shook under him and he maneuvered his fingers into her cunt, pressing into her in slow even strokes. With every in and out thrust she moaned into Big Jay's mouth and eased her thighs wider.

The sound of her juices covering his fingers stimulated his senses as Sandman lowered his chest between her thighs and replaced his fingers with his mouth and tongue.

* * * *

Big Jay just couldn't seem to get enough of Grace's mouth. He explored her with his tongue, swallowing her moans as Sandman pleasured her down below. He knew that Duke was sucking on her breast and teasing her nipples as she thrust her hips then her chest upward. Pulling slowly from his mouth, she gasped for air then shook underneath them as her first orgasm hit her.

"Oh God, I can't take it." She rolled her head side to side against the pillow. Big Jay laughed.

"Darlin', you got yourself three very hungry, experienced lovers. You gonna take it and then you gonna take some more," he teased her and smiled as the blush exploded across her cheeks and chest.

"Take this off. I want to see all of you," Duke said as he pulled her tank top up and over her head with Big Jay's assistance. Big Jay licked his lips.

"Hot damn, woman, I knew you were built well. You're so conservative the way you dress," he complimented as he lowered his mouth to take a taste of the perky pink nipple. She placed her hand against his head, holding him to her breast and making him desire her even more.

"She sure is perfect," Duke added then licked across her other nipple. Big Jay locked gazes with Duke and they smiled before they aroused their woman even more.

* * * *

"You on the pill, honey?" Sandman asked as he sat up and began to pull off his boxers.

"Oh God, you're huge," she said and he chuckled.

"Baby, I'll fit. You were made for me, and this pussy is nice and wet." He pressed a thumb to her clit and she thrust her hips upward.

"Yes, I'm safe. I'm on the pill."

"We're safe, too, baby. It's been forever," Duke admitted to her and Sandman felt that bit of something different inside of him. It scared him momentarily as he tried ignoring the meaning of his brother's words and what this first ever ménage session would come to mean to all of them.

"Oh God, please do something," she begged of him as Big Jay pulled her nipple between his teeth and Duke nibbled on a sensitive part of her neck.

"Yes, ma'am," Sandman said then slowly pushed between her wet folds attempting to penetrate.

"Fuck, baby, you're so tight."

"Oh please, oh God, you're so big." She moaned.

"I'll fit, honey, just relax. Come on now and let me in, sugar." He tried to push slowly into her to take his time but Grace had other ideas as she locked her legs around his hips and pushed upward. He pressed down and into her thrusting all the way and making her moan in pleasure.

"Hot damn she looks beautiful with a cock deep inside of her," Big Jay said as he lay on his side and caressed her cheek. Duke did the same on the other side. The four of them were together, connected from the start of this thing, whatever it turned out to be.

Sandman eased his way out then thrust forward again. He repeated the strokes.

Staring down into Grace's eyes, he sensed the connection, the deep meaning of being inside her like this and making love to her. He sat up, his cock hard as a steel rod moving in and out of her cunt.

"You are gorgeous, baby. Your body is perfect. I told you that I'd fit." He pushed into her again.

"Oh, that feels so good. God, I can't believe how incredible I feel," she admitted.

"You look incredible, too," Duke said then took her arm and held it above her head before taking as much of her left breast into his mouth as he could.

Grace squealed and then Big Jay took her other arm, raised it above her head, and moved it back against the headboard as he took her other breast between his teeth. He pulled on her nipple and the sight drove Sandman wild.

"Fuck, baby, you're hot. I love watching my brothers play with your breasts while I fuck this pussy." He thrust into her harder, faster, and Grace tried to reach out to touch him.

"Keep those hands on that headboard," he ordered and his demanding tone aroused her body. He felt her cream lubricate his cock as he gripped her hips and plunged deeper, faster into her. Over and over again he penetrated as he grabbed her hips and allowed his body to release everything he had into her. Grace took it all, while she moaned and thrust back against him until she screamed her release. Her mouth opened wide, and she pushed her breasts and her hips upward as she came. "I'm there, baby. I'm right there with you." Sandman lost his ability to hold off as he climaxed, filling her with his seed.

* * * *

Grace was shaking from the aftereffects of the best orgasm she'd ever had. She knew that having three men make love to her together was responsible for her actions and her body's obvious display of satisfaction. Everything about them was a turn-on. Their large hands, their big muscles, intricate tattoos, and holy shit their cocks. She gasped as Sandman pulled out of her and that snake of a cock he had kept going and going until finally it fell to the bed. She was amazed that he fit inside of her. But then he kissed her lips as he jumped up and off of her. Big Jay removed his boxers and took Sandman's place. She looked down and knew she was in serious trouble. Maybe this was really why they called him Big Jay?

She felt her cheeks blush and then all three men smiled at her.

"You look sexy as damn hell, woman. Your hands are gripping that headboard, your breasts are full and covered with patches of love marks, and fuck it if you think I can go slow. You're too damn beautiful." Big Jay lifted her thighs up over his thighs and stroked her pussy with his fingers.

He pressed two digits into her slowly, arousing her body, preparing it for penetration.

"I feel so out of control," she admitted and he smiled down at her.

"You're perfect." He pulled one finger from her cunt and caressed it over her puckered hole. She nearly shot off the bed but Duke and Sandman were there to keep her down.

"Whoa, sweetheart, are you okay?" Duke asked as he caressed her lower lip with his finger.

"He, he…" She couldn't say it.

Big Jay did it again. His wet finger moved over her anus as his other finger stroked her cunt.

"Oh!" she moaned.

"What's he doing to you, baby?" Sandman asked while tweaking her nipple.

Big Jay chuckled then pressed both digits into her. One in her pussy and one into her anus. She moaned as she pressed down taking his fingers deeper. "Yeah, that's what I thought," he said then leaned down and took her mouth in a deep, sensual kiss. He pumped his fingers into her and she released the headboard to grab onto his shoulders as she kissed him back. Big Jay felt her thighs widen and her hips pumped harder against his fingers. He released her lips.

"Somebody likes it naughty, huh?" he teased as he pulled his fingers from her body then adjusted his cock against her pussy and pushed forward. She grabbed onto his shoulders while moaning and counterthrusting to his invasion. He collapsed against her, not fully allowing his weight to be released on her. He'd crush the poor woman in an instant. She was petite, delicate, and so damn sexy. He couldn't hold back his desire to claim her as his woman. He'd never felt like this before and it scared him.

She climbed his body higher, wrapping her thighs against his hipbones as he stroked her deeply. They were entwined together as tight as could be when he cupped her ass cheeks and pressed his face against her shoulder and neck, penetrating her as deeply as humanly possible. He inhaled her scent, the smell of her perfume, the way her hands felt as she dug her nails and her heels into his skin. "Harder, Jay," she pleaded. He adjusted his fingers and pressed one to her puckered hole.

"Yes, oh that burns." She moaned and he pressed deeper. His finger was in her ass and his cock deep into her pussy as he turned his head and whispered into her ear.

"I love being inside of you. I want to fuck every hole, baby, claim you as ours forever."

He felt her body jerk then shiver as she came, lubricating his cock and finger right before he exploded with her.

They were both panting for breath as he licked her throat and made his way to her lips. When he locked gazes with her angelic face and she smiled, he knew he lost his heart to her forever.

* * * *

Duke was lying down beside Grace and Jay. He rolled to his side and glided a fingernail along her breast making her shiver. Jay kissed her one more time then looked at his brother. Grace followed his line of sight and stared at Duke.

She watched him move his hand down his body and fist his cock.

"I've got something for you, honey. Come on over here and let me taste you."

Big Jay kissed her lips then her nose before he slowly pulled from her body. He got up and walked to the bathroom. "Come on now, don't be shy, woman," Duke whispered, and she blushed a beautiful shade of pink.

Slowly she rolled to her belly and began to straddle his waist when he lifted her up so fast. She grabbed the headboard as her pussy landed over his mouth, right where Duke wanted it.

"Nice move, bro," Big Jay stated as Duke dove in for a taste of his gorgeous woman. He couldn't wait to touch her, to stroke her pussy with his hard cock, and he was definitely hard. Grabbing ahold of her ass as he plunged his tongue repeatedly into her wet cunt, he felt her curves. He massaged her cheeks, spread them then held her hips. When she reached back with one hand to grab ahold of his cock, he felt the fire rush through his entire body and he nipped her clit. Grace screamed a small release and he licked her clean. Lifting her up in the air by her hips, he stared up into her eyes. Hers were as big as saucers until he moved her down and over his shaft. Once she took him inside, her eyes closed and he thrust up into her.

"Damn you're strong." She panted with her face against his neck. Duke smiled to himself, glad she was impressed with his abilities thus far in bed. He wanted to please her. It was a first for him. Not that any woman he bedded ever complained, but this was different. It had been a long time coming and now that he had Grace, he was going to give it his all. Spreading his thighs wider, he began to thrust upward, while he used the palm of his other hand over her lower back and ass to keep her in place.

The sound of her soft purrs of pleasure fed his ego as he continued to pump up and down at record speed.

Grace lifted up, grabbing ahold of his shoulders as she countered his thrusts. It seemed his woman was demonstrating some act of independence and he loved it.

"That's it, baby, ride him hard. Let me see that wet pussy smack against his cock," Big Jay said as he pulled on one of Grace's nipples. She squealed and continued to ride Duke as fast as she could.

"You're so gorgeous, baby. I love your breasts, your toned arms and thighs." Duke cupped her breasts and countered upward to her downward thrusts.

"I love her ass," Sandman stated then swiped a finger down her back and over the tight bud.

"Oh God, you guys are crazy," she said.

"You think we're crazy?" Big Jay asked as he leaned up and nipped at her shoulder.

"Or maybe this is crazy," Sandman said, taking position behind her and touching her. Duke didn't need to ask what his brother was doing. He could tell by the way Grace tightened up then closed her eyes with her lips parted that Sandman was playing with her ass.

"Ever have a man play with your ass?" Sandman asked her.

She shook her head wildly from side to side.

"Good." He helped her move lower so she would be chest to chest with Duke.

"Look at me, baby," Duke told her and she slowly opened her eyes. She definitely stole his heart with that look of passion, hesitation, and innocence. She was young and she was exceptional. How the hell did he and his brothers get so lucky?

* * * *

Grace could not believe how high-strung she was or how experienced and sexy Duke, Sandman, and Big Jay were. Three exceptionally dominant, sexy men who individually could rock her world were currently turning her into whatever they wanted. She didn't care what. All she knew was that she wanted more of them. She wanted to kiss, lick, suck, and explore their bodies and make herself theirs. She wanted to love them so good and so perfectly that there would never be another woman in their lives who came even close to her. Silly, but these possessive feelings struck her like a bolt of lightning. They had her and she was ready and willing to do or try anything with them including anal sex.

At that moment Sandman pushed a finger into her anus making her moan. She was so wet that Duke's cock was slipping in and out of her pussy. She was moaning as her body tightened up. Duke grabbed her, pulling her down and kissing her as they both exploded together. Sandman pulled his finger from her ass and gave it a slap, snapping her out of her sexual daze.

"Hey." She turned toward him with her face plastered against Duke's chest. Duke was caressing her back and her ass.

"Hey, yourself," Sandman said.

"You slapped my ass," she replied.

"You have a great ass, Grace." Sandman got up from the bed and walked to the bathroom.

"Sure do, sugar. Can't wait to get me some of that ass," Big Jay stated then winked.

"Me either," Duke whispered as he stroked a finger down the crevice between her ass cheeks. She closed her eyes and held in her excitement.

Son of a bitch, I can't wait to let you three try it.

Chapter 9

Maggie Sheridan lay handcuffed to a pole in some abandoned underground tunnel, her own handcuffs no less, and as a cop she should have been more careful, more cautious. But she wasn't and now her life was in jeopardy. She couldn't see a thing and the tape that the killer placed over her eyes was pinching her lids and giving her an instant headache. She could feel her eyelashes and eyelids sticking to the tape. She was perspiring, practically dripping with sweat from unsuccessfully trying to fight off her attacker and from pure fear. His voice and every move he made echoed in the wet tunnel that reeked of garbage and decaying roadkill.

She knew the man before her was the killer, the one everyone was looking for and she recognized the man's voice. She knew she'd heard it somewhere before.

She wondered if John knew how much she loved him. She never told him and she was so busy acting tough, trying to be so damn unaffected by him that he probably didn't love her, too. The fault would be her own, all brought on by the pressure of her job, being a respected female officer, and being sure everyone knew she earned her position and she hadn't used the weapon between her legs to obtain it. John respected her and valued her feelings as he hid their relationship from everyone. That was the way she wanted it and now she may never see him again.

The killer approached her now and she felt the sharp object lightly cut her chest.

He's going to kill me, just like he killed the others. I know what he did to them. Oh God, John, I love you and I'm sorry.

* * * *

He held the ice pick in his hand, and glided it along the lovely white skin of his latest adventure. He laughed at his victim. A beautiful young cop and girlfriend of SWAT team member John Thompson. This was a special kill. It would enter him into a whole new category. He could see the headlines in the newspapers already. "COP KILLER."

He chuckled at the thought and stood tall, filled with pride and assurance.

No one can catch me. No one knows who I am. I live among them, socialize along with them, and they haven't a clue. But you've all been so tight-lipped about where Grace is hiding out. Perhaps this will send a clear message to return her to me.

He was confident he would get away with this kill as well. But most importantly it sent an even stronger message. Especially to Grace and the investigator that whisked her off to hide her from him.

"I will have you, Grace. I will go after you any way I can," the killer said out loud as Maggie Sheridan struggled to free herself.

His original plan had changed so much over the past few years.

What was once his motivation, his hobby, had now become his purpose in life, his meaning for living. Getting away with the first dozen kills gave him confidence and power. *I'm so fucking smart. My mind is amazing. My plans of attack, to evade capture, to plant evidence are so fucking awesome.* He felt his blood pumping through his veins. He sensed that need to finish this act and move on to his next strategic move. He wanted Grace so badly now, he could taste her. She had become his obsession and when he thought about how close he had gotten to her so many years ago, it killed him inside to think he had lost his opportunity. She left, but he was always aware of where she lived, who she was with and that she would one day return.

"With love to Grace," he whispered as he grabbed Maggie by her hair and kissed her, biting her lip.

She was pleading for him to stop, and the killer enjoyed this part of the game, the fantasy. He loved to hear them beg and scream from the pleasure that he brought them.

"I am your master, you are my slave. Do as I say before you go to the grave."

* * * *

John was in Donald's office. He was telling him about his relationship with Maggie.

Although they had only been dating a couple of months, he was unsure whether or not they should continue seeing one another.

After all he was a SWAT Team Commander and she was a patrol officer studying for the sergeant's exam.

People were already starting to talk and he wasn't sure he was up for the hassle.

"John, she's a great woman, and so what, that she works in the department. It's not like you're both in SWAT team or working side by side," Donald said as he looked at John from across his desk.

He thought of Sarah's kids like they were his own. They had become so close and he was honored when her sons came to him for advice.

"I know that, Donald, but I'm not sure she's right for me. Take yesterday for example. She didn't return any of my calls and her roommate said she never came home last night. I know she just broke up with her boyfriend only a few days before we started dating. I'm getting too old for this cat-and-mouse shit. I want commitment, maybe get married, and stop living the bachelor life." John paced back and forth in front of Donald's desk.

Donald got up, walked around his desk, and put his hand on John's shoulder.

"I'm happy to hear you're ready to settle down, John, and maybe Maggie's not the right one, but don't jump to conclusions. Find out the truth from her then move on if you have to," he told him and John agreed.

"I'm glad I have you to talk to, Donald. You know you're like family right?" John said as Donald smiled.

"Have you heard anything from your sister or Sandman yet?" Donald asked as he leaned against his desk.

"Not since yesterday. She said she was safe but no details. I hope to hear from her soon. My mom's freaking out and Eric's been busy with work so Aunt Betsy and Aunt Grace have been keeping Mom company."

"Well Eric does have a business to run and the promotion for this November's upcoming elections. I'm sure Aunt Betsy has brought along plenty of those delicious blackberry preserves she makes. I may just have to stop by and visit," Donald said and John laughed.

"You should, Donald. I know my mom would love to see you," John told him before he left the office.

Chapter 10

Grace climbed into the shower and let the hot water cascade over her body. When she closed her eyes, all she could see were three strikingly handsome men. She smiled to herself. She felt happy. As ridiculous as this was, to feel this way while her life remained in jeopardy was insane. She smiled as she began shampooing her hair, rinsed it, then added conditioner. As she started lathering up the soap, she remembered last night, well early this morning. Then the memory of her nightmare came rushing back. In an instant she felt the fear grip her heart. She rinsed the conditioner and felt the tears roll down her cheeks. She wiped them away with the water. Why was she crying? Why, after being so strong and willing away the fear and the memories of her sister's murder, was she crying now?

Grace turned off the faucet, stepped out of the shower and wrapped the towel around her hair and then another one around her body. The mirror was fogged up, as she stood there frozen in place. She thought about Sandman, Big Jay, and Duke. She longed for their company, their embrace. That was what took her mind off of these morbid thoughts. She gripped the bathroom counter and lowered her head.

He's out there. He continues to kill, to cause fear, and make the public worry about their loved ones' safety. He's looking for me. What does he want from me? Wasn't it enough that he took my sister?

The tears rolled down her cheeks and she felt the hands on her shoulders. She screamed, turned abruptly and shoved at the person.

"Whoa, Grace, it's me." *Sandman.*

She went from feeling frightened to embarrassed so quickly she felt dizzy. She leaned back against the wall, closed her eyes, and tried to calm her breathing. Sandman placed one hand over her shoulder against the wall behind her and one against her right hipbone.

"What is it, baby? Why are you so scared?"

She couldn't open her eyes and face him. Sandman was strong, a soldier, a man to be reckoned with. She on the other hand was weak, defeated, and so overstimulated with emotions and anxiety she didn't have an answer.

He caressed her cheek. He towered over her, his size even more dramatic with her standing barefoot in only a towel and him fully dressed, boots and all.

"Relax, baby, and just breathe. Listen to my voice and know that I'm here to protect you."

God, he was so amazing. She would die if anything ever happened to him and his brothers. One night of lovemaking and she was so attached and possessive. She needed to put some space between them. She needed slow, not fast. Her mind needed to catch up with her body and its wants and desires.

"Please, Sandman, just let me be. I need to handle this alone." She opened her eyes, knowing they were filled with tears and emotions. His deep blue eyes bore into hers, and when he licked his lips then stared at hers, she knew he wouldn't comply with her wishes. In an instant he was kissing her and she was kissing him back.

* * * *

Grace's fear and need to put space between him and her was not so easily accepted by Sandman. He came upstairs to check on her but mostly because he missed her. Wasn't that a fucking crazy insane thing? He was going to scare her if he came off as immediately possessive. Even his brothers wanted to visit her in the shower, but they knew this whole ménage thing was new to all of them. They decided that they would slow things down as much as they could handle. Grace was going through enough emotional turmoil and they didn't want to add to her anxiety. It seemed they were too late. As quickly as the thought hit his mind, he reacted and kissed her. God, she tasted like heaven and sunshine.

When she wrapped her arms around his shoulders and returned the kisses, he felt triumphant as well as needy. He had been a man with a heart of steel. Many called him cold, unemotional and heartless after he returned from war. He didn't give a damn. He had experienced so much death, violence, and desert heat to last him a lifetime. So what, that he never dated or let his emotions show? Grace touched him like no other and he couldn't believe how his body, his soul craved more.

Caressing his hands along her thighs, he lifted her up. She straddled his hips as he pressed her hard against the bathroom wall. The feel of her fingernails pressing against his scalp as she fought for control of the kiss made his dick hard and desire strengthen.

He tore his lips from hers so he could pull back and remove the towel from her body.

"Fucking beautiful. I want you, Grace. I want you right here, right now."

Her eyes still glistened with unshed tears but the emotion changed. No longer looking fearful and defeated, they shined with passion and hunger. "Yes," she whispered and began to pull his shirt up and off of him.

"Hold on tight," he said and felt her legs lock around his hips, her arms around his shoulders then her lips and teeth sucked against his neck.

He wanted to touch her everywhere but he also needed to get his pants off. Sandman ran the palms of his hands along her toned thighs then to her calves that were tight against his ribs. He somehow undid his pants and pushed them down as she continued to lick and kiss his skin from neck, to shoulder, to chest. She dipped lower, taking a nipple into her mouth and pulling.

"Fuck, Grace." He pressed her harder against the wall, aligned his cock with her wet pussy, and shoved in to the hilt. Her head fell back, her chin tilted up as she gasped, and he immediately began to stroke her cunt.

"Mine. All fucking mine." He dipped and thrust, dipped and thrust, wanting his cock to reach her womb and seal the deal that she belonged to him, she belonged to the Sandstone brothers.

"Harder, yes, like that Sandman, so good." She cheered him on which only made him grow harder and wilder to satisfy their hunger. The sloshing sound filled the room and she screamed her release as he ground deeper, pelvis to pelvis. He spread her ass cheeks, trying to go even deeper. He could feel his balls against the crack of her ass. She was so fucking wet, so needy for his cock.

"Yes, so good, Grace. So fucking perfect." He slammed into her in three quick strokes then grunted as he exploded inside of her. Breathing heavy against her neck, he absorbed the scent of her skin, the delicate flesh of her femininity and relished in the fact that they were one.

Her fingers ran through his hair and his heart came alive in recognition that she was the one and the only for him. She was his amazing Grace, his everything and he would protect her with his life until his last breath.

Chapter 11

Grace and Sandman headed downstairs, and when she entered the kitchen, she thought she would find Big Jay and Duke, but they weren't there.

The disappointment must have shown on her face as Sandman hugged her from behind then bent down to whisper into her ear.

"Big Jay went into town and Duke is doing some computer work in the office. I need to make some calls. Can you hang out in the library for a bit?"

She turned in his arms, placed her hands up on his shoulders, and smiled at him. "How about I look through that freezer of yours and find something to make for dinner. I'll cook tonight."

He raised his eyebrows at her and she wasn't certain if he assumed that she couldn't cook. She squinted her eyebrows up at him. "What? You don't think I know how to?"

He ran his hands down her back and over her ass, giving it a squeeze. "Honey, you have the body of a supermodel and you photograph them. I figured with your type of schedule, you probably eat out a bunch and order room service and nibble at fancy parties." She was surprised at his evaluation of her.

She pulled from his embrace and walked over to the freezer. She opened it up as she spoke to him.

"I'll have you know that I am a very good cook. You'll be impressed considering I order out all the time and nibble at fancy parties," she said sarcastically and he chuckled as he crossed his arms in front of his chest and stared at her. The man was a sexy god. She could totally imagine him in military fatigues and weapons with sand coming off his big, heavy military-issued boots as he stalked toward her. Her pussy leaked and she knew she had it bad. Licking her lower lip he followed her tongue with his eyes and she knew she had his complete attention.

"You can call me a domestic goddess. I'm that good." As she turned to look into the freezer and reached for some packages of chicken cutlets, he swooped in fast, pulled her into his arms, and kissed her hard on the mouth.

His dominant, sexy action caused her entire body to warm up and she knew she would never be the same again. Sandman, Duke, and Big Jay had a part of her she could never get back and hopefully nothing would take them away from her.

* * * *

Grace had put on a green tank top and khaki shorts along with a pair of white sneakers. She pulled her hair back into a ponytail then applied a little lip gloss to her lips and some light makeup to her eyes. When she was satisfied with her appearance, she puttered around the house a bit and became bored. She hadn't thought about work at all and hadn't remained in contact with her boss about her scheduled trip to Milan in another two weeks, and she was panicking. She opened up her laptop, plugging the wire into the phone jack to take a look at her e-mails.

"What the hell do you think you're doing?" Duke asked her as he rushed across the room, grabbing the laptop out of her hands.

"Duke, what's wrong with you? I was just checking my e-mail messages," she replied, shocked by his abruptness and anger.

"Did you go online yet? Did you open up any e-mail's?" He opened the laptop and saw the power wasn't even on yet.

Duke looked at her in a dead stare. It gave her the chills to see him like this, so fierce and concerned. What was the big deal? Then he appeared as if he felt bad for raising his voice and overreacting.

"I'm sorry, Grace, but you can't use your laptop. You can't open your e-mails. Not on this house line. You need a secure line. We can't take any chances. Remember, the killer is not stupid."

Duke still showed the anger in his voice.

"You really think he could track me down like that? Through my e-mail?"

"Remember, he's crazy, not stupid," Duke replied then ran his fingers through his hair. He seemed extra uptight. She didn't want to add to his anxiety. Whatever else was going on with him?

"You're right, Duke. I'm sorry. I just didn't think. It won't happen again." She stood up from the bed and tried to take the laptop away from him.

He held it there a moment and their eyes met.

"I believe that my brother told you it's our way only," he added in the same stern voice, wanting her to know how serious he was.

She let go of the laptop.

"Damn it, Duke, I said I'm sorry. I will have to check my e-mails and get in touch with my boss. I have a photo shoot in less than three weeks. I need the itinerary and I have a few other people I need to contact," she told him as she stepped back.

"You're not going to contact anyone, Grace, until we have a secure line. We're not taking any unnecessary chances. Your life, your profession is officially on hold," he told her with his face red with frustration. He was getting angrier with her.

"I have to contact my boss and the magazine I'll be working for or I could lose this job," she told him, not backing down from a fight. She wouldn't allow anyone to talk to her this way. Attraction or not, she would stand her ground.

"If the killer finds out where you are or where you're headed, then you won't make the photo shoot because you'll be dead," Duke said in a strong, harsh voice as he looked into her eyes then lightly dropped her laptop down on the bed.

Grace turned away from him, taking a deep breath and wanting to punch the man behind her. God, he made her so mad. He really got under her skin. The way he just spoke to her, controlling her, she wasn't used to that and she hated it as she released a long breath and tried to control her anger.

Duke called her name.

"Look at me, Grace." She slowly turned toward the commanding voice.

"Why don't you understand the danger you're in? I know you know the details of these murders and what the killer did to his victims. God, I want to shake you, you've got me so angry."

He pulled her closer and stared down into her eyes. Duke was ginormous. He was so much taller than her and big like his brothers. She swallowed hard. She knew that there was more to his upset. God, she had heard the details about the bodies, about what the killer had done. She swallowed hard. "I'm sorry, Duke. I feel so out of control of my life right now. I'm trying to hold on to what I have, in hopes that there's a future for me, with my profession, with my family."

"And what about us?" he asked, shocking her and sending her head in a whirlwind of emotions. She was going to respond but she didn't have an answer. Instead he swept down covering her mouth with his as he lifted her up against his chest. She kissed him back, ran her fingers through his hair, absorbing his strength and his masculinity as he held her so easily against him.

That kiss grew deeper as she straddled his waist and he lowered her to the bed. His weight, the thickness of his body pressed her deep against the soft mattress and comforter.

Pulling from her mouth, he trailed kisses against her throat, eliciting moans of pleasure from her lips. God, he made her feel so wild and needy.

"Oh God, Duke, you're so big and strong, I love the way you feel crushing me with your body. This is crazy."

He lifted up, taking her comment to heart and taking off some of his weight. He rested on his left elbow and forearm. "Crazy? You got that right, Grace. You drive me crazy. You get under my skin and make me want things and need things I've never wanted or felt before."

He was so damn serious, and before she could respond, he lifted up, undid her shorts, pulled them down her thighs and tossed them onto the rug. He divested her of her tank top and bra then pulled off his clothing so quickly she hadn't had time to absorb every bit of beauty before her.

"You're mine, always." He spread her thighs, aligned his cock with her pussy, and shoved into her. She gripped his shoulders, felt his need, the desperation to consummate their affection, their bond as one. Their gazes locked and he gripped her hands then placed them above her head in a controlling and dominantly sexy fashion that had her creaming and moaning for more.

"Yes!" she said loudly, and he thrust into her. He was relentless in his strokes. Over and over again he somehow moved deeper, penetrating her as she felt like his cock hit her womb and scraped against her inner muscles.

"Oh God, Duke, it's too much. I'm going to come."

"Fucking come then. Spread that cream all over my cock, baby. I want every bit of your sweetness." He lowered his head to her neck and shoulder, grabbed hold of her hips and ass, spread her cheeks, and thrust into her hard and fast. She was moaning and coming and shaking in excitement and overload.

"Duke!" She screamed his name and he thrust two more times before following suit, growling her name against her ear and neck as he exploded inside of her.

Duke kept kissing and licking her neck and ear, he lowered to her breasts then back up to her chin and lips while she continued to try and catch her breath.

"So perfect. Never like this, baby. Never like this." He licked across her nipple, pulling the tip and making her jump.

"Hey," she reprimanded. When they locked gazes, she saw a playful side of Duke she would love to bring out in him again and again.

"I could stay inside of you forever," he whispered.

She was about to respond when his cell phone rang.

"Yeah?" he said into the phone as he slowly pulled out of her.

He grabbed his boxers and pants as he walked toward the doorway trying to listen to the call. Grace started to get dressed as she watched him. He gave a few noncommittal yesses and no's then closed up the phone. He released a not so quiet sigh then turned to her. The smile on his face was forced.

"Sorry, baby, but I have to get back to work." He walked over to her, lifted her up so she was standing on the bed, and helped her get her shorts on. When he held her hips and looked down into her eyes, he smiled.

"Stay off the laptop. I'll have Big Jay set up a secure line and go over your e-mails with you."

"Go over them with me? I may need some privacy."

His expression once again was stern and that wall he kept up except when making love to her returned.

"No secrets. We need to be aware of everything and everyone in your life. Anything could become a potential threat." He kissed her lips then picked her up, placed her feet on the rug and caressed her chin before leaving the room.

Grace stood there after he left and couldn't help feeling as if she were in prison or perhaps were the one under surveillance and monitoring.

* * * *

Sometime later she recovered from the confrontation with Duke and headed downstairs to take some pictures. She figured doing something she enjoyed would help to stay positive and not get bored.

The men got caught up in some work and had given her a large yellow folder filled with hundreds of pictures of potential suspects. He told her to take her time looking at each one to see if any of them looked familiar. A couple of hours passed and she was unsuccessful. After a while she thought a lot of the pictures looked familiar. It was no use. She had looked at all of them and came up with squat. She washed her hands and face in the bathroom sink and applied some facial lotion. She felt rejuvenated and decided to go downstairs to start dinner.

There was a nice Bose radio in the kitchen and Grace turned it on.

The sounds of doo-wop and the old rock 'n' roll music echoed through the kitchen and Grace hummed along to the sounds of Jackie Wilson and "Lonely Teardrops."

Grace opened the maple cabinet to the right of the stove and found some pans to begin cooking. She located the spice cabinet and searched through the various McCormick and Napa Valley spices until she found all the ingredients she needed.

Apparently either the men really did know how to cook or someone cooked for them when they were up here at their cabin. She was surprised by the instant jealous emotion she felt thinking about Duke, Sandman, and Big Jay with another woman or women. God, could they have done this kind of thing before? She sure did jump into bed with them quickly. What would come of this situation? She called it a situation because she couldn't call it a relationship. It was based on lust, sex, and five days alone in a house in the middle of the woods somewhere. Maybe they weren't so deserted and alone. Sandman said that Big Jay went into town. Town couldn't be far. She thought about why he went there. The refrigerator and freezer were well stocked along with the pantry. Could he have gone to see someone he knew? A woman perhaps.

That thought annoyed her a little but she had no right to be. Grace tried to ignore her own thoughts. She dipped the cutlets in egg mixed with Parmesan cheese then into a bowl of seasoned breadcrumbs. She understood this was a difficult situation for all of them. They didn't really know her and she didn't really know them. It was merely a week and these were not normal circumstances. Now here they were thrown into living together, fighting a natural and spontaneous chemistry that continued to build between them. Getting emotionally and sexually involved with them during such an extreme and dangerous time could be a huge mistake.

Throw in the entire ménage thing and what the hell was she thinking? A relationship like this one was only something she read about. Sure they existed but still, when she thought of having a potential future with a man, it was just that, with one man not three. In all honesty she had thought she would remain alone forever. So what did it matter? The end result would be her alone. They were men. They could move on. She on the other hand would be mortified, heartbroken, and damaged goods. What other man would want her after she'd slept with three men at once? Oh God, only another set of men who liked the same thing, sharing a woman. She felt like vomiting. She didn't want other men. She wanted Duke, Sandman, and Big Jay. Her own thoughts angered her. She wanted to ignore her emotions and attraction and simply blame the confusion on the current stress in her life. Any of the events alone could lead someone so rational like herself to react irrationally. But she needed them now, wanted them so badly, and it both excited her and annoyed her. No one got under her skin the way they did.

By the time the last chicken cutlet was lightly fried and placed in the large glass baking dish Grace felt like she needed to put on the brakes and slow things down.

She smiled to herself as a bottle of white wine was presented to her from behind. Once again, one of the men snuck up on her undetected. It scared her, thrilled her, and made her smile up at Big Jay.

"I thought this might be good with the chicken. It smells great." He placed the bottle down onto the counter. He kissed her cheek and then her neck as he wrapped his arms around her from behind. She read the label, "Meridian chardonnay," until he turned her around.

In a flash he lifted her up, placed her onto the counter, and stepped between her thighs, pressing them open.

He kissed her harder on the mouth as he ran his hands up her shirt to cup her breasts, Big Jay was very dominant and always in charge. He released her lips.

"I want you. Couldn't wait to see you, kiss you, and, ah hell." He pulled her shirt up over her head, and then undid the button on her shorts. She lifted up and he removed her shorts and undergarments then his pants. She was turned on by his aggression and sex appeal as she ran her hands up his shirt and against his pectoral muscles. She pinched both nipples while holding his heated gaze before he lifted his shirt up over his head. A moment later he was pulling her ass and pussy over the edge of the counter.

"You're glistening already, goddess."

Even though she was up high, it was the perfect height for Big Jay to align his cock to her pussy and shove in.

She gripped his wrists as he maneuvered his cock through her pussy muscles before reaching as deeply as he could go. He closed his eyes and remained still a moment as if he really had been waiting all day to be inside of her. The thought fed her ego and washed away earlier thoughts of him going to town to see some another woman. There was no way he did that.

He pulled out then shoved back in before he reached down and held her hips in place. He pulled her a little further off the counter then stroked her pussy slowly.

"So fucking tight and wet. I love watching my cock disappearing into your pussy, woman."

When she glanced up toward him then down where her pussy and his cock met, she felt the cream drip down her ass.

She widened her thighs.

"I want to try something, baby. I want to fuck your ass, just like this," he said as he pulled out then slowly pushed back into her pussy. He ran a finger down her thighs and below to her puckered hole.

"Fuck, you're wet. I don't have any lube, baby. Me and my brothers have never shared a woman before or brought any women up here."

"Oh God, try it. I want to, please," she begged. His words meant more to her than he would ever know. This was special. This thing between them was incredible. She wanted to try anal sex. She wanted so much right now it was almost painful.

He pressed a finger to her ass as he pumped his cock into her pussy.

As he pushed into her, she moaned louder.

"Do it, Jay. Do it," she told him. He pulled his cock from her pussy.

"Nice and easy, baby. Fuck, you've got me so hard, baby." She felt the tip of his cock against her puckered hole. She tried to relax but she was so thrilled with trying this and holding on to the connection and emotions she felt right now. He pressed deeper and she felt her inner muscles pulling him, trying to get him in deeper.

"Oh God, it burns," she said but then reached down to touch her pussy. It felt so swollen and needy.

"Holy fuck, we're having Grace for appetizer," Duke said as he walked into the kitchen.

"She needs us both, Duke. Fuck, her ass is so damn tight."

In a flash Duke was by the counter and his finger pressed into her pussy as he licked and sucked a nipple into his mouth. She thrust upward as she screamed sending Jay into her ass balls deep and lubricating both passages.

"Holy shit," Duke said.

Grace looked at Big Jay's intense red face.

"Fuck, she's too tight. I'm too turned on. Fuck." He pulled out, pushed back in then exploded inside of her ass.

"Fuck, baby!" he yelled as Duke pulled his fingers from her pussy while Big Jay pulled Grace into his arms.

She was panting for air but heard Duke behind her.

"I need her. Now."

Big Jay kissed her nose and then her lips while she embraced his shoulders, and she felt complete and ready for Duke next.

Big Jay turned her toward Duke who looked almost savage as the need in his eyes dominated all the other emotions on his face.

"Bend over that table, Grace. Make it fast."

She didn't hesitate even though her legs shook.

She lay over the table and felt his hands on her hips then his cock between her wet folds. In one swift motion Duke pressed his cock to her pussy and shoved in.

She gripped the table, her breasts flat against the wood and moaned in pleasure. "Oh God, Duke, this is wild. Holy crap," she said and both he and Big Jay chuckled. Duke was relentless with his strokes just the way she needed him to be. She had such a desire inside of her as she pressed back, counterthrusting to his strokes.

"So fucking good, baby. You're gorgeous and I love this ass," Duke said, and she felt the palms of his hand move up and down her back and spine then over her ass. He squeezed the cheeks as he spread them, pulled out of her pussy and thrust back in. He kept doing that, making her body cream and erupt with tiny explosions. When she felt his finger against the tight bud she thrust back, wanting it.

Duke pulled out, drew her hips back off the table farther then pressed into her ass slowly. He was so big, too big to fit in such a place and she moaned and tightened.

"Easy, baby. Nice and slow." He panted and then pressed a finger to her pussy. As Duke applied pressure against her clit, he pushed a little deeper into her ass. She wiggled her hips and felt the flow of cream release again.

"Oh God." She moaned and he thrust all the way into her ass with his cock while his fingers thrust into her pussy. Both holes were filled and somehow the man maintained a sequence of thrusts with fingers and cock into both holes. Over and over his hips and cock shoved into her. She wiggled and thrust back and down, trying to fill the need swarming around her.

They were both moaning and so in tune to the connection that they lost control together. He thrust and exploded. She followed suit then he hugged her from behind as he kissed along every bit of her skin from shoulders to spine and ended kissing her ass cheeks as he pulled out from her body.

* * * *

Duke pulled Grace into his arms and hugged her to him. Big Jay kissed her shoulders and held her as well. Sandwiched between them Duke realized that the more they shared her together, the more he was committed to making this type of relationship work. He spoke with Big Jay and Sandman this morning while Grace showered. The energy and connection between the four of them was spectacular. He never felt so close to his brothers or to another human being like he did when they were all together with Grace. He didn't want to lose this connection and bond. And even though it had only been days into this exploration, he was beginning to panic that it could not last. Especially after his conversation with Grace about an upcoming photo shoot in Milan. What if the killer wasn't caught yet? Did she think they would allow her to leave? She couldn't. They wouldn't take the chance in losing her.

Slowly they released her and helped her get dressed as Big Jay looked for a wine bottle opener. Then Sandman came into the kitchen. He didn't look happy, but immediately put on a happy face for Grace. Duke felt his gut clench. His instincts were never wrong.

* * * *

Big Jay located a solid silver wine bottle opener from the small fancy wooden box that sat on the counter.

He poured them each a glass of white wine then leaned across the counter to take a piece of sliced mozzarella cheese.

Big Jay watched her as she cut and diced, sautéed and located everything she needed in their kitchen. He admired her ability to adapt quickly and focus all of her attention on the task at hand. She seemed to be enjoying herself a little and he smiled hoping it was because she felt safe with him and his brothers. The way she awoke in such a fragile and frightened state last night had done a number on his insides.

She covered the chicken with the concoction she created in the frying pan then added a jar of gourmet baby peas. As she closed the oven door, she turned to look at him and Duke who were both staring.

"You're going to love this," she said as she began preparing a bag of chicken-flavored rice. Then she started slicing mozzarella again and handed a piece to Big Jay and then Duke.

Duke took a piece of mozzarella and fed it to Grace.

"Do all of you know how to cook or do you have someone that cooks for you?" she asked them. Was she trying not to sound like she was being nosy or asking straight out if they were involved with someone?

Big Jay smiled then took her hand and brought her knuckles up to his lips to kiss them. He looked down into her eyes.

"Why don't you just ask us directly if we're involved with someone? You've been pretty direct so far, Grace," he challenged as he released her hand then reached to the counter to take a sip of his wine. She was silent as she did the same.

"I assumed that the three of you must be very popular with the ladies. Perhaps one of them comes over from time to time and cooks for y'all when you're here." She shyly looked away, placed her glass onto the counter and began to wipe down the counter with a dishtowel.

Big Jay put down his wine glass and took Grace's hand from the towel. He put it up to his lips and kissed the top of her fingertips. Then he reached around her waist and pulled her toward him. She felt so petite and delicate in his arms, yet her curves were obvious and his body reacted.

Looking into her eyes, he smiled softly. "We're not involved with anyone, Grace, and we all enjoy cooking. It's actually one of my hobbies, but I like the fact that you were a little jealous," he teased her then clutched her waist firmer, causing her breasts to collide with his belly.

"Who said I was jealous? I have no right to be." She looked up into his eyes.

"I make you nervous, don't I?" Big Jay asked her.

"No you don't," she said, voice quivering as she stared up into his eyes. He placed his finger gently against her lips to stop her from trying to deny it.

He took a moment to look at her closely. She was shy and gorgeous.

She had perfect skin, perfect white teeth, and an infectious smile.

"You're so stunning, so young and sexy." His hand brushed against her cheek then to the back of her head, which he cradled in his hand.

Big Jay sensed Duke moving behind Grace and placing his hands on her shoulders. "You're the only one, Grace. We've never brought a woman here," Duke stated. Her eyes widened as if she were unsure if Duke were lying or not. "The three of us have never shared a woman before either," Big Jay told her then leaned down and kissed her lips. He had been with other women, none as young as Grace and none more compelling. Grace was strong, independent, and acted as though she needed no one to help her.

There was so much about her that he admired, and he wanted to know her better, learn everything about her. For the first time in years he was the one pursuing instead of the one being pursued.

"Is dinner ready?" Sandman asked.

"Yes, and I'm looking forward to dessert," Big Jay said then winked at Grace, making her blush before she shyly turned away and checked on the meal.

* * * *

The four of them sat around the island in the kitchen eating and talking. Grace was happy that they complimented her cooking and truly seemed to be enjoying themselves. It was funny to watch the three tough, big men banter over silly things like who was responsible for what chores. It was crazy when the conversation turned to who could shoot a gun farther and with more accuracy.

She chuckled as she took a sip from her wine glass.

"Hey, Grace, you have brothers. Did you argue with them or did you always get along?" Duke asked and the others became silent.

"We had our moments but for the most part we got along great."

"Oh sure, you never argued or stopped speaking to any of them for days?" Big Jay asked. She shook her head.

"My dad got sick with cancer when I was young. It was tough on my mom trying to raise five kids herself. We didn't want to make matters worse so we really tried our hardest to behave. I think that's why we're so close to one another now, too."

Big Jay smiled at her but Sandman looked serious.

"Your family does seem very close. I didn't know about your father. If you don't mind me asking, why did you leave them, Grace?"

She took a deep breath then looked at each of them. "It wasn't an easy decision. My sister Clara and I looked like twins. So often people would confuse us, calling us by the other person's name. We were only fourteen months apart and were very close." She paused a moment.

"After she was murdered, my family life turned into a complete mess. It's not something everyone can understand or comprehend. There's a big difference between someone dying from an illness, disease or even an accident, than someone being murdered. Clara was alive one moment and the next she was dead. She was robbed of everything. The rest of us were alive." She looked away from him.

She felt Big Jay place a hand on her knee. She turned to look at him.

"You shouldn't feel guilty because Clara was killed and you're alive."

"You don't understand, Big Jay. I can't help but to feel guilty. Part of why I left was the guilt I felt looking like her, feeling I had to act like her. It's what my family wanted. Everything I did was compared to Clara. The way I even combed my hair, or walked down the street. Everyone including my family did that to me. At first I didn't mind, believe me it made me feel even closer to Clara, but then it got crazy. I started to feel as if I didn't exist. Can you understand what I mean?" she asked him.

"Yes. I think I do. You were feeling smothered and controlled which made you feel out of control and dependent. You started to give in to them treating you like Clara instead of remembering that you were Grace, your own person," Sandman said.

She was shocked at his response.

She smiled at him softly.

"Exactly. God, I wish I met you two years ago. It's like you understand because you feel or felt the same way yourself once," she said to him.

"I think I kind of felt that way before I called it quits with the Marine Corps. I had no idea who I was when I returned after fighting in the war multiple tours. It was like I became a name and a number. I'm not sure if we would have hit it off if we met back then, Grace. You needed those years to become so independent. To figure out who Grace was and what she wanted." Sandman gently brushed a piece of her hair away from her eyes.

"You're right about that, it was a tough move. I cried a lot and even went as far as buying a plane ticket home only two weeks after leaving. I talked myself out of it and decided that was exactly what my family wanted and expected. The new me wasn't going to be like that. So that became my new motto. Every time there was a decision to make in my new life, I'd ask myself one simple question. What does the new me want to do? And in doing so I became who I am today."

"Well I think you did a great job. I definitely like the new you, although I suppose one would say I'm biased considering the intimacy we just shared," Duke said then winked. She of course felt her cheeks warm as she shyly looked down to her lap.

"I'm so glad that I met you guys. I'm not glad that these circumstances brought us together, but the one positive is the three of you."

Big Jay leaned over and kissed her on the lips. She placed her palms against both of his cheeks and kissed him back. When they finally ended the kiss, they leaned foreheads together and smiled.

"I think I'm ready for dessert now," Big Jay whispered and Grace chuckled as her pussy clenched and her heart soared to the highest level she'd ever felt before.

* * * *

Donald couldn't stop thinking about Sarah. He called the house, surprised that Eric wasn't screening the calls. He would be doing that if Sarah were his wife. Donald ran a hand through his hair. He knew that was never going to happen. She was with Eric, despite his attempts at letting her know he had wanted her. Being best friends with her husband Frank Sr., who died suddenly, placed him right beside Sarah during the mourning process until Eric arrived on scene. The man came out of nowhere and swept Sarah off her feet. He knew how to control the media. He knew how to gain Sarah's full attention. Donald failed in that department.

"You sound funny, Donald. Are you holding up okay?" she asked. Sarah was the one who was suffering.

"I'm good, Sarah. I was just worried about you. I wanted to see if you heard from Grace at all." She was quiet a moment.

Then she whispered, "I'm not supposed to say anything. But yes, I did. She's safe. It doesn't mean I'm not worried though."

"I know. That special investigator is really good. More thorough than any of us ever expected or considered being detectives in this small town. I'm sure he'll keep her safe."

"There's others with them, too. He's being very cautious."

"Others?"

"That's all I know. I'm sorry, Donald. I need to go. Eric just got here and he's giving me that look. I know it was safe to tell you. I'll talk to you soon."

"Later, Sarah."

Donald hung up the phone and leaned back into the chair. That guy was never too far from her side. Eavesdropping on her phone calls. One thing was for sure, Eric hadn't been hamming it up with the media as much as when Clara went missing. God, he remembered those days. That guy had the media everywhere. It was difficult to ditch them so he could get his personal business done. Donald ran his hands through his hair. He didn't like being out of the loop. He wanted to be part of

Sarah's life. Her sons came to talk to him about their personal lives and about their professions, not Eric. Donald felt his blood pressure rising. There wasn't a thing he could do about that. He had to lie low and observe from afar. After all, he loved Sarah.

* * * *

The following morning Grace awoke alone in bed. She was a little sad they hadn't stayed in bed with her, but when she turned over and saw the time she was shocked.

Grace couldn't remember the last time she slept until 10:00 a.m.

But she was so comfortable and felt so safe in their arms. She hadn't even had a bad dream last night and she knew it was because of Sandman, Big Jay, and Duke.

She took a quick shower then headed downstairs. As she came around the corner to where the kitchen was, she saw Sandman and Big Jay standing around the large rectangular kitchen table.

Sandman was on his cell phone and Big Jay looked at her as if he was shocked to see her but recovered nicely.

"Good morning, Grace. Did you sleep well?" Big Jay asked her as Sandman spun around with the same surprised look that Big Jay had.

"Yes, I did, thank you. Now why don't you tell me what's up?" she asked Big Jay who turned to look at Sandman.

Grace watched him and she could tell the news was bad as the little veins by Sandman's temples pushed out. His teeth clenched and his shoulders tensed up as he looked at her. He gave a nod with his head indicating for Big Jay to take her out of the room. She shook her head. "What's going on? What's wrong? Tell me." He continued to listen attentively to the caller and ignored her demands.

"Come with me into the living room, Grace. Let Sandman finish the call."

She looked up at Big Jay. He caressed her arm and then her back with one hand then took her other hand and led her out of the room. She planted her feet. She wouldn't leave the room.

"No, damn it. Something is wrong. I can tell by his face, his body language. Something happened. Tell me please?"

* * * *

"Her eyes were taped closed, she was raped and tortured. The medical examiner's report isn't back yet but her throat appeared to be cut open with some sort of thin, sharp weapon. We'll know soon enough, Sandman, then I'll call you back," Jim told Sandman.

He couldn't respond and Jim got the message.

"Grace is there now?"

"Yes."

"Shit, she's going to take this badly. This could send her over the edge."

"I know. I'll handle it," he responded.

"Good luck and I'll call back soon enough. This is terrible. We have to find this asshole and soon."

"I know."

Sandman disconnected the call and turned toward Big Jay and Grace.

"Well?" she asked in a shaky voice.

"Sit down, Grace."

She shook her head, refusing to listen. "Just tell me. Tell me what happened now."

Big Jay had his eyebrows scrunched and his hands were on Grace's shoulders.

"Your brother John's girlfriend…Maggie."

"Oh God…Oh no." She shook her head and she covered her face with her hands.

"She was found off the side of the road somewhere along Allington Way. She's been murdered, baby." He walked toward her.

Grace turned away. She pulled from Big Jay's hands. She was angry and upset. She would want to go see her family, to see John and be there for them. But she couldn't. That was exactly what the killer wanted.

Sandman grabbed her arm and pulled her into his embrace despite her attempts to stop him.

Grace was crying. "I want to go home. I need to go home. Now."

"You can't go, Grace. You know I can't let you."

She tried to push away from him, still crying with her hands against his chest. "I want to go. I need to see John. I don't care if I die. Maybe everything will just stop if he kills me already."

Big Jay caressed her hair. "Baby, that's not an option. This guy wants to hurt you, cause you pain and make you come back to him."

"It's all my fault. He killed Maggie because of me."

"No, baby. He's the one committing murder. Whether you're in Houston or out here, he's got an agenda and we need to figure it out," Big Jay added.

Sandman was at a loss for words. He was angry and pissed off and he felt so awful for Grace his heart actually ached, indicating it was still functional with emotions. He thought he had grown coldhearted and unaffected and he was wrong. Grace came into his life and his brothers' lives and changed them.

"You can't leave, Grace. It's not even an option. What we need to do is sit down and go over the information I have. Maybe together we could come up with something concrete. As far as your family's concerned, we'll set up your laptop in my office. You can e-mail Donald. That's where the other secure line will be set up."

"What's going on?" Duke asked as he walked into the room carrying a bunch of papers. Big Jay explained as Sandman tried to get through to Grace.

"Son of a bitch. Damn, honey, I'm so fucking sorry," Duke said then placed the papers down onto the island and pulled her into his arms. She allowed Duke to hold her and to Sandman it was a step in the right direction.

She stepped from Duke's arms and rubbed her tears away from her eyes. Sandman took her hand and pulled her against his chest.

"We'll set up the secure line right away, baby. You'll be able to talk with your family," Sandman told her.

"Let me go, Sandman. You said you would set that line up. You haven't even done that for me? What were you waiting for? Something like this to happen? I need to be alone." She pulled from him and walked out of the room.

"I want this guy's head on a fucking platter," Sandman stated with fists by his sides.

"We do, too, but we need to be rational," Big Jay said.

"Fuck rational. If this continues, we'll lose her," Sandman said.

"He's right, Jay. Grace is not going to be able to handle much more bad news like this," Duke stated.

"Let's start off with the material you have, Duke, and then we'll see what our next move is. There is more to this guy. I know it. His MO is changing regularly. Just as I think he's some sick serial killer out for personal pleasure, someone else pops up dead. I think there's a definite connection to those other murders of those men. There's a link there somewhere. We need to find it."

"You're right, Sandman, but first, let's get Grace through this current situation. She'll need us," Big Jay added, and they agreed as they went in search of her.

* * * *

"Damn it. I should have known something was wrong. She would have called, should have called. How could I have been so stupid? What now?" John asked, rambling on and on about Maggie.

"It's not your fault, John. How could you know? You said it yourself you thought she might be with her ex-boyfriend. Listen it doesn't matter now. We have to help these detectives find out who's responsible. We need to stay focused. The word is that they're calling in some federal agents. This guy is now a cop killer, too," Donald stated to John, and Frank agreed as he placed his hand on John's shoulder.

"You know Maggie's family, John. Take a few days off and help her parents with the arrangements. Take as much time as you need," Donald said.

"What about Grace? Does she know yet?" John asked.

"Probably. Jim called Sandman about ten minutes ago. He figured better to find out from Sandman than the media," Frank told his brother

"God, this is probably killing her. I wish I could talk to her," John said

"Sandman said he set up a secure line for her to e-mail us here in Donald's office. We should hear from her soon," Frank added.

Donald opened up his e-mails to check to see if Grace had e-mailed yet.

Donald, it's Grace. I heard about Maggie. How is John doing?

I'm so sorry this is happening. If I could stop it I would.

I wish I was back in Europe where everything was normal and my family was safe. God, how I wish so many things were different. How are my mom and Eric doing? Please tell them I love them. Tell John I'm so sorry and that I love him so much and Frank and Peter, too.

I'm racking my brain. I feel so alone, out of control, weak, and this killer is doing it to me. I want to be strong, I need to be strong but just as I feel a little strength, a little confidence, he strikes again. I want to be there with all of you. I want to be there with John. Oh God, Donald, please tell him I'm so sorry. So sorry.

Donald read the message and felt heartbroken for Grace. She felt Maggie's murder was her fault. She was blaming herself for the killings and was losing her confidence and control.

Her brothers read the message and felt the same way. They had tears in their eyes as they each responded back to her. They told her how much they loved her and that it wasn't her fault. They told her to be strong and positive that together they would stop this killer. They told her not to blame herself and they prayed they would see her again.

* * * *

Grace sat in the office and read the return e-mails from her brothers and Donald. She was crying now and wondered how she could stay strong. Her brother John didn't blame her for Maggie's death. He blamed the killer and his warped, demented mind.

"How are you doing, baby?" Sandman asked as he entered the office.

Grace looked up at him, trying to wipe her tears away with her hand.

"They don't blame me. They're so worried." She wiped her tears then stared at the last line on the page. The words "We love you, Grace" were typed in at the end.

"Why would they? It's not your fault. This guy is sick, Grace. He's playing a game. There are no rules, only his. He wants to be in control." He sat on the edge of the desk next to Grace.

"He is in control. He is winning this sick game. I don't want to play it, Sandman. I can't take this. I need to be with my family. Can't you protect me there at home? There are three of you."

He let out a long sigh as he looked at her.

"You're better off here where we can go over everything and keep you safe. I know it's hard."

Grace stood up and cut him off as she moved around the desk.

"You know it's hard? How do you know how I'm feeling? You couldn't possibly understand. This is killing me. I'd rather he just find me and kill me than just drag this thing out. He's hurting people I love. He wants me and I don't know why. I don't know who he is. I'm racking my brain, Sandman, and coming up with nothing. I can't handle this. I need to be in control. I want to stop this asshole and I can't do anything. My arms are tied behind my back, he's winning, Goddamn him, he's winning!" She raised her voice as she turned and faced the doorway.

Sandman grabbed her shoulders, stopped her from walking out, and turned her toward him.

"You have to keep that anger you have, baby. That's your strength and your power. He's not winning. He's just ahead a few points. Together we can do this. You're not alone, Grace. I'm here for you. Big

Jay and Duke are here for you, too."

He hugged her tightly and she grabbed onto him, loving the feel of his strength and conviction in his tone, his words.

He held her in silence and she realized how much he and his brothers had come to mean to her so quickly. But she was used to handling things on her own and right now, it would be too much to talk with Sandman, explain her emotions, her memories and fears. She would feel like she was giving up all of her layers and taking a chance that he and his brothers would never hurt her. In this fragile state, she just couldn't find the belief and power to do that.

She slowly pulled back from his embrace.

"I think I need to be alone, Sandman. I need some time alone."

He nodded his head and accepted her request. He was too good to be true. Too perfect for the likes of her and this situation.

"Call me if you need anything." He softly kissed her lips. She watched him leave the room then touched fingers to her lips. She loved his kisses. She loved the connection she felt for him, Big Jay, and Duke.

Grace walked back to the desk and sat down, reading over the e-mails again. It was too much to take in and to accept as reality.

She laid her head down on the desk and closed her eyes as she began to think about growing up with her mom and dad, brothers, and Clara.

Grace was only three years old when her father Frank Sr. had passed away from cancer. She had a good memory and recalled a lot of good times with him and her siblings.

He was a sheriff for many years until he got sick, became weak and had to retire early. He loved being a lawman. It was in his blood. She guessed it ran in the family considering John, Frank, and even Peter's choice of careers.

Her mom had a hard time dealing with the loss of her husband. It took her more than ten years to finally start dating. One day her mom told her that since Grace was fifteen years old, she could start to focus on herself. Her wants and needs in life.

That was when she met Eric. He was a nice man who was married once before and had lost his wife to cancer as well. They met at some community volunteer event and that was how they began dating.

He opened a hardware store in town, after buying out and taking over the small, beat-up old one Henry Tucker used to own.

Eric tore the building down and renovated the whole place. It was very well known in the area and he actually opened up two others.

They got married that same year after Grace's sixteenth birthday.

They made a very nice couple and Eric was pretty decent. He did, however, want the kids to call him dad, but they refused.

As far as they were concerned, they had a dad. His name was Frank Thompson Sr. and he was their only dad.

Finally after many discussions they opted for "Eric" and that was final.

As the years went on Eric traveled a lot between stores and her mom would sometimes travel with him. Then they decided to get involved with politics.

Eric figured with Mom's great personality and his good business sense they would make the perfect local, political couple.

Grace's mom started getting involved in charity organizations and was Eric's campaign manager. She also helped Donald out a lot with different fundraisers and community welfare programs.

Grace remembered one time she and Clara got mad at Eric because he told them they couldn't go out on a double date with these two boys they liked.

He said he didn't trust them and that she and Clara were way too young to date. They laughed at him saying they were seventeen and eighteen years old, old enough to live out on their own and do as they pleased. Grace laughed as she recalled her and her sister's stubbornness.

Eric wouldn't budge. He sent them to their rooms and of course, being defiant teenagers they snuck out.

Eric found out and was furious and unfortunately their mom agreed with him. They were so upset with Eric that they snuck out again and drew funny faces on all his political posters that hung near the hardware store.

At the time it was very funny and they both felt they achieved their revenge on him. Eric was really angry.

As time went on Eric became a little more controlling of their mother, wanting her to be the best-dressed politician's wife, have the best car, act a certain way…and so on. Grace's mom didn't have a day off but she claimed she wouldn't have it any other way.

When Grace's brothers made their achievements, graduating from the police academy, passing the bar exam, and becoming first grade detective it only added to their perfect political family.

Then that early June only three years ago, when her older sister Clara disappeared, their perfect little family fell apart.

The media went crazy. The town was swarming with investigators, reporters, camera crews, and television vans. It was crazier than when the carnival came to town and it pulled in just as much attention and people.

She didn't want to relive any of it as she changed her thoughts back to Clara.

She went over their conversations in her head. First when she called to say she was coming home, then after she arrived and they hung out together talking about Alan. Poor Alan was even investigated and was called a possible suspect in Clara's murder by the media before the police even questioned Alan.

He was heartbroken, devastated, and emotionally distraught just as Grace's family was.

He nearly lost his job with the amount of time he took off from work even after Clara's body was found and Stew Parker was arrested.

Stew Parker. Grace said his name to herself. That had been a shocker.

Then she thought once again about Clara and how she and her would play in the woods and fields around their house all the time.

As a matter of fact, Clara went on some pretty dangerous hiking trips in college that were planned through the university. Which now made

Grace wonder.

She didn't know why she hadn't thought of it before.

Clara knew that woods inside and out and she was very resourceful.

Plus she would have put up a fight, struggled with the killer especially if he was a stranger. Grace recalled a conversation her brothers were having about the crime scene. The police said she was stabbed to death. The thoughts disgusted her but she had to face this situation head-on. She needed to see the report, ask Sandman questions because she was now thinking that Clara knew her killer. There was no other explanation for it. Clara had to have known who her killer was. She needed to find Sandman.

When she walked into the dining area, she saw Sandman sitting at the large wooden table looking at some pictures and reading a file. Big Jay was leaning against the wall staring at a pile of papers and Duke was scrolling with the mouse as he stared at the computer screen

"Sandman."

They all looked at her.

"Hey, gorgeous. How are you doing?" Big Jay said then placed his palm against her cheek. She leaned into it and allowed him to hug her. She looked back at Sandman.

"I'm sorry about before. I was upset and angry and I'm used to being alone. Dealing with things on my own. I know you care and you want to help me. I'm going to need your help. It's going to be hard for me. I know this so please bear with me, okay?" she said. She would always be amazed at these three men's height and superior appearance. Even now as Sandman approached, she felt her belly quiver and the anticipation of his big strong arms embracing her and taking away her fear.

"I understand that, baby. Just remember that you're not alone and that we can do this together, okay?"

He smiled before he pulled her into his arms. He held her close and she loved having all three of them there with her.

Big Jay caressed her hair and she turned to look up toward him.

"We're here for you, baby."

She smiled. "I know."

Sandman released her and Duke took her hand and brought her fingers up to his lips. He kissed them softly.

"We'll get through this."

"I know and I need all three of you to help me." She took a deep breath then released it.

"I was thinking about my sister and I was wondering about the crime scene. I need to see her file."

Sandman crossed his arms in front of his wide chest and showed no emotion when he said no.

"Please hear me out, Sandman. I was thinking about her and a part of her disappearance that I ignored, or blocked out, or maybe simply didn't want to face."

"What is it, Grace?" Big Jay asked.

Grace took in a deep breath and looked into Sandman's eyes.

"I want to see her file. I need to know how the killer got her to the woods. What was the cause of death? Everything."

"That isn't necessary. Leave it to us, baby. It's our job and it's something we're used to viewing," Duke said very firmly but also with compassion and empathy.

"I need to see it. I know I can help. I can't just sit around and do nothing but wait for him to strike again."

"This is going to be difficult, to say the least, Grace. The pictures are pretty bad. Maybe I can just read you the report, tell you what the detectives' and the coroner's findings were?" Sandman asked her as she sat down at the table. If he was suggesting that, then the pictures must be horrific. She needed to trust his judgment, and the fact that he was letting her in on this much was surprising. She needed to take what he gave her in this situation.

"Okay," she said as Sandman took a seat next to her and began reading and explaining the findings.

Chapter 12

Frank, John, Peter, and Eric sat around the kitchen table in their mother's house.

Sarah was working at the kitchen sink peeling potatoes for potato salad.

"I wonder if Grace still likes my potato salad?" Sarah asked, as she looked out the large window above the kitchen sink.

She missed her daughter something terrible. She wanted her here with her. She wanted to hold her and love her.

"I'm sure she does, Mom. She'll be back home soon. You'll see," John said, as he looked at his brothers.

"I'm sure she's fine, Sarah. After all she is with that special investigator," Eric added, as he gave his wife a loving squeeze.

"Yeah that guy is something else. The way he used his own body to protect her. I'm real curious about his confidential files. I wonder what that guy is capable of?" Frank asked, and the others added similar comments indicating that they all wondered as well.

"Can't you find out more about him, Frank? Something to make us feel even more confident that she's safe?" Eric asked.

"No, I can't. Whatever he's done in the past that's labeled confidential stays confidential. I did hear Detective Jim Warner say something about Sandstone being the best. He had been assigned to a lot of high-profile government officials in the past. Supposedly he came pretty close to getting killed. The position he has now is supposed to be less dangerous. Then add in his years in the military as a commando and I'd bet he's the best we could ever ask for in protecting Grace," Frank told them.

"Yeah the word around the station is that he's an expert in arm-to-arm combat. He actually prefers it to the use of a gun. But who knows if that's just talk. He's so mysterious, people tend to make up stories when they can't find out anything about someone," John told them then took a slug of beer from the bottle.

"Well, I just hope he can protect your sister. Grace must be so scared right now. Having to wear a disguise to escape the precinct undetected," Sarah added.

The guys laughed a little.

"What's so funny?" she asked as she looked at her sons.

"You should have seen her in that police uniform," John said with a smile on his face then shook his head as if he were remembering the scene.

"Yeah, I've never seen a female patrol officer who made the uniform look that good before," Frank added.

"I thought Sandstone's eyes were going to pop out of his head when Grace first walked through the door," John added.

"Donald and our eyes popped out of our heads when we first saw her, too. The guys are still taking about it." Frank and John began laughing.

"I hope she'll be safe with this Sandstone guy. He's a very attractive man and big, to say the least," Sarah stated.

"Maybe you'll get that son-in-law you've been wishing for, Mom," Frank teased and the others began laughing.

"What? You guys think something is going on between those two? He's only known her a few days," Eric said, sounding concerned. Sarah knew that Eric cared for Grace as if she were his biological daughter. Even when she was away, he made sure he was home whenever Grace planned on calling.

Sarah put her arms around Eric's waist.

"Honey, you didn't catch their reaction to one another when they first met?" Sarah told them and the men hadn't seen exactly what she had. The instant attraction, the chemistry, and if a relationship emerged between them she would recall both of their first reactions to one another. She would never forget it and would cherish the fact that she was able to witness it. She often wondered if Grace had any relationships while she was in Europe. She never wrote about any or mentioned any over the phone. She knew her daughter was old enough to be sexually active and responsible enough but she worried about her handling the emotional part.

Grace closed herself off when Clara died. She put up a wall around her heart and she resisted emotional commitment. It would take someone strong and special to tear down that wall. Grace was stubborn, independent and strong willed. She felt she could do anything and everything on her own. She preferred it that way and probably felt content and in control relying solely on herself. Sarah was sure that Grace and Sandstone would bash heads in that category but she hoped he could keep her safe.

Sarah laughed as she went about adding the fresh celery to the potato salad. The men continued to talk about the case and still wondered who the killer could be and what he wanted with Grace.

"How are Maggie's parents doing, John? Do they need anything?" Sarah asked as John leaned against the kitchen counter.

"They're doing all right I guess. They have a lot of family in the area so they've had a lot of company the last few days. Once things settle down I'm sure it will start sinking in more." John looked down at his shoes with his hands in his pockets.

Sarah wiped her hands on her apron and took her son's hand.

"We know it's going to be hard for them. It's tough to lose a daughter, a sister, anyone you love, to murder. You be there for them, Johnny, just like people in the community were here for us," Sarah told her son and John gave his mother a hug.

* * * *

"The medical examiner's report shows a blow to the head just above the right temple. She was stabbed with a long, sharp weapon, twenty times," Sandman told Grace as he read certain parts of the medical examiner's report.

Grace took a deep breath as a tear fell from her eye.

"What kind of object do they think she was hit in the head with?" Grace forced herself to ask.

Sandman looked at her a moment, amazed at her strength. He could see the fight in her eyes. She was determined.

"Well let's see what it says here." Sandman scanned over the documents. "The medical examiner said a possible weapon used was something made of hard metal, thin like a tire iron. The evidence found at Stew Parker's house contained one tire iron with your sister's blood on it."

Sandman looked through the file.

Grace thought about it for a minute and felt she knew her sister really well.

"What are you thinking?" Big Jay asked her as he looked up from the laptop. Even Duke sat nearby. He didn't look happy at all about the situation.

Grace put down the file.

"My sister knew those woods inside and out. We used to always play in those woods then walk that same highway to get back home. Everyone in town knew Stew Parker. He was the poor guy who lived in the shack off the highway. Kids made up stories about him and a friend of our father's who was the sheriff told us to stay clear of Stew, that he wasn't mentally fit and we did," Grace told them.

"Would your sister have given him a ride if she saw him walking the highway? That would explain the fibers from his coat that were found in the passenger seat," Big John asked.

"No, she would never do that and the killer probably planted that evidence, too. At the time I was so distraught I didn't know one day from the next, we were all confused, and scared. It was terrible. The entire town was on lockdown and in pursuit of a killer. I don't think there was a person alive in our town that hadn't been affected by the incident," Grace replied, looking toward the slider doors instead of directly at the men.

Sandman figured she had a hard time talking about what happened. Sharing her feelings and experience with them was difficult for her.

"Clara would have never picked up a hitchhiker, a stranger, or Stew. If someone needed help, then she always carried her cell phone. She would call someone else to come help the person. My brothers taught us to be street smart, be aware of our gut feelings, and know when circumstances seemed wrong or unnerving. I think my sister knew the killer," Grace stated confidently and Sandman moved forward in his seat.

"Other people were questioned in the area. All other suspects were accounted for, including her boyfriend at the time. The detectives checked their alibis, confirmed their whereabouts at the time of the murder," Duke added.

"I'm telling you that Clara knew the person she let into her car. I should have known this then. I just wasn't thinking clearly and then the detectives and the police found out about Stew and the evidence in his home. What exactly was found in his house?" Grace asked.

Sandman stared at her a moment before he looked down at the paper. He was utterly impressed with her strength. She wasn't the type of woman to sit back and have everyone do all the work. She was a team player and it made him feel proud. That was an odd feeling to have, considering his other thought was how badly he wanted to sink his cock into her sweet, tight folds and make love to her for hours. He wanted to take her mind off of all this blood, gore, and heartache and just hold her, get lost in her body as he and his brothers explored what was theirs. He knew he sounded possessive, obsessed in a way, but he didn't care. When all this was done and over, he and his brothers would take Grace away for a while and get lost in themselves.

"Sandman?" Big Jay said, interrupting his thoughts. Sandman cleared his throat and looked back at the papers.

He looked at the list from the file again as he read it off to Grace.

"One tire iron with blood stain, one set of plastic adjustable ties, one winter coat, a set of leather restraints with blood stains and some rope."

Grace put her head down on the table. She was trying to think. She felt in her heart there was something there but she just couldn't see it.

They had been working on the file for a couple of hours. They went over the other cases and Grace looked exhausted.

"Let's take a break for now, Grace. I'll call Donald and find out who else was on the detective's list as a possible suspect at the time. My agents will find out more about them and recheck their alibis. If you think she knew her killer, then we may have something to work with. Good job, honey," Sandman told her as he gave her a kiss on the cheek.

* * * *

Grace stepped outside for some fresh air. Her ears absorbed the sounds of the pond and waterfall as well as the birds singing and peacefulness in the isolation and safety of the men's home.

She took a deep breath as visions of her sister's body kept flashing in her mind. The evidence that was found in Stew Parker's home disgusted her. The ideas of what the killer had done to her made her stomach churn. She knew her sister suffered, she knew she was raped and tortured like some animal. This killer had no respect for human life, for body or soul. He had no soul of his own. Though after listening to the similarities in the cases and the way he killed each of his victims, Grace couldn't help but feel the killer was killing with conviction. To him he had a purpose, a rationale. Kind of like a hobby. He was exact in all the killings. The way he tied them up or used the handcuffs to control them and keep them in place and then placed tape over their eyes. He tortured each of them the same way and he didn't deviate from his pattern. The only exceptions were the males that were found murdered in a similar fashion that Sandman, Big Jay, and Duke thought were connected somehow. Those men weren't raped but they were left on public display and exposed naked. *What the hell did that mean?*

Although she couldn't handle looking at most of the crime scene pictures, she did notice that there wasn't a lot of blood. The killer may be meticulous.

Grace shook her head in amazement and shock. What the hell did she know about police work or homicides, crime scenes or any of the gruesome procedures and skills that went along with it? She was a civilian, a photographer. Maybe that was it. She was used to looking at a scene or subject in a different way as a photographer. The person was an object that she had to portray and make them come across in certain ways.

She made models look even more beautiful, goddess like, or like fine art. That was why she had the reputation she did. She was an expert in the field and the models wanted Grace to take their pictures, beautify them, enhance their qualities, make magazines want them over other models and Grace did just that.

Sandman, Big Jay, and Duke stepped out onto the patio to join Grace, and she explained her thoughts and feelings with them.

"It's amazing how in tune you are to this. You do come from a law enforcement background. Maybe it's in your blood?" Big Jay asked as he took her hand and placed her palm against his lips. She smiled at him and wondered if he was right.

"Technically, you've come up with a profile for this killer without even knowing it. We'll work on that next, right now there's something else I could really use," Duke stated then pulled her into his arms and kissed her deeply.

In a flash, Duke was lifting her up and she was straddling his waist.

* * * *

Grace grabbed ahold of Duke's cheeks and held his gaze. "I feel desperate," she told him as he pressed her back against the wall of the house. Sandman and Big Jay stood on either side of Grace, staring down at her. She absorbed their facial expressions, their ginormous sizes and how attracted she was to all three of them.

"Desperate for what?" Big Jay asked then pressed a strand of hair back behind her ear. She closed her eyes as she absorbed the tingling sensation from his touch, combined with Duke's cock that was pressed hard against her mound.

"Desperate for all three of you to always be with me, part of me…in me." She immediately saw the change in Duke's eyes.

"In you is where I need to be right now, baby." Duke covered her mouth and kissed her deeply. She wrapped her arms around his head and thrust her pussy against his cock. She felt every sensation and sensed the movement around them and the sounds of the small waterfall descending into the Koi pond. There was the beat of their hearts, the scuffling of clothing, and belt buckles banging to the porch wooden flooring. She ravaged Duke's mouth, felt the hands moving up both thighs, and knew they belonged to Sandman and Big Jay.

Duke released her lips and kissed along her throat as he undid his pants, shoved them down as fingers ripped her panties from her body.

"Oh God, yes, yes, please," she begged of them, head tilted back, and legs wide. Suddenly a cock shoved into her pussy.

"I need you so badly it hurts, baby. It actually fucking hurts." Duke thrust into her hard. He stroked her pussy repeatedly, grinding his cock through her vaginal muscles as she gripped his shoulders and counterthrusted. She wanted to get lost in the intense need and desire these men brought on.

"More. I need more."

Duke pulled her from the wall and turned then sat down in a long chaise lounge. He spread his thighs and increased his thrusts as she fell to her back on top of the cushion. She locked gazes with him and then Sandman and Big Jay who stood there naked with their cocks in their hands stroking themselves and watching her.

"I want you, too," she said, and Duke paused in his strokes.

"Together, baby? Are you sure?"

"I've never been more sure. I want to feel you all everywhere. I want to taste you," she said to Big Jay.

Duke stood up then lifted Grace up, too. He took position on the chaise lounge, spreading his thighs over the edge. Big Jay pushed over another chair and kneeled on it. She wondered what they were doing then understood as Duke turned her in his arms so that she straddled him.

"Ride my cock, baby," Duke whispered as he pulled off her shirt and Sandman unclipped her bra, removing it while his thighs tapped against her shoulder blades. She lowered herself onto Duke's shaft, sucking in a deep breath because his cock felt so hard. "Come down here." He cupped her breasts and tweaked the nipples before kissing her lips. The kiss was so sensual she felt her body release small spasms and lubricate Duke's pathway in and out of her pussy.

"Oh yeah, baby. You like when we play with your tits don't you?"

"Yes."

She felt Sandman's hands pressing her back lower and Big Jay scooted the bench closer. As she thrust her hips up and down, she turned to see Big Jay holding his cock. She stared at the size of it and wondered how the hell that fit inside of her. She licked her lips. "That's right, darling. This is for you." Big Jay moved his cock closer and she stuck her tongue out to take a little taste. Duke thrust upward and Sandman began to play with her anus.

"Oh." She began to moan when Jay pressed his cock between her lips. She accepted his move, relished in the sweet, musky taste of male flesh, then tried to remain calm. Sandman was pressing a second digit into her ass and Duke was playing with her breasts.

"We want you at the same time. Each of us inside of you together, connected as one," Sandman whispered. She moaned a response, and Big Jay chuckled. He caressed her hair then stroked his cock deeper.

"Just like that, baby. Suck it all in. Make me yours." Big Jay's words were shockingly arousing. She began to find a rhythm, a way to accept his length and girth without feeling panicked for air. She relaxed her throat just as Sandman replaced his fingers with his cock.

The three of them took over control of her body and she wasn't complaining. She felt so feminine and comparable to some sex goddess who could satisfy three men's hunger with her body alone. The three of them made love to her in such a way she wondered if they had some magical powers only brothers could have.

Duke held her hips as she moved her mouth back and forth over Big Jay's cock. Sandman gripped her hair and leaned over her, his cock deep in her ass.

"Damn, Grace, you drive me fucking crazy." He nipped her ear as she moaned against Big Jay's cock.

"Fuck, brother, keep it up. Her mouth feels so incredible sucking my cock. I'm coming, baby." Big Jay thrust faster and Sandman held her there while Duke thrust up and down.

She was losing her strength, her ability to remain upright as Big Jay exploded inside her mouth. She swallowed as quickly as she could, wanting to taste every bit of him and satisfy him. He made a noise as he pulled from her mouth. "Damn, baby, that was fucking hot." Big Jay sat down on the bench and leaned back. She was trying to catch her breath when she felt Duke begin a series of hard upward thrusts while Sandman remained still in her ass.

"Oh God, I can't take it. I'm losing my strength," she admitted.

"Hold on, baby, we're almost there," Duke said as he pumped faster. She fell to his chest. He wrapped his arms around her and continued his thrusts as Sandman grabbed ahold of her hips and pounded into her from behind. They were all moaning and panting. "Oh!" She screamed her release.

"Damn." Duke roared and Sandman continued his strokes then shoved into her hard, exploding into her ass. The three of them lay still, catching their breath as the sounds of water flowing, birds singing, and the peacefulness of the seclusion around them took place of their moaning and thrusts.

"Sweet mother of God, you're incredible. That was incredible,"

Duke said as he cupped her face between his hands and kissed her hard on the mouth. She started to lift up as Sandman began to ease out of her.

"Slow down, sweetheart. Let Duke carry you inside," he said in that commanding bossy tone of his. But this time, she accepted it and allowed him and his brothers to take care of her while she closed her eyes and rested.

* * * *

Sarah and Eric turned on the news after breakfast. The reporters were talking about Maggie and the serial killer. He had put himself in a new category of Cop Killer and the public was scared. It hit Sarah hard as the reporter stated that the killer was looking for Grace Thompson.

"Sources close to the investigation say that Grace Thompson has been placed in protective custody for her safety, and our sources say she is still in the state of Texas and merely a half an hour's plane ride away. More information is being verified at this time and I will have the latest for you as soon as I can," the reporter said as she continued the news report.

"Oh my God, Eric, someone found out where she is. The killer." Sarah began to say but Eric cut her off.

"It's all right, Sarah, she's going to be fine. She's with the investigator and the reporter didn't say they knew Grace's exact location," Eric told her as the phone began to ring in the kitchen.

Sarah picked it up and Frank called to see if she'd heard the report.

"Donald is pissed off right now along with the agents. We don't know who's leaking the information, Mom. Sandstone made sure none of us knew where she was headed. As far as I know, Grace doesn't even know where she is," Frank told her as he continued to calm his mother down.

"What about Grace? Does she know about the reports?" Sarah asked.

"No she doesn't. Jim is going to contact Sandstone and let him know. I told him they should keep the information from Grace. If she finds out, then she'll want to come home," Frank said.

"You're right, Frank. She would want to come home. Do you think she'll be safe with him?" she asked her son.

"Yeah, Mom. He'll keep her safe, I'm sure of it," Frank stated confidently. They talked a few more minutes, then he hung up the phone.

* * * *

"This is bad news, Jim. Does Sandman know about the news report this morning? How could this happen?" Agent Burbank, the senior investigator with the FBI, asked Detective Jim Warner.

"I just got off the phone with Sandstone, sir. He's going to keep the information away from Miss Thompson. She's having a hard time dealing with her brother's girlfriend's death. She wants to come back home. Sandstone said he could handle it. I don't know who leaked the information, but I'm going to find out," Jim stated.

"This case is getting worse by the week. Now this sicko kills a cop. Have you got any other leads?" Senior Investigator Burbank asked.

"No, sir. Not right now. Sandstone did say that Grace was possibly onto something. He'll call with more updates as they become available. Meanwhile we're still looking closely at her sister's case. We're going to reinterview some of the people who were questioned the first time around. Maybe we'll find something there. Also, those other murders that Sandstone think may be connected were all associated with one another through volunteer communities. Either they helped organize, gain funds, or fought for government funding for projects together. Not sure if that's a link or if they just all happen to be good citizens," Jim explained. "It's something Sandstone was figuring out."

"Well, I've known Sandman for quite some time. The man knows how to solve the unsolvable. If he thinks there's a connection then let's start putting some serious manpower on that idea. Let me know if you need the agents' help."

"I will, sir. Thank you."

"Okay. Give Sandstone my best when you speak to him next. If you need anything else just call me."

* * * *

Sandman listened as Grace talked to his brothers about photography and working with models. He listened to the way she described her profession and the environment she worked in.

She was an amazing young woman. She had gone through so much in such a short amount of time. She was strong and independent, not wanting to rely on anyone for help or get too close for that matter.

He did though. He was slowly beginning to tear down that wall. She was so beautiful, so sexy, and he wondered if any relationship would continue after the case was over. He had his fears about commitment as well but that was before he met Grace. He had been so afraid to get close to any one woman. He saw the struggles in the relationship between his father and his mother. He didn't want that kind of life. His father put the Marine Corps first and there was always another mission. While other husbands were beginning to plan for retirement or slow down a little, his father was determined to volunteer for more missions. One more dangerous than the next. He had no problem leaving his wife and he never gave it a second thought. His mother was very strong and so supportive, yet she cried continually fearing for her husband's life, having difficulty dealing with the loneliness.

He felt that was what actually killed her. She became depressed and eventually mentally unstable. She didn't have any problems with her heart but it just gave out on her one day. The doctors said it was a stroke but he felt she died from a broken heart. His father hadn't even made it to her funeral. He was on some crazy mission and there was no way to contact him. The thoughts angered Sandman all over again. The relationship between him and his father began to weaken and he lost respect for him. While others would compliment Sandman on his father's heroic accomplishments, he would just nod his head, give a courteous thank-you, and hope he wouldn't turn out to be just like him. His brothers felt the same way. It must have really sent his mom over the edge when all three sons decided to follow in their father's path. They were young. They weren't committed to anything other than the Corps. That was life as a Marine.

He could have easily become his father. Sandman loved taking on any and every possible mission or extra training missions he could. He wanted to stay clear of his father and clear of any intimate relationships. They saw each other briefly between missions and avoided any conversations that involved their emotions or his mother.

Big Jay and Duke were all Sandman had in the world. They decided to retire from the service and settle down, commit to one location. So what that it was amongst other service men and women in a community of first responders? They loved their jobs and that was what scared him about Grace.

The way she described what she did and her desire to continue put any ideas of long-term commitment out of the equation. She traveled to work in Europe. The last time he was overseas, he was nearly killed by terrorists.

He looked at Grace again, grateful that their lives were thrown together. She was a lot like him and his brothers. She was so strong on the outside but inside she was afraid, not wanting to take chances with herself physically or emotionally, yet she still left her family, left the country, and pursued an exciting career. He wanted to know everything about her but they needed to focus on the case. He needed to protect her and he would do more than that. He was in love with her and would have to submerge those feelings if he was to stay focused and alert.

That thought was clarified when he got a call from Jim Warner informing him that information was leaked about Grace's whereabouts. He agreed to keep Grace in the dark but he wouldn't be able to stop her from watching the TV. She would want to go home, and of course he would refuse to take her. Sandman smiled to himself as something she said made both of his brothers laugh.

"What kind of stories are you telling them?" Sandman asked.

"She is one funny little lady. I'll tell you," Big Jay said then wiped the tears of laughter away from his eyes.

Grace was smiling as she helped Duke with the tray of sandwiches.

"What did Jim want this morning?" she asked as she sat down next to Big Jay at the wooden table on the porch.

"He just wanted to update me on the investigation back home. Nothing's new," Sandman replied as he avoided eye contact with her. Lying to Grace was more difficult than he thought it would be.

Grace took notice and so did his brothers.

"Sandman?" She touched his hand, stopping him from lifting his sandwich.

She looked into his eyes and he knew he was in for it.

"I know you're not telling me something. What's going on? What happened at home?"

"Nothing happened at home, Grace. I told you that," he said to her but she wouldn't budge.

"You're afraid I'll make you take me home, aren't you?" she asked him as Duke and Big Jay watched and listened.

"You can't make me do any such thing. Now leave it alone, Grace. If there's something you need to know, I'll be the one to tell you," he replied firmly.

Grace stared at him a moment and realized he was serious and she dropped the subject.

"I think we should focus on Grace's profile of the killer," Big Jay said.

"My profile?" she asked.

Sandman explained her theory as well as the similar patterns in each crime scene.

"I asked Jim to look into the other suspects from the other cases. Maybe something will come up from that," Sandman said, still recalling that conversation and also how Grace's location could have been compromised.

"What about the letters? Anything ring a bell there for Grace?" Duke asked.

Sandman never told Grace about the letters. He knew the latest one would upset her.

"What letters?" she asked, and Duke looked at Sandman, knowing he fucked up.

"Oh I must be thinking about something else. I'm sorry," Duke said as he rose from his chair to clear his plate.

"Nice try, Duke. What letters, Sandman?" Grace asked. She held his gaze and he wished he could lie to her.

There was no use in lying now, so Sandman told her about the poems left at the last few crime scenes.

She was hesitant a moment and he hoped for a second that she would decline seeing them. No such luck.

"Can I see them?"

"I don't think it's a good idea."

Grace cut him off. "I think it's a good idea. Maybe I'll see some kind of connection there. Why didn't you show them to me earlier, Sandman?" She was angry with him for withholding the information.

He stared at her a moment. Part of him didn't want her to experience the sick, demented obsession the killer had with her. Another part of him did, so that maybe she would drop the idea of getting further involved and just let him and his brothers protect her.

"Because the latest one mentions you. I didn't want to upset you more, Grace." Her eyes widened.

"What do you mean mentioned me? What did it say? I want to see it."

Sandman rose from the table. He knew she would be even more determined to get her hands on them. "Maybe later, Grace. I think you need a little break from this. Enough for today." He cleared his plate.

He heard her slam her hand down on the table.

* * * *

"Don't tell me what I need. I want to help as much as I can. I want to see the damn poems." She raised her voice now as she stood in front of him with her hands on her hips.

Sandman walked away toward his office as Duke spoke to Grace.

"I'm getting a headache just watching you two bash heads like that. You have got to be the most stubborn people I've ever laid eyes on. Damn," Big Jay stated.

"I'm getting turned on by it actually," Duke added as he leaned back in his chair and gave Grace a wink.

She shook her head.

"He makes me crazy. I looked at the files from my sister's murder. How much worse could these letters be than that? Why is Sandman acting like this?"

"It doesn't take a genius to see the sparks flying between all of us. Sandman's the one who brought us together. You get to Sandman more than I've ever seen anyone, man or woman, get to him. I'm sure the same thing goes for you. Those letters are pretty intense, sweetheart. When you're not used to seeing such things, it could be very upsetting. I think Sandman just wants to protect you as much as he can," Big Jay told her just as Sandman turned the corner.

He walked up to the counter and dropped the papers onto it.

"You want to read them so badly? Here you go," Sandman said as he went to the refrigerator and poured himself another glass of ice tea.

Grace took the letters and walked up to her room leaving the men to talk.

* * * *

"Damn she is so stubborn." Sandman banged his fist on the table.

"Just like you. Although I didn't think you'd give in that easy," Big Jay teased his brother, trying to make light of the situation.

"Easy? You think I gave up easy? She wanted to see the damn things. Let her. I don't think she realizes how crazy this guy is, Jay. Jim called and the news reports are claiming to know Grace's whereabouts. Of course Grace doesn't know that either." Sandman put his hands in the pockets of his blue jeans.

"Don't you think she has the right to know? Why shouldn't she? It's her life being tossed around and turned upside down. She's not going to leave. It's not an option," Duke sated, suddenly not so quiet anymore.

Sandman stared at both of his brothers. "Well I'll tell her later. Right now I want to look over these files some more."

Sandman walked out of the room, but his mind was really on Grace and what her reaction would be to the letters.

* * * *

Grace sat in the bedroom. She was getting sicker and sicker to her stomach with each line she read. The killer was after her, wanting her. He spoke of making love to her and thinking about her as he killed.

She thought about Maggie and the way she died. This killer wanted to send a message and he knew Grace's family and her loved ones, and he could easily get to any of them.

Suddenly Grace was in a panic as she paced the room, her mind spinning out of control with every thought. She was dizzy and nauseous all at once, her body was sweating, perspiring, her blood felt like it was boiling as she grabbed the wooden bedpost. Her head fell forward and she collapsed to the floor, passing out.

* * * *

Sandman was walking up the stairs to check on Grace. He shouldn't have given in so easily. He should have refused to let her see the poems. He thought about how angry she got him with her persistent attitude. He was used to being in charge and having people take orders from him.

What did she know about investigative work, about murder and death? The majority of his life as a soldier and as a special investigator forced him to become almost desensitized to it. Grace didn't need to be exposed to such things.

Just as he got to her bedroom door, he immediately saw her lying on the floor next to the bed. He was in a panic as he called down to his brothers.

She looked pale and her clothes were damp. He knew instantly she had passed out as he glanced at the poems that lay strewn across the floor.

"Goddamn you, Grace. Why do you have to be so damn stubborn?" he stated with his teeth clenched.

He picked her up and placed her on the bed then went to get a cold washcloth.

"What the hell happened?" Duke asked as he and Big Jay entered the bedroom.

"She fucking passed out. I knew I should have followed my gut. Fuck." Sandman walked over toward the bed with a cold washcloth.

He sat next to her gently pushing the loose, wet strands of hair away from her face. He placed the washcloth on her forehead and spoke softly to her, trying to wake her up.

"Come on, Grace. Wake up, baby." He ran his index finger gently along her cheek and jaw. He watched her chest rise and fall with even breath. She would be okay. She just passed out. He looked at his beautiful woman. The emotions, the fear that something could happen to her struck him hard to the chest.

"Sandman?" Big Jay said his name.

"Yeah."

"She'll be okay. She probably had information overload and panicked. Her coloring is already getting better." Sandman felt both his brother's hands on each shoulder. He eased his breath, and took comfort in their support.

He thought he would never need anyone. He was wrong.

* * * *

As her body cooled down Grace slowly began to open her eyes, unaware of what happened to her.

"You must have passed out, baby. I found you by the bed on the floor." He told her as he held the washcloth to her forehead.

"I knew this was going to happen. It's been so long." She spoke slowly, still a little groggy.

"What do you mean? This has happened before?" Big Jay asked her and she didn't answer him. She didn't want them to worry more. She had passed out a few times in her hotel rooms in Europe as she thought about her sister Clara, her family and all that had happened to her. She did it mostly when it was close to the anniversary of her sister's death.

Then it hit her that tomorrow was the day. Three years since her sister was killed. Grace began to shake and tears filled her eyes as she tried to turn away from Sandman and lie on her side.

Duke stopped her, holding her arms as he looked at her face. She was scared and sad and she said she had passed out before. What was Grace not telling them? He wondered as he spoke to her.

"Grace, what is it?" Duke asked her. "You're shaking."

She tried to open her eyes. They were red and filled with tears that now escaped down her cheeks, past her neck, and onto the comforter. "I can't breathe, Duke. The pain in my chest, in my heart, I can't breathe. I just can't take it," she struggled to say as she began to weep.

Duke's heart ached, and one look toward Sandman and Big Jay and he knew they felt it, too. They surrounded her on the bed now and tried to calm her. Each of them began to caress her thigh or her cheek and make her focus on them and nothing else.

As Duke watched her cry, he saw and felt her sadness, her pain, and her loss. He lay down next to her on the bed and wrapped his arms around her, pulling her close against him as she continued to cry.

"It's okay, baby. Everything's going to be okay," Big Jay said as he lay down on the bottom of the bed and caressed her ankles.

Sandman moved in behind her on the other side, pushing strands of damp hair away from her cheek.

Duke held her tight, rubbing her back softly, spreading tiny, gentle kisses across her forehead.

* * * *

Grace cried for a while as she thought about her sister Clara, Maggie, and the other victims. Why was this happening to her? What did the killer want? Who could he be? So many questions scattered through her mind, her head was pounding, and her stomach was in knots.

"Sandman," she began to say but he interrupted her.

"Don't talk, sweetie. Just rest. We're right here with you."

"We're not going anywhere," Duke added then kissed her cheek.

Grace closed her eyes.

* * * *

Duke awoke a while later still holding Grace in his arms who now lay sleeping. She said something about it happening before. Then she wouldn't tell them everything. She still didn't trust them completely.

He looked over her toward Sandman who was in a dead stare at Grace as her eyes fluttered open. He knew that both his brothers were feeling her pain.

* * * *

Grace awoke and felt the dread of having to face Sandman, Big Jay, and Duke. They'd seen her at her worse. They saw her break down and lose it, and now they would keep her out of the investigation. She started to get up when strong hands pressed her shoulders down. Opening her eyes, she stared up at Duke.

"How are you feeling?"

"Better," she whispered in a shaky voice. Her body was completely aware of these men and their bodies. Duke pressed his thigh over her legs and between them. He adjusted himself so his weight was mostly off of her but she was still pinned to the bed.

She swallowed hard as he gently traced her jaw with his fingertip.

"You gave us a scare, darling. I take it this type of thing has happened to you before."

She heard his intense tone and knew that lying to him would be stupid and ridiculous. These men were professional interrogators anyway. She nodded her head.

"It's been a while though, hasn't it?" Sandman asked and she turned to look at him. He scooted closer and was now pressed against her other side.

"Not so often as before."

"You scared me," Duke repeated then lowered his mouth to hers and kissed her softly. She immediately reached up to hold on to his shoulders as he deepened the kiss.

She couldn't help her reaction. She didn't want to talk about it now. She wanted to make love with them. She wanted them deep inside of her taking all her fears and worries away.

Duke slowly released her lips, and they were both breathing heavy.

"I need you," she whispered and he nibbled his bottom lip as he stared into her eyes with the most serious expression.

"We're going to make love to you. Slowly, deeply, darling. You're going to allow us in. Enough of not trusting us fully, Grace. You're ours and we're yours."

She felt the sincerity and power of his words as a tear escaped her eyes.

Duke lifted up to remove his clothing as Sandman caressed the tear from her cheek.

"You're more important to us than anything. Let us show you."

She nodded her head and allowed them to divest her of her clothing.

In no time at all the four of them were naked.

Duke pressed between her legs as Sandman lay on her right side and Big Jay lay on her left side.

She was sandwiched between three large, robust military men, filled with muscles and enough of an arsenal of abilities she knew nothing about. It gave her peace of mind, security, and hope that one day there would be only happiness in her life, in their lives.

Duke caressed his palms over her shoulders, down her arms to her hands as he scooted his cock closer to her pussy.

She gasped at the chills that ran up her inner groin and in response, spread her thighs wider.

Duke pressed his cock between her wet folds as he held her gaze and brought her hands up and above her head to the pillow. Their fingers locked and slowly, deeply, he made love to her.

As Duke glided his cock in and out of her pussy, she absorbed every sensation including the way his wide hips moved and dipped downward then into her. She felt both Sandman and Big Jay's hands on her thighs, spreading her wider as they trailed fingers along her curves and to her breasts.

She gripped Duke's fingers tighter and thrust her hips upward meeting his thrusts. It was too much. Their lovemaking was overwhelming as tears rolled down her cheeks.

"Look at me, baby," Duke commanded and instantly she opened her eyes, vision blurred from her happy tears and she smiled at him.

"That's better. You feel it, baby? You feel how into you I am?"

"Yes. You have to move faster," she begged of him.

"I want to make love to you, baby. I want to brand you my woman for eternity." He thrust deeper, faster into her.

"Do it then. Do it harder, faster please, Duke."

He leaned down and kissed her passionately. When he released her hands and grabbed her hips, she reached for his hands and he pounded into her. Duke looked so intense and wild with the veins in his neck bulging out and his head tilted back. She knew she was deeply in love with him as she exploded, screaming his name, and he followed suit.

"Grace. I love you, Grace!" he yelled then thrust three fast, hard times into her before he fell to the bed and held her tight.

He was crushing her but she didn't care. "I love you, too," she whispered then kissed his shoulder while she held him, her big SWAT team commander in her arms, and for once she felt like she could give Duke what he wanted and needed in life.

* * * *

Sandman got up off the bed. Big Jay saw the tears in his brother's eyes as Sandman shook his head, pulled on his boxers, and walked out of the room. His brother was so used to being alone despite the fact that Big Jay and Duke were in his life. He didn't have any romantic relationships. None of them did until now. Big Jay stared at Grace holding Duke in her arms. It touched him, too. He felt the power of their love, of all of their love, the four of them together. It was un-fucking-believable and it was all because of Grace. She was amazing.

He crawled up next to her and Duke. Duke must have sensed him as he lifted up, kissed Grace a few more times, then smiled at her.

"I'm going to go take a shower. I'll see you in little bit, okay?"

She smiled as she nodded her head.

Big Jay watched her eyes glaze over as Duke pulled slowly from her body. Duke got up and walked toward the other room, grabbing his clothes.

"Hey, beautiful," Big Jay whispered, and Grace turned toward him smiling. She lay on her side, knees slightly bent and she covered her breasts with her forearms. He chuckled, then took her wrists in one hand and placed them above her head. She gasped as she rolled to her back.

"Don't you know that you shouldn't be shy around us anymore, baby? This is all ours." He leaned down and licked across her breasts. The tiny pink flesh hardened under his tongue, and he drew in a deeper suck.

"Yummy." He moved across to her other breast and did the same thing.

He remained holding her wrists with one hand above her head making her body appear like a feast just for him.

"I like restraining you. You know, in the service I was best known for my intricate, complicated knots. They came in handy when we had to propel down from rooftops and crash through windows."

He watched her eyes widen and her breathing grow rapid. This turned Grace on.

"Is that why they call you Big Jay?" she asked as he trailed his fingers from her breasts to her cunt. He pressed a finger up between her slick folds as he smiled at her.

She parted her lips and moaned.

"No. Ain't it obvious, baby?" He lifted up to get between her thighs. His long, thick cock tapped against her thigh.

"Oh, you mean your...cock?" she asked, sounding so shy and inexperienced. He chuckled.

"That, too. I guess I'm big all over."

She looked at him as he hovered over her body, thrusting his fingers in and out of her wet cunt. He still held her wrists above her head, restraining her, and she appeared to really enjoy it.

"I have plans for you, woman."

"Oh, you do?" she replied with a little spunk. He hid his chuckle.

"Oh yeah, big plans."

"Such as?"

"You tied up to my bed on your belly. I'd place a pillow under your hips so that your beautiful, round ass was lifted nice and high."

"Oh." She moaned as he applied pressure to her pussy with his fingers then pressed his pinky against her puckered hole. She thrust her ass down and then her pussy hard against his fingers as she tried to get her wrists free.

"You're a naughty little thing, aren't ya, darling? You like being dirty. You like a cock in your ass and the idea of me tying you up to my bed and spanking that ass of yours."

"Oh God, yes, yes, I want that." She thrust her pussy against his fingers.

He used his thighs to spread her thighs wider then pulled his fingers from her pussy.

"That's what I'm going to give you soon enough. Right now, you've got my cock so tight I won't last long. I love you, Grace."

"Oh God, Big Jay, I love you, too. I need you inside of me. Do something now."

He lined his bog cock up with her wet pussy and shoved in to the hilt.

He felt on fire as he stroked down deeply, repeatedly into her wet pussy. Over and over again he pounded into her, wanting to brand her his woman and leave his mark. He released her wrists, entwined his hands with hers and stroked her over and over again, dipping his chest all the way down to her chest with every thrust.

She locked her legs around his waist and counterthrust until he released her hands, wrapped his arms around her like a grizzly bear, and squeezed her tight. He spread her ass cheeks with each stroke and felt their pubic bones collide together. This was the closest he could ever get with Grace, with anyone.

"Fuck, Gracey, I love you, darling. I love you." He exploded inside of her as Grace joined with him, shaking and screaming her release against his neck.

* * * *

Grace squeezed Big Jay to her even though he was crushing her body. He was so big all over, she felt lost in his embrace. She loved how close she felt to him and was shocked at how deep he penetrated her body. She loved him and his brothers so much she wished she could be lost inside them like this forever.

Big Jay lifted up and kissed her along her jaw and then her lips. She ran her fingers through his hair, absorbed the smell of his cologne and the feel of his manly chest.

"I don't want to crush you. I'm sorry, baby," he whispered.

"I don't mind. I was lost inside of you. I love making love to you." He smiled at her.

"That's a good thing, 'cause we'll be doing it a lot and for the rest of our lives."

She swallowed hard as the tears reached her eyes.

"Big Jay, I'm scared this won't work out. I fear this killer."

He placed a finger over her bottom lip."

"The killer will get caught. The four of us will work this whole relationship out and be together forever."

She looked past his shoulder, realizing that Sandman wasn't there.

"Where's Sandman?"

Big Jay appeared upset but then he smiled as he placed his hands against her cheeks and slowly pulled out of her.

"He's scared, baby. He loves you so much and watching all of us make love got to him."

"You mean he was jealous?"

He chuckled.

"No, of course not. He was…scared."

"Sandman, scared?"

"He felt the connection, the bond and love between the four of us. I think he's closed off his heart all these years after his experience in the service and the missions he went on. You've changed that for all of us, Grace. Hey, that's it. You're our amazing Grace." He kissed her deeply before he lifted up and offered her a hand.

She thought about what he said. Sandman was just like her in more ways than either of them could recognize. No wonder why they argued and banged heads. *He's just like me. He's scared to feel and open up his heart.*

"Where is he, Big Jay?"

"Probably in his room," Big Jay said with a smile. She knelt up on the bed, gave him a kiss, then very proudly walked out of the room naked and in search of her soldier, Sandman.

* * * *

Grace heard the shower running. One peek into the bathroom and she saw Sandman standing under the flow of water in the huge tiled shower with his head hanging down. She tiptoed over, wanting to sneak up on him.

"I'll be out in a little bit," he said, making her jump. Son of a bitch, he was good.

"Can I join you?" she asked, not giving him the chance to decline, hoping he wouldn't anyway as she got in behind him. There were multiple sprayer heads, shooting streams of water from around the shower. It was an impressive setup and it instantly wet her entirely. She eased her way closer to him then underneath him so she was now between his arms. Grace cupped his face between her hands, and when she looked into his eyes, she was shocked to see them red and almost bloodshot.

"I missed you," she whispered.

He kept his hands flat against the wall behind her. He wasn't budging. Big Jay was right. Sandman was scared to open up his heart.

"I wanted to make love to you, like I did with Big Jay and Duke." She leaned forward to kiss his chest. She lowered herself down his body, kissing along his muscular chest, his belly, his ribs, and then his cock.

He pulled up slightly to give her better access to his long, thick cock. She immediately pulled it into her mouth and drew in his shaft.

His hands fell to her head. He gripped her tightly then stroked his cock slowly into her mouth.

She held on to his chiseled thighs and allowed him to set the pace. He was awfully big, and there was no way his entire cock would fit down her throat, no matter how relaxed or hungry she was.

As if sensing her inability to take it all in, he slowed his strokes, only giving her half his cock.

"That feels good, baby." He moaned and slowly moved his hips back and forth.

She caressed his thighs, massaged him as she explored his body all the way to his ass. He was thick, wide with muscles, and she pressed her mouth closer, so she could reach halfway behind him and squeeze his ass. The man had an amazing ass.

She caressed her way back, using her hands to massage his tight muscles before she cupped his balls in the palm of her hand and was soon lost in pleasing her man.

Sandman suddenly pulled from her mouth, lifted her up and placed her against the wall. She wrapped her legs around his waist, felt her thighs trembling as she locked gazes with him.

He held her face between his hands as he looked down into her eyes with love and compassion.

"I've never." He swallowed hard.

This was difficult for him.

"I love you, Sandman. I want to be with you and your brothers. I want you inside of me. It's where I feel perfect and where life is perfect."

"Damn, Grace. That's it. That's what I feel, too." He pressed his cock between her wet folds and pushed into her.

She gripped his forearms as he pulled out of her then pushed back in. They held gazes and she saw the deep emotion in his eyes. She felt the connection to him with her heart and soul.

He must have felt it, too, as he increased his speed and stroked her pussy over and over again, bending his body to penetrate her deeper. She was screaming his name, panting for breath when he exploded inside of her.

"I love you. You're mine forever." He held her to him as the water sprayed over their bodies. She didn't care how long they stayed in this position with him inside of her, just as long she could have him and his brothers forever.

In the back of her mind, she sensed the feeling of foreboding. It was there, just at the edge of their happiness. The four of them wouldn't have a future until the killer was found.

Chapter 13

"Are you kidding me? Of course she trusts us or we wouldn't be in the position we are right now or feeling the way we do. She needs us, as much as we need her. That poor girl has been running scared for years and rightly so, I might add. She finally decides to come home and she's faced with her sister's murder again, nearly has her head shot off, touches evidence from a murder, is hauled off in disguise from her family and friends. Then she comes here and falls in love with us, starts pushing herself to solve these crimes along with us, never mind the anniversary of her sister's death is tomorrow. No wonder she fainted," Big Jay stated as he, Duke, and Sandman stood in the kitchen. It was late in the evening and they all dreaded what tomorrow may bring for Grace emotionally.

"I feel like I don't know what else I can do for her. I'm not sure she holds the key to catching this guy. I'd rather be protective and keep her out of the loop of everything. Ya know? Isolated from the entire case until this guy is caught," Sandman admitted.

"We feel the same way, but that's not an option. She was good the last few days, coming up with a profile, trying to find something to help in the investigation. We can't put a wall up now or that wall will go up between us and our relationship, too," Duke said.

"Yes, we have to stay focused. We need to be there for Grace because we're in love with her and together we can protect her. Wrap things up so we can start focusing on each other. She obviously feels like she can help in some way. If these killings continue, you know what your superiors are going to want to do. This guy killed a cop. The feds are right there itching to take over this case," Duke added.

"I know that. I've been avoiding that thought for days. I also know who they sent in and he doesn't give a shit about anyone or anything he has to bulldoze over or use to get to the killer," Sandman added. "They'll want to use Grace as bait." He rose from the chair.

"You're damn straight. You know you'll have no control over that decision. We won't be able to stop them, and knowing Grace, she'll do it. She's emotionally distraught and wants to be with her family. She wants a normal life," Big Jay said then pushed an envelope across the table toward Sandman.

"What's this?"

"I picked up these pictures Grace took last week. She had asked me to get them developed for her. She's a great photographer. I've never seen pictures like these before," Big Jay said.

"She took some nice candid shots of us, but some amazing ones of you," Duke added.

Sandman sat at the island thinking about Grace as he opened the envelope.

She had taken gorgeous pictures of the landscaping around the property along with individual pictures of the Koi in the pond as well as candid shots of Big Jay cooking and working and Duke trying to act cool. He chuckled as he scanned through the pictures. As he viewed each photograph he saw some of him that he hadn't even known she had taken. The first one showed him sitting at his desk looking over some files. One showed him talking on the phone, holding his laptop on his lap, and drinking a cup of coffee.

There was even one of him cooking in the kitchen, talking to his brothers.

The pictures were great and he was impressed with Grace's talent. He also had an instant thought that brought on worry and fear. She was a professional photographer. She had a career, a life in Europe. This visit to her family was for a wedding and she hadn't planned on staying in the United States long. He couldn't stand in the way of her career and what she so obviously loved and enjoyed doing.

He looked at his brothers.

"Once this is all over, we'll work things out. We'll figure out how she can continue her career as we continue ours." Duke seemed as if he were trying to convince himself as he said the words

"We need to stay focused. You can handle this, Sandman. You're one of the best." Big Jay gave his brother a squeeze on his shoulder.

Sandman looked at the clock. They needed to head to bed. Tomorrow was going to be a doozy of a day.

"We should get to bed. Grace doesn't like to wake up alone," he said as he numbly headed upstairs. His heart was heavy. His mind consumed with the case, with a future for his brothers, him, and Grace, and with finding the person who held the cards in his hands and ultimately held their fate.

* * * *

The agents were questioning suspects all night and had just begun a new list this morning. They were coming up with dead ends and wondered what to do next.

Sarah walked into the police department and received warm welcomes from everyone that knew her. She headed toward Donald's office to see if she could talk to her daughter or perhaps e-mail her.

"Sarah, how are you?" Donald asked, as he rose from his chair and greeted her.

Sarah smiled at Donald as she walked into the room. He was a handsome man and had become such a close friend of the family. She knew he would always be there for her and her children. God knew how much they adored him.

She said hello and took a seat across from Donald's desk.

"Excuse the smell in here. The room was painted a few days ago but you can still smell the paint fumes," he told her, and then gave that charismatic smile that was so Donald.

"I thought I might e-mail Grace or perhaps call her? I'm not sure what I'm allowed to do. Would that be all right?" she asked hesitantly as Donald rose from his chair.

"You can use this laptop right here, Sarah, and I think Detective Jim Warner is about to call Sandman soon. I have to leave for an hour or so but I'll check with him and I'll have one of the agents check up on you in a little while. How does that sound?" Donald asked as he pulled out his chair, offering for her to sit down.

"Thank you, Donald. I'm so glad that you're part of this investigation. You've been part of the family for years and all the kids look up to you," she said, and he held her gaze. Donald was truly a handsome man. She often wondered why he never remarried after his wife had died. He held her gaze and a funny sensation filled her gut. She shyly looked toward the laptop on his desk

"Let me go check with the detective and you get started." He began to leave.

Sarah grabbed his hand to stop him.

"Thank you, Donald, for everything." He smiled back, squeezing her hand.

"Sarah, you know that you can always count on me right?" he asked her as she smiled and nodded yes before walking away.

* * * *

Donald felt his chest tighten as he stared at Sarah before leaving the room. He ran an unsteady hand through his hair. He was in love with a married woman. It was instant and happened the moment they met. She was way too good for Eric but there was nothing he could do about it. He heard they had some troubles and there was a rumor going around town that Eric had cheated on her on multiple occasions. He didn't know if there was any truth to these rumors but he knew that if she were his, he would love her, cherish her, and dedicate himself completely to her. He glanced back toward his office before heading to the elevator. Her heart was breaking and all he wanted to do was hold her, comfort her.

Donald bumped into Jim and asked him to assist Sarah. He of course obliged as he headed into Donald's office.

* * * *

"Thank you for your help, Jim. I can take it from here," Sarah said as Jim gave her a soft smile. He was a good man. He was married and shared his wife with his best friend. Of course Sarah found it difficult to believe such relationships existed, but who was she to judge? Her own relationship with her husband was questionable. She had been denying the fact that he truly didn't love her anymore. She even believed that Eric was cheating on her. She couldn't confront him though. Then she would be left completely alone. Instead she submerged herself in her volunteer work and pretended pure happiness with Eric.

She thought about Donald. Donald was so handsome, so kind and understanding. He always knew what she was thinking and what she needed. She couldn't help but be attracted to him but she was a married woman and Eric was her husband. She pushed the thoughts from her mind as she sat down and began typing.

* * * *

Grace's cousin Jamie had arrived home after food shopping. She was enjoying her new role as wife and career woman. It was her day off from the accounting firm where she worked as an office manager. She had taken the day off to go visit Sarah. It was the anniversary of Clara's death today and she knew Grace was in protective custody. There was no way Sarah could speak to her on the phone and Jamie felt she should spend some time with her aunt. Sarah had planned to go by the police station to e-mail Grace and talk to Donald.

Jamie had left Sarah's house around an hour ago and decided to get the supplies she needed to cook dinner. She was planning on making a gourmet meal for her new husband Tod who was due home at around five this evening.

As Jamie unpacked her shopping bags placing the fresh spinach into the vegetable compartment in the refrigerator and putting the butter and eggs away, she heard a noise come from the upstairs. It sounded like Precious, her Siamese cat, had knocked over the planter in the hallway again.

Jamie stopped what she was doing and headed up the stairs. She noticed the planter lying on the floor and this time the cat made a big mess.

Jamie yelled out her name as she bent down and began cleaning.

"Damn it, Precious, why do you always have to do this? I have a dinner to get started," Jamie said as she gathered up the broken pieces.

She never heard a sound or felt the presence behind her until it was too late. Suddenly she was grabbed from behind and Jamie began to scream.

The man sprayed something into her eyes and she couldn't see. Her eyes were burning as the attacker covered them with masking tape.

She was screaming now, scared out of her mind as her attacker punched her in the mouth, trying to shut her up as he pulled the tape tightly across her mouth then patted it closed making sure it would stay put.

"Shut up, bitch. Or I'll kill you right now." He hissed at her as he threw her over his shoulder and carried her to the bedroom.

* * * *

The killer tossed Jamie onto the bed and then walked over toward the window where he had already closed the blinds.

This was real risky doing this in the daylight. He was taking a big chance. He was desperate and as they said, desperate times call for desperate measures.

He looked at his latest victim. This would send the message to Grace. *Come home or your family and friends are next.*

He began to tie Jamie's hands to the bedposts as she kicked her legs and grunted at him through the tape.

He laughed out loud at her. She was a tough one. He wouldn't expect anything less from a cop's wife. It would give him such great pleasure to do what he wanted with her then kill her right here.

He began to rip her clothes off, pleased with what he saw, claiming it with every touch, igniting all the fantasies and desires he had inside for Grace.

He would pretend she was Grace for a little while. There would be nothing better than the real thing and soon he would have her.

Grace was his goal. His ultimate prize. He would retire from his murder spree soon enough. By the time the cops figured out who he was and why he killed, it wouldn't matter. Grace would be his to have forever.

He stared at Jamie. She was Grace's best friend and cousin. She didn't have shit on Grace, but she was quite appealing to the eyes. He closed his eyes a moment and envisioned Grace lying there, bound, naked and ready for him.

He moved closer and removed the tape from Jamie's mouth.

"Don't scream, my love. Don't cry, don't yell, just do as I say and maybe you'll live."

* * * *

Jamie shook with fear as the killer whispered to her. Her arms were aching, her eyes were burning and the killer was on top of her, touching her.

"I've missed you, Grace. You've been on my mind constantly." He rubbed Jamie's stomach with his hands. Her heart ached and tightened. This was definitely the killer. He came after her. Why?

"I'm not Grace," Jamie began to say as the killer smacked her across the face.

"Shut up. You speak when I tell you to speak or I'll kill you right here."

Jamie couldn't believe this was happening to her. She was going to die and her husband Tod, a seasoned detective, would be the one to find her. She was shaking with fear as the killer taunted her, acting like she was Grace. She tried not to freak out as the pounding sound in her head continued. She focused on his voice and it hit her. He sounded familiar. *Do I know him?*

Her chest tightened and she gasped as different people's faces passed before her eyes, but his words, the sick tone of his voice cluttered her thinking.

"I love you, Grace. I have for many years. Especially after Clara died. I wanted you then, but I couldn't have you. Why did you go away?" He kissed her neck, her shoulder bone.

I know him. No, it can't be?

"Do you love me, Grace? Tell me you love me."

"No, you sick son of a—"

The killer began hitting her, punching her, and suddenly she felt his gloved hands around her neck. He was choking her, taking the life out of her.

"Tell Grace I'm waiting." He punched Jamie and she fell unconscious.

* * * *

Grace slept until midnight. She couldn't believe she slept through dinner and that the guys never woke her. As she looked around the room, she saw Sandman there, sleeping in the armchair.

His laptop was still on and she assumed he spent the day watching over her.

"Hey, sleepyhead, how are you feeling?" Sandman asked as he turned off his laptop and stood up to stretch out.

"I feel tired."

He smiled at her as he approached the bed.

"We had an eventful evening," he said, and she felt her cheeks blush. She remembered making love to them.

She remembered passing out.

"You were upset after reading the letters. I shouldn't have pushed you like that," he told her and she shook her head at him.

"No, don't go back to that and start thinking I couldn't handle the poems. I've had issues with anxiety and passing out before. And it's usually around the anniversary of Clara's death."

Sandman held her face gently in his hands.

"Which is today, but you're not alone, honey. I'm here for you. Duke and Big Jay are here, too." He kissed her softly.

Grace kissed him back and loved the way his kisses soothed her.

"Why don't you come in here where it's more comfortable?" she asked him as she lifted the blanket and scooted over.

Sandman slid next to her and began kissing her lips then her neck and shoulder. Grace closed her eyes and leaned her head back with anticipation as Sandman moved on top of her then down lower and under the blanket.

She giggled and shivered at his every gentle touch wanting him inside her, making love to her, healing her pain.

"Sandman, please…I want you," she whispered as he removed the remainder of their clothing, wanting to make love as much as she did.

They were naked in no time and she felt the thickness of his cock against her inner thigh and the weight of his upper body as her breasts pressed against his chest.

"I'm so ready for you," she whispered, feeling assertive. He smiled at her in such a seductive manner. Her heart leaped with joy that this man was hers to love and cherish.

He gently adjusted his position between her thighs. They shivered and quaked in anticipation of the first touch of his cock to her entrance. He pressed into her and she released a sigh of relief. The desperation she felt prior to penetration rocked her mind. She was so in love with him and his brothers.

He was inside her now, rocking into her slowly, sharing the rhythm, staring into one another's eyes. This time it was different. It was even more meaningful, deeper, more passionate. She silently realized that this was what true love really felt like. Giving all of yourself, willing to do anything for the other. They kissed one another simultaneously as if knowing they were thinking the same thing at the exact same time. No words were necessary as they continued to make love, their bodies, souls and spirits uniting, merging into one, feeling complete at last.

* * * *

She spent the morning in bed, then took a shower and headed downstairs in anticipation of having lunch with her men. *My men. I can sure get used to saying that.*

Grace headed to Sandman's office. He had told her she had a few e-mail messages that came from Donald.

She was actually in a good mood considering what day it was. It was Sandman, Big Jay, and Duke who did it to her.

She never imagined that falling in love would be so wonderful.

Grace sat down at the desk and began reading her messages. Her brothers wrote to her first thing this morning and she instantly replied to each of them.

Her mom had written her an upbeat note that told her how much she missed her and loved her. Grace had tears in her eyes and wished she could hold her mom in her arms.

Suddenly, she heard someone by the office door and looked up. Sandman was standing there holding his cell phone.

"Here, baby, it's for you." He stretched his hand out to give her the phone.

Grace wondered who it could be. Sandman, Big Jay, and Duke hadn't let her near a phone since she arrived.

"Hello."

"Grace, baby, is that you? Oh God, it's so wonderful to hear your voice," Sarah said as Grace looked at Sandman, then Big Jay and Duke as they stood in the doorway smiling. The tears rolled down her cheeks.

They were about to walk out of the room when Grace stopped them.

"Yes, Mom, I'm doing great. Actually I'm in love," Grace said and her three men stood there in shock. She chuckled.

"You are? Oh my God, I just knew it. I could tell by the way Special Investigator Sandstone looked at you and you at him."

"Well, actually, Mom, he has two brothers, Duke and Big Jay. I know it's unconventional, but I'm in love with the three of them."

Her mom gasped.

She was silent a moment and Grace felt her heart sink. Would her mom hate her or be disappointed?

"I've heard of relationships like that before, Grace. Just be careful and be sure. You're special and a man or men should love you entirely, not just for now."

"I know, Mom. It's all new to me, to them, too, but we're taking it one step at a time."

"I'm happy for you, Grace. Just be sure. So, how are you holding up, honey?" she asked her as Grace continued to talk to her mom for about fifteen minutes. Then John got on the phone along with Frank.

By the time Grace hung up the phone, she was in the happiest of moods.

She prayed to her sister Clara, thanking her for keeping the family together and helping her find Sandman, Big Jay, and Duke.

Grace came out of the office and found all three men standing by the table. They looked at her with big smiles on their faces.

She ran to them and jumped into Big Jay's arms.

"I love you so much. Thank you. Thank you." She hugged him tightly. Big Jay kissed her deeply and began to caress her ass as he squeezed her body closer to his.

"Hey, I want some of that 'thank you' loving, too," Duke teased and Big Jay reluctantly passed her off to Duke, who held her close and kissed her deeply. When he released her lips he smiled at her.

"It was Sandman's idea," he whispered.

Grace looked over toward Sandman who stood with his arms crossed and smiling at her.

"I needed that, Sandman. How did you know how much that would mean to me today?" she asked him. He stepped closer and Duke passed her over to Sandman who held her tight in his arms. He stared down into her eyes and she held his gaze.

"I'll do anything for you, Grace."

She smiled before she kissed him then hugged him tight.

* * * *

Back at the Houston Police Department, Detective Federal Agent Lancaster and his team were going over some leads and kept coming up with the same name, connecting the person in minor ways to the Clara Thompson murder and two other women after that.

"Take a look at this, Justin. This guy was at every crime scene, he was one of the first to respond, he kept in contact with the family and friends. He's been right next to them from the beginning and he knew that we were going to the Thompson place to question Grace," he told his partner Justin and their team of agents.

"It can't be anything, sir. He's a cop, a Lieutenant. What would be his motive? Yeah, he has easy access but still he's like family," Sullivan added as Agent Lancaster stared at the papers.

One of the other agents spoke up.

"It could explain why he's evaded capture for so long. The killer uses handcuffs, he knows everything about the family. Friedman would have access to all that."

"You're reaching, sir. I'm telling you he's not the guy," one of the others added.

"It won't hurt to ask him a few questions. Donald is Tod's father. Where is he anyway? He left over an hour ago," Lancaster said as he looked through the office windows and toward Donald's office.

Chapter 14

Grace was sitting at the dining room table looking over the files. Big Jay told her she didn't have to look at them today if she didn't want to but she felt it was the right thing to do. She wanted to catch this killer as bad as anyone and move on with her life. See her family again and be with Sandman and his brothers.

"What about the cases before Houston, the ones dating back nearly ten years ago? Were there any suspects at the time, anyone who seemed suspicious or hanging around?" she asked as Big Jay handed her a pile of files. Then Duke and he kept the rest.

"What are you thinking?" Duke asked her.

"Well, maybe those were his first time. Maybe he messed up somewhere and the detectives didn't catch it at that time. They weren't looking for something minor. We are." She opened up the first file.

They were at it for a while until Duke got up to start making some cheeseburgers.

"Do you need help, Duke?" Grace asked and of course he told her no as he went about preparing dinner.

Big Jay's eyes were getting tired as he closed the last file.

Grace stayed focused on the file in front of her. She found a photocopy of a small typed note that was found inside the jean pocket of the young woman who was murdered nearly nine years ago.

"Look at this, Big Jay. It states here under artifacts found with the victim's clothing were a small typed note and a four-digit telephone number."

"So the Detectives at the time would have checked for fingerprints and asked around about the telephone number, or maybe looked into it being a date, or even a passcode for something," Big Jay stated.

"What if they didn't? You're assuming they did, but we're talking over nine years ago and it says here that the woman's face was covered when they found her. Doesn't that usually mean the killer can't face what he's done and he tries to separate himself from the act?" she asked.

"Honey, have you been watching some detective shows or reading some off-the-wall books?" Duke asked as he tossed a salad.

"She may have a point, Duke. They may have been unable to get a print off of them at the time," Big Jay said.

"Today, our fingerprint and forensics equipment is even more precise than it used to be. Maybe this half a phone number or code or whatever it is, might lead to something?" She sat forward looking at Big Jay.

"Hey what have we got to lose? I'll call Jim and see what he can come up with. Let's put this stuff away for now. Give me that file and I'll go call him," Big Jay said.

"You're doing a good job, sweetie. I'm sure it's been tough not having your family around," Duke said as he stood next to her chair.

Grace got up and put her hand on Duke's arm.

"You're just like family, and when this is over, you have to come meet my family. I have an aunt that makes her own homemade blackberry preserves. It's the best," Grace said and Duke smiled.

Grace began to set the kitchen table for dinner and was thinking about the killer's letters. She had read a lot of the other files and there were no letters or poems left at the crime scenes. Only the first one contained a note and she wondered if Sandman could get his hands on it.

Maybe there was a connection between the first murder and then Clara's.

Grace often prayed to her sister for guidance. She still felt such a strong connection to her and now she was feeling that it was her sister pushing her to work this case and find her killer.

All those poor, innocent women killed so brutally. It was meaningless, wasteful, unfair but not through the eyes of the killer. To him there was great meaning and purpose behind them. They were somehow all connected and she could see the similarities between the victims. They were beautiful, all brunettes, tall and thin, they had good professions. What was it about Clara and now herself that the killer wanted? Could it be the simple fact that they were sisters, almost twins? They looked so much alike when they were younger it had to be someone they knew from the area.

The killer knows my family.

He was so easily able to track her down at her mom's house then at her brother John's. She wondered if he was connected to the police department somehow. Or maybe he had some connections there, people who found out information for him. Maybe there was more than one killer?

"You got awfully quiet. What are you thinking about, darling?" Duke asked as he began to uncork a new bottle of wine as she set the table. She explained her way of thinking and about her connection to her sister.

"It's not a far-fetched idea. If the killer is someone from your town, a known person who your family is friends with, then surely they would have had access to your whereabouts," he told her.

"Maybe I'm thinking too much. I should take a break and relax a little. You know, clear my head. Then we can look at the files some more later on."

"Sounds like a plan." Duke gave her a kiss on the cheek then offered her a glass of wine.

* * * *

It was 5:20 p.m. and Tod was just pulling into his driveway. He was twenty minutes late getting home to his new bride and he couldn't wait to see her. The house looked dark as he arrived and he wondered what kind of surprise she had in store for him.

A smile formed on his face as he thought about Jamie, her gorgeous face and fabulous body. Oh, how he loved to make love to her, discover every tiny freckle, every little spot that made her giggle or plead for more of him. She was so wonderful the way she cooked for him and catered to him when he arrived home from work. He couldn't wait to get inside as he unlocked the front door.

Tod put his keys on the long, narrow wooden table by the front door. Jamie had found the old piece of furniture at a garage sale, refinished it, and turned it into a unique conversation piece. She was so talented and so creative. He loved that about her. The house was far from completely decorated and they both agreed to take their time choosing pieces of furniture, art, and decorations carefully. They wanted their home to be perfect.

Tod headed into the kitchen and was surprised to see grocery bags still filled with food sitting on the kitchen counter and it didn't look like Jamie had started cooking yet. The large gallon container of milk was sitting on the counter near the kitchen sink and he assumed she forgot to put it in the refrigerator. He lifted the container and headed across the kitchen when suddenly he stopped.

The milk was warm, too warm. His gut was telling him something was up as he tried to remain calm. He instantly took out his revolver, looking around the living room and first floor of the house, and then headed up the stairs.

The first thing he noticed was the warm heat that hit his face and body as he entered the hallway. The air-conditioning wasn't turned on. It was very warm. His eyes were pulled toward the broken planter that lay scattered across the floor. Did Precious knock it over again? Where was Precious? He wondered as he became more frantic, practically running toward the bedroom.

The bedroom door was slightly ajar and he pointed his gun allowing his training to take over as he pushed the door opened with his other hand.

It was dark and he could hardly make out the figure on the bed.

Something jumped toward him but he didn't shoot as he heard the cat cry out as Precious jumped off the bed.

"Freeze right there," he told the person as he reached to the sidewall to flick the light switch on.

As the dark room instantly turned bright his mouth dropped at the sight and his arms fell to his side as he saw Jamie tied to the bed, beaten and bloodied.

He ran to her, screaming her name, praying she wasn't dead as he went around the side noting the path he took, trying not to disturb any possible evidence. He was thinking like a detective, even at a time like this. First he had to see if she was alive then take the next step.

As he reached toward her neck placing his two fingers gently against it, he felt the slightest pulse. She was alive but just barely.

He reached for his cell phone first calling 911 then the police department. As he spoke to the homicide commander, he noticed the letter lying next to his wife. He didn't touch it but knew it was from the serial killer. The one who was after Jamie's cousin Grace.

"Jamie, Jamie, can you hear me?" Tod kept repeating, but his wife was unresponsive. He untied her wrists from the bedpost, gently placing them at her side.

As he looked at her, his heart ached. He felt helpless and scared. He carefully pulled the tape from her eyes and she didn't move at all. He feared the worse. Her eyes were swollen, there was some kind of brown oily liquid pooled around them and her cheeks were cut and bruised. The slightest smell of motor oil filled his nostrils. She lay there, clothes torn off of her, cuts on her chest and belly. Tod closed his eyes as tight as he could.

This can't be real. I can't lose Jamie.

He heard the sirens in the distance. Then the front door opened. There was stomping up the stairs, and he turned to see the police officer's guns drawn until they caught sight of him. He recognized the cop. It was a friend of his, Billy Butler.

"The paramedics just pulled up. Is she alive, Tod?"

Tod nodded his head then stared at his wife.

Not long after the other detectives, his friends showed up along with Frank.

The paramedics were taking care of Jamie as the detectives were snapping pictures trying to maintain their professionalism and not contaminate any possible forensic evidence left behind. If Jamie died, they would need as much evidence as possible.

Tod followed the gurney out of the bedroom and met Frank in the hallway. One of the patrol officers was explaining the situation.

"It was the killer, Frank. He went after Jamie. She could die," Tod told him as he combed his fingers through his hair and blinked his eyes trying to stop the tears from escaping.

"How do you know, Tod?" he began to ask, but Tod cut him off.

"There's one of his sick fucking poems on the bed. He was going to kill her. I didn't touch it but I could read it from where I stood. He knows how close Jamie and Grace are. He's trying to make a point. She might die, man," Tod repeated as Frank put his hand on his shoulder.

"You go with Jamie. I'm going to make sure everything goes smoothly here. Then I'll come to the hospital. She's going to make it, Tod," Frank said.

Tod looked around his house as he descended the staircase. His house was swarming with police. His home was being invaded, violated and he thought of his young twenty-five-year-old wife and what she must have gone through. He prayed she would survive this as he jumped into the ambulance with her.

* * * *

"What do have so far, guys?" Frank asked as he stood in the bedroom doorway.

"Well we have the note bagged, we're gathering some fingerprints off of the dresser by the bed as well as the cord that opens the blinds. Tod said they were closed when he entered the room. Tod really kept it together, man. I don't think I could have done that," one of the detectives said and the others around the room agreed.

Frank took the letter from the Detective.

"Are you sure you want to see that?" the other detective asked and Frank nodded as he began to read.

My dearest Grace, a gift for thee,
I could have killed her so easily.
She's not like you, none of them come close,
You're the one I want, need, desire the most.
I will continue to pursue my hobby, my pleasure,
Until your safe return home, my love, my treasure.

Frank stood there disgusted and angry. This guy had no fear. He was determined to get to Grace. His poor sister, what would she do when she found out? He thought about his family and about poor Jamie. Detectives continued to gather possible evidence and then Federal agents arrived on the scene. Agent Lancaster and Agent Sullivan along with Jim and Teddy.

"What's that you have, Detective Thompson?" Agent Lancaster asked Frank.

Frank was a bit annoyed with the agent. They didn't hit it off very well from the start.

"A letter the killer left. It's been bagged, noted, and we have established a chain of custody for all evidence. This is the searching officer who's in charge of it." Frank pointed to one of the patrol officers, Billy Butler. The young cop moved forward but Lancaster didn't acknowledge him. Instead he took the evidence out of Frank's hands and read the letter. Frank rolled his eyes at Lancaster and the officer shook his head in agreement. Apparently Frank wasn't the only one the agent pissed off.

Just then Lieutenant Donald Friedman entered the house. He went directly toward Frank and the agent.

"What happened, Frank? I heard over the radio that Tod called for an ambulance and that the killer was here. Is Jamie all right?" he asked, worried about his new daughter-in-law.

"She's at the hospital, Donald. Tod went into the ambulance with her. She's alive." Frank didn't add anything more.

"Where were you before, Lieutenant?" Agent Lancaster asked Donald. Frank and Donald looked at him funny.

"What do you mean? When?" Donald asked defensively.

"You left the office as soon as Sarah Thompson came in around lunchtime. Where did you go? I was looking for you," Lancaster asked. Frank thought Lancaster sounded like he didn't trust Donald one bit.

"What do you think, Agent Lancaster, that Donald had something to do with this?" Frank asked the agent, speaking rather loudly.

At this point the room and hallway became quiet as the detectives and patrol officers looked on.

"I think you need to go back to the office. I have a few questions for you, Lieutenant," Lancaster said, not backing down from his suspicion.

"Well, your questions can just wait. I'm going to the hospital to be with my son and daughter-in-law. I'd be careful if I were you." Donald pointed at Lancaster's face. Agent Sullivan stepped between the two men.

"Just go to the hospital, Donald. We'll take care of things here," Frank said as Donald gave the agent a dirty look and headed down the hallway.

"What the hell is wrong with you, Agent Lancaster? Donald?" Frank asked.

"You're not in charge of this investigation, Frank. I am and I don't need to inform you about information I might have. Remember who's in charge." Agent Lancaster and Agent Sullivan walked away from Frank.

"What an asshole," Frank said, as he looked toward the bedroom where other detectives and police officers stood watching him.

* * * *

Grace, Sandman, Big Jay, and Duke were sitting on the porch enjoying the beautiful clear night along with some coffee. Grace was telling them about Europe.

"My mom told me to be careful when I left. That many Europeans were interested in marrying American women so they could get to the United States and become citizens. Anyway it was my first month in Venice. I was supposed to meet some friends after dinner at a local dance club in town but first I was in the mood for lasagna." Duke caressed her shoulder. She was leaning against him as they sat on the porch swing.

"The night was beautiful, kind of like tonight. You could hear the echo of police sirens in the air. You know they drive ridiculously fast in Europe? There are constant automobile accidents. Anyway a bunch of us decided to treat ourselves to a gourmet, four-course Italian feast. What better place to go than to a four-star Italian restaurant? The atmosphere was amazing, so authentic and cultural. Italian opera music filled the air and not from some stereo unit. It was the real thing. A twelve-piece orchestra played beautiful music, we drank wine, and tried to speak Italian," she said, giggling as she remembered the night's events.

"Sounds delicious," Duke whispered then kissed her shoulder. She smiled at him.

"We started off with some stuffed artichokes, homemade roasted peppers in extra virgin olive oil, fresh baked Italian bread, rolls, and specially seasoned dipping oil. It was fantastic. By the time the entrees came we were stuffed and the waiter, a very handsome young man, was catering to me hand and foot. The others picked up on it right away but it wasn't until I received my piece of lasagna that I noticed something was up.

"Three of my other friends ordered the same thing but my piece was huge. It was so delicious that I ate the entire thing and noticed the waiter stood and watched me.

"He asked my friend in Italian and broken English if I enjoyed the meal and of course I told him how wonderful it was and he was extremely pleased.

"Our espresso arrived along with dessert containing fresh,

homemade Italian cookies and pastries. There were cannoli, cream puffs, you name it and the waiter brought over some gelato that was out of this world. It was so delicious and as I finished it another waiter and a busboy came around and placed two more servings in front of me. My friends were laughing and of course I was so embarrassed. I declined the other dishes of gelato, laughing and wondering what was going on.

"My friend Marcia spoke Italian and just as she was going to ask why the waiter and everyone were paying so much attention to me, the waiter emerged from the kitchen with the cook, an older woman, and two other young men in their late twenties.

"The other patrons in the restaurant looked on, some saying hello and waving to them, obviously knowing the people.

"It turned out they were the waiter's brothers, mother, and father.

"They asked my friend Marcia if I was betrothed to anyone and if I would be interested in accompanying their son the waiter to the local dance club down the street," Grace said then laughed.

"You've got to be kidding me? That sounds like something out of a movie," Duke stated.

"I thought of my mom instantly and what she said about the men wanting to find American women to marry and I freaked out. I was going straight back to the hotel, alone and unbetrothed," she said and Big Jay, Duke, and Sandman laughed.

"It must have been an amazing experience living in Europe, learning about the different cultures and language. You probably have a lot of stories," Sandman said and Grace smiled.

"I guess I do have a few. It was great. I hope to go back someday. But not alone. The cities are too romantic. Venice, Florence, even Paris and Madrid. It would be wonderful to share it with someone special."

She smiled at the thought.

"Do you ever think about settling down here in the States? You know, trying to find a photography gig that's closer to your family?" Duke asked, and she swallowed hard. She never thought about returning home. She was in the midst of an amazing career. She was young and at the top in her field.

"I still have a lot to accomplish. I've won some awards and I'm considered one of the best at my job. I'm supposed to go to Milan in a week. I haven't even spoken to my boss about it."

"You can't go if this killer is still out there," Sandman stated and she heard the hint of regret in his voice.

"I have a career. If I don't go and do that job, I might as well kiss my entire profession and the last three years good-bye."

"We were kind of hoping that you would consider staying with us. This house is an hour's drive from Houston. You could visit your family anytime and they can even come stay here. We have the extra two bedrooms," Duke said.

"What about your careers?"

"I would still work SWAT and train. Big Jay can still do his private investigator stuff and Sandman can pick and choose when he wants to take on a job," Duke stated as if he had everything planned out. Grace felt her belly tighten. This was going too fast.

"So what you're saying, Duke, is that you three get to keep your careers while I have to change mine?" She sat forward in the seat.

"You wouldn't have to change careers, just change locations and stay locally instead of overseas," Big Jay said.

"I photograph models. That means major exotic locations. Houston does not fit into that category. Models in bikinis on beaches with tropical surroundings."

"There's no need to get upset over it. We'll work it out," Big Jay said.

"Where are we anyway?" she asked them, trying to change the subject. It seemed she had a lot to think about, including whether love was enough to make this relationship work out.

"An hour outside of Houston. We have a small town a few miles down the road. There's a bus stop, a deli, diner, hardware store, et cetera. There are miles between properties, the way we like it," Duke stated.

"It's a vacation place for us. We do have a house not too far from the city. It's more suburban like with shopping centers and restaurants," Sandman added.

"Yeah, some close friends of ours own a bar restaurant called Casper's. That's the main hangout. We have a nice place there and the area is surrounded with ex-military types, like us," Big Jay told her. She absorbed what they were saying, but her gut felt as if it were in knots. There was so much to be concerned over. She was in no position to make plans for the future.

Just then Sandman's cell phone rang and he answered it while walking out of the room. Grace watched him walk away, smiling at the thought of sharing Europe with him and his brothers, but they seemed to have different plans. Would this be what would tear their relationship apart, before they even got fully started?

Duke and Big Jay were quiet as they all sat there. She wondered if they were thinking what she was and that maybe this relationship wouldn't work out. She didn't like the feeling she had.

Just then, Sandman walked back into the room.

He didn't look happy, his face was flushed and he was having a hard time keeping eye contact with Grace.

"Is everything okay?" Big Jay asked.

Sandman walked over to her, knelt down on the floor and took her hand into his.

"That was Frank who called. The killer went after Jamie," he said and then looked down.

"What? No! Oh God. Oh my God. No. Please tell me she isn't…"

"She's alive, Grace. Just barely but she's alive. He didn't kill her."

Both Big Jay and Duke were next to her, too.

"It's okay, honey," Big Jay said and Grace looked up at him with tears rolling down her cheeks.

"Where is Jamie now, Sandman?" Duke asked and Grace was grateful, because she couldn't speak. She was crying and her heart ached something terrible. *Poor Jamie.*

"She's in intensive care. Tod is with her as well as Donald and your family." Sandman placed his hand over hers and squeezed it.

"Tell me everything. Don't leave anything out." She wiped her tears.

"Grace, I don't think—"

"No! You will not keep this from me," Grace interrupted as she stood up and pushed their hands away from her.

He remained silent as he stood there towering over her with one hand on his hip and the other running through his hair.

"You don't think what? For God's sake, Sandman, he's going after my family. Jamie's my cousin. What does he want? What did they find?" She raised her voice. The anger, the frustration was getting to her.

* * * *

Sandman tried to remain calm and empathetic. He knew Grace was going to take this badly. She was on to the police procedures, the practices, the way they collected evidence. She was so smart but he wanted to protect her. The letter this time was taunting her. The killer wanted her to come home and there was no way Sandman would allow that.

"No, Grace. It's not important right now. Your cousin is alive."

He glanced at his brothers. They looked pissed off but hopefully would save their questions for later. Sandman didn't want Grace to know about the letter.

"This isn't the killer's MO. Jamie should be dead. He didn't kill her and there's a reason. Did he leave another poem?" she asked and Sandman looked at his brothers for help.

"She has a right to know. Tell her, Sandman," Duke whispered.

Sandman remained silent. The information could send Grace over the edge. Grace begged him to tell her more, but this time Sandman held his ground.

* * * *

The words from the killer's letter stared out at Sandman, Duke, and Big Jay from his laptop. Frank had e-mailed the note along with the other evidence found at Jamie's house.

The killer wanted her, wanted to perform sick sexual acts as he had done with the others. He said he desired Grace and that she was his treasure. The sick son of a bitch had killed over thirty young women.

"We can't let this sick fuck get to Grace," Duke stated firmly.

"We need fucking answers," Big Jay added.

They heard the door open and knew that Grace had returned from going to the bathroom. Sandman closed down his laptop.

* * * *

Grace overhead part of their conversation. The killer did leave another letter. He mentioned her in it. He was taunting her and wanted Grace to return home.

"Can I talk to Tod or Donald? What about my mother? Any word from her or my brothers?" she asked.

Grace couldn't stand being away like this. She wanted to be home. She wanted to stop this guy. What was Sandman not telling her?

"Frank should be calling me back soon. There's something you should know, Grace, about Donald." Sandman looked at Big Jay and Duke. Neither man looked happy. They kind of appeared pissed off to Grace.

She was shocked when he explained how the federal agents believed Donald was the killer. Just as Sandman and Duke explained why the agents believed Donald was part of the investigation and a potential suspect, the phone rang.

Big Jay took her hand and led her out of the room. They were blocking her out, keeping her from the investigation. She wanted to go home. She wanted to help. The situation was out of control.

Chapter 15

"Peter, I just don't get it. Why would the agents be looking at Donald?" Frank asked as John joined his two brothers. "There's no way he could be the killer."

"Apparently Agent Lancaster has enough evidence to obtain a search warrant," Peter told them.

"What? When did this happen?" John asked.

"Just a little while ago. I got a call from a friend of mine. He knows how close Donald is to the family. He was giving me a heads-up," Peter stated.

"This has turned into a major mess. There is no way it's him. No way," John said, and both Frank and Peter agreed.

"What did Sandman tell Grace? You know she'll want to come home," Peter said.

"Well that's not an option. She's staying put in the safety of Sandman and his brothers' arms for all I care, but far from here. This killer means business and now we have our family to protect. I think Mom should have one of us by her at all times or maybe one of the agents," Frank said.

"Donald had stationed a guy there already," John told them. He didn't want to think Donald had something to do with this. He was like a father to him.

"We can believe in our hearts that Donald's not the killer but we have to be smart about this. I don't think we should trust anyone," Frank added.

"I agree. I know you don't want to consider this but the FBI may want to use Grace as bait. The killer wants her, he's killing other innocent people because of it and they might feel it's the only way to smoke the guy out," Peter said.

"You've got to be kidding me? There's no fucking way our little sister is going to be bait for this monster. The FBI can just kiss my ass." Frank raised his voice as he stood up from his chair knocking it over onto the floor.

"Calm down, Frank. I'm just telling you what they're going to say. She'll be safe with Sandman and his brothers and I'm sure that Agent Lancaster will keep her there while he's investigating Donald. When that turns up to be a dead end, Grace could be coming home sooner," Peter stated.

"I don't believe this. We lost one sister to this fuck head. We're not going to lose another. And Donald is innocent. The killer probably planted some evidence on him just like Stew Parker," John said to his brothers.

"I'm sure Lancaster covered that already. I spoke to Donald a little while ago. He was going to cooperate and speak to the agents first thing in the morning," Peter told them.

"He might need you to defend him, Peter," John said.

"I've already offered my services but he says he doesn't want to go that far yet. 'One step at a time' were his exact words." Peter shook his head.

Both Frank and John smiled. That was Donald all right, very easygoing, always taking his time, never in a rush to make a judgment.

"I'm going to head over to the hospital and see how Jamie's doing. If she regains consciousness soon, maybe she'll be able to help with the case," Frank said, sounding hopeful as he headed toward the door.

"Give them our best and tell Tod I'll be there in the morning," Peter said then he looked at John who nodded his head.

* * * *

"Peter, you keep someone on Lindsey. There's no telling if this asshole is liable to go after your wife," Frank said.

"I thought about that already. Your roommates volunteered. I think they still feel responsible for Grace getting that envelope when she was staying with you guys."

"They're a good group of guys and they do feel responsible. They'll help out. We all will. Have you spoken with Jim and Teddie?"

"Yes, they asked me to look into something they came across. Well actually, Grace picked up on something with Sandman and his brothers while going through some files. There was this old case and a letter left behind. I think Jim and Teddie are looking into the connection between the other victims and real estate property."

"Real estate property? What do they think that has to do with this case, Pete?"

"Not sure, but it could make matters worse for Donald. They found a link between the three victims and a charity group. Not sure where it may lead, but hopefully not as more potential evidence in a case against Donald."

"Well, Pete, they don't have enough to lock him up. Let's hope for the best."

"Let's hope that we can find the real killer and get Grace home where she belongs."

"At least she's with Sandman. He's a good guy. Jim and a bunch of guys swear he's the best."

Frank stood up.

"You heard what Grace told Mom the other day."

"No, what?"

"She said she was in love."

"No shit? With Sandman?"

"Her exact words were Sandman and his two brothers."

John was shocked.

"Holy fuck. Big Jay and Duke are huge. Plus they always look so damn pissed off."

"You aren't worried about the whole ménage thing?" Pete asked.

"Hell no. Look at Jim, Teddie and Deanna. Never mind a bunch of our other friends. It happens. I just hope they truly love her."

"If they don't and they hurt her, we'll kick their asses."

"I think we'll need our own army to try. I have hopes that this will work out. Grace could use a happily ever after."

"Do they really exist?" Pete asked and John nodded his head.

"I sure hope so, for Grace.

* * * *

"Donald is not the killer," Grace told Sandman, Big Jay, and Duke as they stood in the office. Sandman just got word that some other evidence pointed to Donald.

"Wasn't he in the office when that bomb went off?" Big Jay asked.

"Yes, he was. What, did the Agent forget that little tidbit?" Grace asked with an attitude.

"You and I both know, Big Jay, that he could have planned it that way. It would cover him for an alibi at the time," Sandman replied.

"Sandman, you don't actually think Donald could be the killer? Jamie is his daughter-in-law and Tod is his son," Grace added.

"Maybe that's why she's not dead," Duke said, sending Grace into shock.

"Damn you. I see now how easily you could turn your back on someone." She turned her back toward the wall.

The men knew how upset she was.

"I need to look at this from an investigative perspective, Grace. He has the capability, the resources, and after a full investigation there may be more evidence that can connect him to the other killings," Sandman stated firmly.

"It's not true, Goddamn it. It's just not true. You're wrong, Investigator Sandstone." She stormed out the slider doors and onto the porch.

"Just give her a few minutes to cool down. She has every right to be pissed off," Duke stated as he stopped Sandman from following Grace.

"She's not the only one who's pissed off. I want to get this guy and kill him myself," Sandman said then slammed his fist down on the table.

"I'm right there with you, partner, but what you need to do is stay professional, stay focused," Duke told his brother.

"I'm trying. Really I am but this guy is getting to everyone. I don't really think Donald is guilty. But as investigators when evidence emerges we have to look into everything. Every tiny detail or possibility. That's how we're going to find the real killer," Sandman said as he headed toward the porch.

Grace stood by the railing staring out toward the woods.

"Grace. We need to talk." He closed the sliding glass door.

"There's nothing to talk about. I want to go home and I want you to take me there first thing in the morning. It gives you plenty of time to make the arrangements," she said to him, still not looking at him.

"No," he stated firmly, making her jump. She was startled as she turned toward him.

"You are staying right here with me where I can protect you and keep you safe." He moved closer.

"You can't make me. If I want to leave right now, I can. You have nothing to legally hold me here," she told him, not backing down.

"Legally hold you here? For Christ's sake, Grace, there's a Goddamn killer out there who's raping and torturing women. Tying them up like some kind of animal, beating them...Damn it. You only think you're tough enough to handle this. Well you're not." He was so angry all he wanted to do was shake some sense into her.

"I'm tough enough to handle this. He went after Jamie. What about my mom or my sister-in-law Lindsey?"

"They're being protected. He wants you. Only you. He wants you to come home so he can have his way with you," Sandman told her.

"Is that what you didn't want to tell me? He said it in the letter, didn't he? He left a letter next to Jamie. Sandman, tell me?" she asked as she grabbed his arm.

Sandman grabbed Grace, putting her hands behind her back, pulling her close to him.

"I love you, Grace. I'm not going to hand you over to him like some piece of meat." He slowly let go of her hands. He looked into her eyes and he could see that her anger was overpowering her fear. She wasn't thinking straight and he knew that he needed to calm her down. Any decisions made out of anger were never the right ones.

"I need to go home. If there's even the slightest way I can put a stop to this. I have to try," she told him as she stared into his eyes.

Sandman took a deep breath as he held Grace close to him, hugging her against his chest.

"We'll talk about it. Let's not make any rash decisions. I'll call Jim and Agent Lancaster in the morning and we'll take it from there," Sandman told her as he held her in his arms and kissed the top of her head.

* * * *

Early the next morning Sarah turned on the television as she made Eric his breakfast.

"The attempted murder of Jamie Friedman is being investigated currently by the FBI, specifically Agent Lancaster and Agent Sullivan who're in charge of the case. We caught up with Agent Lancaster early this morning on his way into the Houston Police Department." The reporter turned the microphone toward the agent.

The reporter began asking the agent questions starting off with why he felt the killer let Jamie live.

"I'd rather not give my personal or professional opinion at this time. However, I do strongly believe by this afternoon we certainly will have more for you," Agent Lancaster said as he headed up the stairs.

"Well there you go. It looks like there may be a possible break in the case. More information in thirty minutes." The reporter continued to talk as they went to another report from the main news desk.

"What was that all about? Do they have a suspect?" Eric asked, fastening his tie. He had a board meeting this morning at city hall. Everyone had been very supportive to him and his family during this time, and the election was looking promising because of it.

"I don't know, Eric. That agent sounded like he might know something but the boys haven't called," she said as she prepared the scrambled eggs.

Eric went over to the refrigerator and took out the butter for his toast.

Sarah placed the plate in front of Eric, and then poured his coffee.

"Thanks, honey. Come sit down and join me," he told her with a smile.

"I can't eat, Eric. I'm so worried about Grace and Jamie. I'm going to the hospital to stay with Tod all day. The poor thing is still out of it." She kept busy cleaning dishes in the kitchen sink.

Eric patted her hand. "You're so wonderful, you know that." He pulled her hand to his lips and kissed her fingers.

"Are you nervous about the meeting today?" she asked. She knew the elections were just around the corner and he didn't want his competition catching up to him in votes.

"No, I'm not. I really think I have a good shot at this, Sarah. I know it's negative and a real bad situation that's going on right now, but our family name is out there. The people are backing us up, they're backing me up. I think they figure I'm the real thing. Everything that's happened in our lives, the tragedy, the loss of Clara and now Grace being chased by some madman. The public feels for us and they're showing their support in the polls," Eric said then continued to eat.

Sarah could understand what he was saying but it didn't make her feel any better about it. This was not the way to win an election. She couldn't lose her only daughter to the same person who took Clara.

"I don't like that, Eric. People should not vote for you because they feel sorry for us or because we lost Clara and now Grace is not safe. It's just not right." She threw the dishtowel down on the kitchen counter.

"I would like to win this election, Sarah. I want to be town councilman and who knows, maybe mayor or governor next. You know this is my dream. Don't ruin it." He rose from the table and headed out the door.

Sarah was not surprised by his attitude. He did want this position. He had been after it for the past two years and finally it was looking promising. She went about clearing the table. She wanted to clean up so she could get to the hospital. Thank God the man hadn't killed Jamie, too.

* * * *

"How's she doing, Tod?" Frank asked as John shook Tod's hand.

"She's the same. No change since I found her," Tod told them as he looked at Jamie. Her face was bruised and her eyes were swollen shut. The men couldn't even imagine what she went through.

"My mom's on her way over. She wants to keep you company," John said as he looked at his poor cousin. He was so angry and he didn't know what to do or how to handle it.

"My mother-in-law is a mess. She can't handle looking at Jamie like this. She just keeps crying," Tod said as he put his hands in his pocket.

"My aunt Julie is pretty tough but seeing her own daughter like this has got to be the worst. That's why my mom wanted to come. She figured she could help both of you," Frank told Tod.

"I don't know how she's being this strong. She must be worried sick about Grace. Hey Grace isn't coming back, right?" Tod asked.

"As far as we know Sandman's going to keep her in hiding. We told him not to tell her everything but I'm sure our sister will get it out of him," John said.

"She shouldn't come home with this guy on the loose. You guys read that letter. He's obsessed with Grace. Make sure she knows we don't want her to take a chance and come home," Tod said and Frank and John agreed.

The hospital door opened and Sarah walked into the room.

"Hey, Mom." Frank greeted his mother, kissing her on the cheek.

"Hi, Frank, Johnny," she said as John gave her a kiss. Then she gave Tod a big hug and kiss on the cheek.

"How are you holding up, Tod?" she asked as she put her purse on the table.

"I'm hanging in there, Aunt Sarah," he told her as the men watched Sarah fix Jamie's covers then gently caress her hair.

"And how is my favorite niece today? I can't wait to hear that beautiful voice of yours. We love you, honey, and you're safe now. Everything is going to be okay." Sarah pulled the chair next to the bed.

Just then Frank's cell phone rang and he went outside to answer it.

He was walking down the hallway and headed out the front door when his brother Peter started rambling on in a panic.

"Okay now I know I heard Donald correctly last night but right now he's an hour late to work. He's supposed to be at the precinct being questioned by Agent Lancaster," Peter stated, sounding worried.

"What do you mean he's not there? Did you try his house? His cell phone?" Frank asked, and of course Peter had done both already.

"This does not look good, Frank. You'd better find him or he's going to be hung alive," Peter said as Frank agreed before he hung up the phone.

Frank and John headed back to the precinct after checking out Donald's house. There was no sign of him and they didn't know what to think.

As Frank and John turned the corner heading toward Donald's office, they heard Agent Lancaster.

"Where's Friedman? If he's not guilty then where the hell is he?" he asked as he motioned both John and Frank to join the others in Donald's office.

The captain was there as well as the homicide commander.

"We were just going over the evidence we have on your lieutenant. As I was saying, gentleman, Friedman had access to Stew Parker's home and opportunity to plant the evidence. He was not at the house when we questioned Grace Thompson. However, he knew we were headed there and most definitely had the opportunity to shoot at her," Agent Lancaster explained.

"Wait one Goddamn minute. There's no way that Donald planted the evidence or took a shot at our sister," John interrupted.

"I can't prove that but I can show that there's enough evidence to prove investigating him as a suspect is justified. Now his fingerprints were found all over the furniture in Jamie Friedman's bedroom," Lancaster told them.

"For Christ's sake, Lancaster, he's her damn father-in-law and he helped Tod move the furniture in there a few weeks ago," Frank told him.

"Where was he during the time of the attack? No one seems to know and he's not here now like he said he would be. Why else would he not show up?" Lancaster asked.

"What's his motive, Lancaster?" Frank asked.

"He a psychopath and he's obsessed with your sister. She looks like Clara who I'm sure he killed as well and he had traveled out of town a lot going to seminars and supposedly visiting his sick mother in Pennsylvania. Might I remind you that the other connected murders took place in New York and Pennsylvania."

"I'd hate to admit this but it looks like he has some good evidence here, boys. We need to put out an APB on Lieutenant Donald Friedman." Their captain reached for the phone and the agents scattered from the room to get moving on their suspect.

"This is crazy," John said as the chaos began.

* * * *

"You have got to be kidding me, Frank," Sandman said into his cell phone.

"No. I'm afraid I'm not. The federal agents are ready to hang Donald and the media has got wind of something going on. I give this until this afternoon tops before it's all over the news."

"Everyone who could possibly be a suspect needs to be investigated. If Lancaster feels that Donald needs to be questioned, just let him."

"The problem is that Donald is nowhere to be found. John and I have looked everywhere. We even broke into his house," Frank explained.

"Did it look like anything was out of place? Any drawers opened or closets emptied?" Sandman asked.

"No. Everything was in order. There were no signs that he left in a hurry or that there was a struggle."

Sandman was asking questions as if Donald made a run for it, but Frank looked around as if Donald might have been taken against his will. Either scenario was possible.

"Let Lancaster do his thing. In the meantime there's no reason why you can't conduct your own investigation. No one needs to know. As far as Lancaster's concerned, just tell him Donald was like family and you're concerned about his safety. It will work out," Sandman told him.

"Before this is over I'm going to tell that guy what I really think of him," Frank said and Sandman laughed.

"Now tell me how my sister is doing? How was she last night?" Frank asked.

"She was pretty upset and still, as of this morning, determined to come home."

"Well she can't come home. You can't let her."

"Your sister is the most stubborn, bullheaded—"

Frank finished his sentence. "Pain in the ass. I know that but you can't give in. I …I also know that you two have become pretty close. Or should I say you and your two brothers as well?"

"Yeah, I guess you could say she got under our skin."

Frank laughed. "Well I'm sure that the three of you want to keep her as safe as possible. So please don't let her come back. Donald's not the killer. I just know it."

"I hope you're right, Frank, but if Lancaster proves otherwise and Donald is the killer, then my superiors are going to make me bring her back. I'll have no choice."

"Let's hope that doesn't happen," Frank said.

Grace walked into the office.

"Hold on a second. Grace's here. Why don't you talk to her?"

Sandman handed the phone to her.

"Hello. Oh God, Frank, I'm so glad to hear your voice," she said into the phone as Sandman gave a small smile.

"I'm fine…really, Frank…no…stop worrying. How's Jamie doing?"

She continued to ask about her family and then about the investigation.

* * * *

"Grace, don't even think about coming home. It's not an option. It's not safe here for you," Frank told her.

"But I feel so responsible, like I could be doing more instead of running away, hiding."

"You didn't run away and you're not hiding. I don't want you to worry too much. It's all going to work out. We'll find this killer and then you'll be home again," Frank said.

"What about Donald? How is he handling this? How did the questioning go this morning?" she asked Frank.

Frank was silent a few seconds. "Don't worry about it, baby. I have to go. John is waiting for me downstairs. I love you, baby."

"I love you, too." She hung up the phone and handed it to Sandman.

Grace walked toward the window in the office. Her brother was hiding information from her. Something was wrong with Donald. Damn she needed to be home, she thought to herself as Sandman approached.

"Grace, what's wrong?" he asked her as he wrapped his arms around her waist from behind.

"Frank wasn't telling me everything. He's keeping things from me, which only makes me think something's not right. What happened at the questioning this morning? How's Donald?"

He released her and leaned against his desk.

"Grace, I told you last night that Donald's being investigated. There's nothing new as of right now."

"Frank sounded like there's more to it than that. Why are you lying to me, too? This isn't right," she told him, and he stopped her from turning away from him by putting his hands on her waist.

"Baby, please listen to me. I know you're trying your hardest to help solve this case and that's part of my reason for having you here but the other part remains priority. Your life is in jeopardy. There is someone after you. Someone who has killed so many innocent women and more recently killed your brother's girlfriend Maggie and nearly killed Jamie."

"I understand all that, Sandman, which should give me the right to know everything that's going on in the investigation. They don't actually think Donald is the killer, do they?" she asked him.

"Let me ask you this, Grace. Try to put aside the fact that Donald has been so close to your family, forget his support during the years, and look at the information we have. Tell me what you would think?"

He moved his laptop and opened the e-mail from Agent Lancaster.

Grace sat down in the chair and read the information.

"Well, first of all he would have been the first on the scene because he was in the search party that day, not too far from the spot where I found Clara. He also would have been the first person to get to Stew Parker's because of his position and because he wanted to find the killer so badly. He made it his personal mission in life."

"From your perspective. But from an investigator's perspective it's not uncommon for the perpetrator to return to the scene of the crime or participate in the volunteer search parties. Because he is in law enforcement, no one would think twice about him sticking around, helping everywhere he could, and engaging your family. You did say he spent a lot of time with your family even after Clara was found?"

"Yes, he did. He even spent his days off with us. But still that's not enough evidence."

"He disappeared the other day on the anniversary of Clara's death. Right after Sarah arrived at the station to e-mail you. He hasn't admitted or proved his whereabouts at the time. It was at that same time that Jamie was attacked."

"She's his daughter-in-law. Tod's his son. There's no way he would hurt her."

"He didn't kill her, Jamie. He kept her alive possibly because of his son."

"Or the real killer's trying to throw you off. Make you think that Donald is the killer. You said it yourself, this guy is crazy but not stupid. This could be one big setup," she said as she moved the mouse to the laptop lower. That's when the words appeared and her heart dropped.

Sandman saw her reaction and knew she was looking at the poem.

"Grace, don't." He put his hand over hers and closed the laptop.

"I want to see it. Let me please?" she asked him as she looked down into his eyes. "I have a right to see them, Sandman. If he wrote these poems to me and kept Jamie alive because of me, then I should be aware of what he's thinking, what he wants from me."

"No one knows what this psycho is thinking, Grace. There's no reason for you to put yourself through this. Just keep it closed."

Just then Sandman's phone rang, and as he answered it, he closed the e-mail and turned off the computer.

* * * *

"Agent Lancaster," Sullivan said as he waved the paper in the air.

"Let's get going, guys."

The other agents prepared for one of their well-known home invasions.

"Search warrant? For the lieutenant's house?" Frank asked.

"You're more than welcome to tag along, Detective. I wouldn't want anyone trying to say we planted evidence," Lancaster stated sarcastically, as he brushed past Frank.

Frank of course followed the circus all the way to Donald's house.

* * * *

When they arrived there fifteen minutes later the agents swarmed the house, each designated to a specific location. They were placing papers and various personal belongings of Donald's into plastic evidence bags and large cardboard boxes. They gathered hotel pay stubs, used airline tickets, and personal expense files. Anything and everything that could possibly leave a paper trail and put him near the location or vicinity of any of the murders.

An hour later they were still heavily into their work and had begun to search the basement.

Frank joined Agent Lancaster and Sullivan and a few other agents in the basement when someone came across an old cubbyhole door behind a large, old, dusty wooden workbench. It was the only thing in the whole basement that was broken down and junky looking. Donald kept the rest of the basement immaculate with each box or wooden chest in a lined position against the walls. In the center were a workbench and some free hand weights. Even his washer and dryer were downstairs and set atop a plywood platform with every detergent bottle, fabric softener, and Clorox bleach sitting in their own positions on a wooden shelf.

He was very organized and meticulous. That was obvious.

"Let's take some pictures of the position of this bench first before we move it," Lancaster said as the photographer who followed them around continuously took pictures of everything in its current position. The photographer began taking pictures and then everything was marked, checked off, and logged.

A few of the agents moved the bench as the loud squealing sound of wood being dragged across the cement floor echoed throughout the basement. Then they opened the door and to their surprise there was enough room for someone to walk in, hunched over, and it looked as though the room continued through the whole house.

"Let's get this room lit up bright so we can see everything before we enter," Lancaster ordered as the others gathered around, turning on flashlights and a handheld spotlight.

As the cubbyhole was illuminated Lancaster became excited at their discovery.

"It looks like the Lieutenant has a naughty hobby," the agent told Frank who looked inside as well as the other agents.

There were centerfold pictures scattered around the walls, all of brunettes, as well as various types of sexual paraphernalia, including whips, paddle boards, handcuffs, and chain restraints.

"Holy shit," Justin said and even Frank was shocked.

As they carefully took pictures and moved forward into the cubbyhole, the ceiling became lower and lower. They came upon a wooden box with a sheet scattered across it.

The photographer took pictures and they removed the sheet.

"What's inside the box?" Lancaster asked.

"There's a few things, sir," Justin said. Then he took the box and moved it toward the entrance of the room.

Frank, Lancaster, and the other agents looked inside and were once again surprised.

"Well what do we have here? Bingo!" exclaimed Agent Lancaster as he held up Maggie's police badge along with various plastic bags containing locks of hair, jewelry, and other personal belongings.

"Let's get this stuff logged and bagged then to the lab immediately," Lancaster said.

Frank knew there was good reason to worry.

* * * *

By the time the 6:00 p.m. news aired everyone was aware of the search for Lieutenant Donald Friedman as well as the agents' interest in questioning him.

The reports were already surfacing calling Friedman a suspect in the case.

"I don't believe this. There is absolutely no possible way that my father is the serial killer," Tod said as he paced back and forth in the hospital waiting room.

"I didn't want to believe it either, Tod, but you should have seen what was in his basement. There was a lot of incriminating stuff in there," said Frank as John sat down in a chair looking just as shocked at the information.

"My dad never used that old cubbyhole. I remember helping him organize that basement and pushing that workbench in front of the door. That's a two-person job," said Todd as he thought about everything Frank was telling him.

"I really don't know what to say except that your father better show up soon or that Agent Lancaster is going to have him tried and sentenced before he knows what hit him," said Frank as the other man looked at him, unsure of what to do next.

* * * *

"I don't believe this, Peter. I just don't believe what I'm hearing. Could it possibly be true? Oh God, what am I saying? There's no way it could be true." Sarah rambled on, not knowing what to think or how to react to the news reports. She gripped the telephone tighter.

"Well, Mom, he didn't show up to work today and he knew that Agent Lancaster was waiting to question him. His house did not show signs of forced entry or that he left in a hurry. However, the agents did find incriminating evidence," Peter told his mother.

"Well what kind of incriminating evidence did they find?" she asked her son.

"I'm not sure, Mom, I'm not privy to that information yet. Frank saw it for himself and I have to tell you that he was pretty upset," said Peter.

"What about Tod? Oh God, poor Tod must be going out of his mind," said Sarah.

"Well Frank and John are with him right now. They've decided to do a little investigating on their own, Mom. None of us believe that Donald is the killer."

They spoke a little longer before hanging up the phone.

"What did Peter say?" Eric asked as he patiently waited in the lounge chair listening to the whole one-sided conversation.

Sarah explained it all to him as she grabbed a tissue and began to cry.

In an instant Eric was at her side consoling her.

"It is going to be all right, Sarah. If Donald is the killer, then the agents or the police will find him. All this worrying will be over and our Grace will come home again," he told her as he hugged her.

"I just can't believe Donald would do this. He was so kind to our family. The boys adore him," she said as she thought about her handsome friend who she had been so attracted to.

"You have always had a special connection with him, Sarah. He helped us through so much when Clara was missing and then after she was found. I have to admit sometimes I was a little jealous," Eric told her as Sarah wiped her tears and looked at her husband rather surprised.

Sarah gently touched Eric's cheek and spoke to him softly.

"There was no need for you to be jealous, Eric. You are my husband, I love you so much, and you were there for me, for all of us when Clara was missing."

He smiled softly as he touched her hair and he tenderly kissed her. "I love the children as if they were my own and I've always felt the need to protect my two girls the best that I could. I promised myself to protect both you and Grace as long as I live, Sarah."

She hugged him. "She's safe, Eric, very safe with Sandman. As a matter of fact Frank may have been right when he said one positive thing we could get out of this whole situation," she told him with a huge smile.

"You mean that Special Agent Sandstone who is supposed to be protecting her?" Eric asked, sounding a little concerned.

"Yes, dear, that one. She told me all about it the other day and she seemed pretty happy. There's more actually. His brothers fell in love with her, too," Sarah said as she turned off the television set.

"Is she out of her mind? A ménage relationship with three men? This could ruin my election, this entire family," he stated, concerned.

"Eric, it happens and the communities know these types of relationships exist. She's in love and she's happy for once in her life."

"I'm not as accepting to this. As a matter of fact, I'm surprised that you're so accepting." He followed Sarah upstairs.

"I want Grace happy and to feel loved. If Sandman and his two brothers bring her that love and can do that for her, then God bless them."

* * * *

It was after midnight and Grace couldn't sleep. She entered Sandman's office and turned on his laptop computer. She was hoping to take a look at the poems from the killer and had tried unsuccessfully to open the e-mail. After a while longer she sifted through the papers in his desk as her eyes lingered toward the locked drawer. She looked for a key but was unsuccessful as she grabbed the letter opener from the desk drawer. She knew she shouldn't break into the drawer and that it was a desperate move.

"Desperate times call for desperate measures," she whispered to herself as she wiggled the letter opener around inside the lock hoping it would work. As she broke the letter opener and the lock simultaneously, she opened the drawer and was surprised at what she discovered.

"You printed them out, of course you did so that you could really look at them and analyze them." She began to read the poems.

They were upsetting but she wanted to continue and she looked at them as a challenge.

When she came to the latest poem her heart ached.

My dearest Grace, a gift for thee,

I could have killed her so easily.

My God, he didn't kill her because of me and he's looking at it as if it's a gift. Something so precious one might give to a lover, a special partner. There was nothing more sacred or more meaningful than life, one's soul and spirit. Grace continued to read.

She's not like you, none of them come close,
You're the one I want, need, desire the most.
I will continue to pursue my hobby, my pleasure,
Until your safe return home, my love, my treasure.

He was threatening her, challenging her to confront him, come home out of hiding. He knew what kind of person she was and that was exactly what she would want to do. She didn't want to show her fear or allow him to dominate her. The killer knew her and he knew her fairly well. He would have to know that she would analyze his poems, his words in attempt to try and figure out his identity.

"My love, my treasure," he called her in his poem. She hadn't been intimate with anyone. Sandman and his brothers were her only lovers, and there was no one she could think of that knew her and her family well enough to know everything about her.

"What the hell do you think you're doing?" Sandman said.

She screamed and nearly jumped out of the chair. "Damn it, you scared the hell out of me. Why did you do that?" she yelled at him as he took the papers out of her hand and eyed the broken lock on the desk drawer.

"Breaking and entering, huh? You know what I should do to you?" he scolded her as he turned her chair around to face him.

"I have a right to look at those poems, Sandman, and stopping me from looking at them is a crime of its own." She crossed her arms in front of her chest.

"Look what you did to my desk, Grace. There was no need to sneak around in the middle of the night either," he told her as he looked her in the eye.

"I wanted to see them, Sandman, and you denied me that right," she began to say as he pulled her out of the chair and into his arms.

"I know that, Grace, that's why I didn't immediately follow you downstairs. I knew you wouldn't be able to leave it alone as I asked. You should receive some form of punishment though," he told her as she smiled and leaned closer.

"What exactly did you have in mind?" she asked him as he held her tighter.

"Well I'm a firm believer in capital punishment, but that seems a bit too extreme for such a minimal crime. However, I also believe in corporal punishment which might make you think twice before committing such a crime in the future." He began to place her over his knee.

"You wouldn't dare!" she yelled at him as she wiggled her way to the floor and Sandman quickly followed.

He was on top of her now, gently holding her arms above her head.

"You're so tough, I know you can handle it." He kissed her neck, making kissy noises into it and causing Grace to laugh hysterically.

"Stop it. Stop it. I'm too ticklish." She could barely get the words out as Big Jay and Duke entered the room wearing only their boxers. She looked toward them until Sandman covered her lips with his.

He moved his legs between hers, pushing up the light cotton nightie she had worn to bed.

Grace wrapped her legs around Sandman's waist and placed her arms around his neck as he removed his boxer shorts.

Instantly he was inside of her, making love to her as he once again held her arms above her head.

"If this is what punishment is like, I may just have to become a repeat offender," she said as she giggled.

"What did she do?" Duke asked.

"Look at my desk," Sandman said through clenched teeth as he stroked her pussy, thrusting his hips until she screamed his name. He followed suit, exploding inside of her.

"You did this?" Duke asked.

Her lips were parted as she tried to calm her breathing.

"So what?" she asked as Sandman pulled out of her then stood up. He reached his hand out, pulling her into his arms. Placing his hand over her ass, he cupped her one cheek.

"I don't think she's learned her lesson."

Grace looked at Duke and Big Jay who had removed their boxers.

"Maybe we can help her learn her lesson."

Sandman released Grace to Big Jay who sat on the chair and placed her on his lap. She immediately took his cock into her and attacked his mouth, kissing, moaning, then thrusting.

Sandman laughed.

"Somehow I think we've released a monster."

Grace was fully aroused as she thrust up and down Jay's cock. She was riding him, completely turned on by getting caught in her so-called illegal activity by Sandman.

He was such an enforcer.

Jay grabbed her hips and thrust upward as she thrust down.

"You feel so good, baby, and you're very wet. I think you like being naughty."

"Yes, oh God, I love having you inside of me," she admitted. Then she felt the hand to her shoulder, and Duke pressed her back down so that her chest was snug to Jay's. He immediately swiped his fingers from her pussy to her anus.

"I don't know why Sandman didn't spank this ass. I bet that would teach you about breaking and entering, vandalism, and engaging in criminal activities."

He pinched her ass and she squealed, feeling her cum drip between her legs. Jay leaned back and she thought they might tumble over but they didn't. Instead, the move caused her ass to lift up giving Duke better access to her ass.

She felt his finger press between the tight bud.

"Oh please, Duke. Please do something." She thrust upward and Jay sucked on her breast, pulling the nipple deeper into his mouth.

"Oh." She moaned as another small eruption hit her pussy just as Duke's cock pressed through the tight rings of her ass.

"Fuck!" Duke yelled then slapped her ass as he thrust into her all the way.

She grabbed onto Jay's shoulders and neck. Her breasts were pressed hard against his face, nearly smothering him, but he didn't seem to mind at all. As she moved up and down along with him, Duke pulled out then shoved back in. She was moving along with them, feeling the fire and excitement as her men filled her with cock.

"Oh God, I can't take it."

She moaned as she lost all ability to hold on as her body tightened then released.

"So good," Jay said through clenched teeth, and then nipped her nipple as he exploded inside of her.

She was trying to catch her breath as Duke grabbed her hips tight and thrust into her, stroking her ass hard and fast. He was pounding into her, causing Jay to moan along with her until Duke hollered as he came. He remained still and deep in her ass, breathing heavy against her neck, kissing and nibbling along her skin.

"Incredible," he whispered.

"Amazing," Jay said then cupped her cheeks as Duke slowly pulled from her.

"In a heap of trouble," Sandman added, and she hugged Jay's neck, not caring about anything but being lost in their arms.

Chapter 16

Camera crews and reporters were swarming around the outside of the Houston Police Department. They were waiting for a statement from the FBI or from the police department but neither was happening.

"This is insane, Captain. I'm telling you why I've been trying to find the lieutenant. He's like family and I'm worried about his safety, sir. All I want to do is find him and bring him in for questioning, so we can settle this matter. He is not the killer," Frank stated as he looked at Agent Lancaster, wanting to wring his neck.

"I understand that, Detective, but this is not your case. The agents have taken it over and will tell us when we're needed," the captain began to say as Agent Lancaster interrupted.

"I don't want him anywhere near this case, Captain. He could know right now where Donald Friedman is and is withholding that information."

"What the hell are you..." Frank began to say as he rose from his chair. So did Agent Lancaster.

The captain immediately wedged himself between the two men before they made contact.

"Frank, just calm down and take a seat. Agent Lancaster, I suggest you do the same. You two have been at each other's throats constantly. This is an intense situation, gentleman, and we need to be professional," stated the captain as neither man took a seat as asked.

"This guy's a fucking idiot. Now he's accusing me of withholding information. Give me a break, you're so wrapped up in trying to play hero and movie star to the reporters, you're chasing the wrong guy." Frank raised his voice as Agent Lancaster moved toward the door.

"Screw you, Frank, and I better not see you anywhere near this case or I'll have you locked up," Lancaster threatened him, before he left the room.

"What the hell is wrong with you, Frank? You can't go around pissing off the FBI. Now tell me what you think you were doing at Donald's house early this morning?" asked the captain.

"Fuck the FBI. All he's doing is screwing up this case and wasting time. I think Donald's in trouble, Captain. You know him as well as I do and there's no way he's guilty. I truly feel that the evidence at his house was planted by the real killer," Frank said, and the captain leaned against the front of his desk.

"You have no proof of this, Frank. I know how close you were to Donald but the evidence is stacked against him. Could you possibly be wrong? I know it's hard to believe. Shit even I'm still trying to accept this and our hands are tied behind our backs. This case belongs to the FBI, Frank, and there's nothing we can do about it. Stay away from Donald's house."

Frank was mad as hell. "So you think Donald could be the killer and you're telling me to stop trying to help clear my friend's name or find him?" Frank asked as he stood up from his chair.

The captain stood next to him and was just as angry as Frank was.

"I'm not going to follow you around, Frank. I can only be aware of what you are doing when you're in my presence," he told him.

"So I'm on my own? You don't know anything?" Frank asked with a smile.

"You're not on your own, Frank. If something comes up where you need my help, you just call me and I'll be there. I don't think Donald's the killer either," he said as he walked around his desk. Donald and the captain went way back and Frank knew they were close friends. They were a few years apart, grew up together and even went to the same schools. The captain would do what he could.

Frank knew the captain supported his efforts, and Frank knew the captain had a game to play.

He said thank you then left the office prepared to continue his solo and unofficial investigation.

* * * *

The killer sat in his house, miles away from everyone on acres of property where screams could echo across the deserted land and not be heard. It was an ideal place to act out his fantasies, take his time, enjoy and savor every moment of pleasure.

The struggling he heard from behind disturbed his thoughts and he turned to admire his latest project. She was beautiful, young, and so naive. He was proud at the way he enticed her to take a ride with him. She knew him and he was so kind and funny. He laughed at his ability to deceive and to manipulate to get whatever he wanted.

He sifted through his pile of toys thinking about his Grace, knowing that his plan was coming along well and that she would come home to him soon.

He wrapped the rope around his knuckles smiling as he turned toward his latest victim.

"We're going to have some fun, my little darling, but first there are some rules," he told her as he jumped on top of her where she lay on the mattress that leaned against the basement wall. In a flash, he turned the rope into a noose and placed it around her neck.

He spoke to her, breathing erratically, becoming more excited with each thought that entered his mind.

His victim lay helpless, eyes red and bruised from her attempt to fight off her attacker. She was having trouble breathing as the killer took the noose and attached it to a solid metal clip on the wall that held her in place like some wild animal.

Initially, he thought about playing with her then letting her go. Knowing that she survived and would live with the terror of the acts he performed on her aroused him somehow. She could identify him now. She knew the serial killer and no one had a clue who he was, except her.

* * * *

She was so stupid to get into this guy's car and take the ride he offered, but she missed the bus somehow, and if she were late getting to work again her boss would fire her. She tried to call her boyfriend, leaving him voice mail message after voice mail message, but he never called. She would die now because of her inability to be on time, fend for herself, and be responsible.

Now here she lay on a mattress on a cold, damp basement floor and no one was looking for her. Her boss would be pissed off and just assume she was a no-show and her boyfriend would eventually answer his voice mail and assume she was mad at him again. It was inevitable. Today would be the day she died.

"Grace, my love, are you ready to play?" he asked Michelle as she stared at him wide-eyed, scared, and trembling. She had nowhere to run. The noose around her neck was tight and with each small turn of her head, she hit the concrete wall. The killer began to touch her and cut her clothes off. She screamed, begging him to stop. She began to kick and punch him, fighting like an animal, choking and gasping for air with each thrust forward. She was scratching his arms and hitting his face but it wasn't enough and he immediately retaliated with much more force and momentum as his fists collided with her face, her body sending her into darkness then light, darkness then light. She was losing it as she tried to fight him off. He was pounding on her, out of control, his eyes bulging. He was a madman, an absolute madman.

Her vision blurred. She was losing strength, struggling to hold on. Right before she passed out, he kissed her softly, gently, so easily he turned his anger to tenderness like turning a switch on then off. "Grace, sweet, beautiful Grace, let us begin, my love," he whispered to her as darkness fell upon her.

* * * *

"Grace, the answer is no. It's absolutely out of the question so just don't ask again," Sandman stated firmly, and when she looked toward Jay and Duke, she knew the question was nonnegotiable.

Sandman stared at the bags. They were packed as if she were about to go home.

"You can't force me to stay here. I want to go home and I want you to call the bureau and have them formulate a plan to capture the real killer. I don't mind being bait. Really, Sandman," Grace said as she stood by the bed.

He grabbed her by her arms. "I'm not going to do it and you are not going anywhere. What the hell are you thinking, Grace? I can't protect you at home like I can protect you here. My brothers and I will not hand you over to the lions," he told her as she stood in front of him angry and frustrated.

"What if I don't want your protection, Sandman? I can ask to be left alone."

"Then you'll die at the hands of that madman. Is that what you want?"

"You saw some of those crime scene pictures, is that how you want to die?" Duke asked as he took position beside her. "Being tortured, raped, beaten to a pulp? He wants you. He has sick sexual plans for you, the unthinkable, Grace."

"Is that how you want to die?" Sandman yelled, squeezing her arms and she began to cry.

Grace was frustrated, angry, and she felt so out of control. All she wanted to do was stop this killer and she'd thought about it all night. She would go back home and that was final, she was saying to herself as Sandman pulled her close to him.

"I love you, Grace, and I won't let you do this because I love you." Her heart leaped and then ached again, having a tug-of-war between happiness and safety with Sandman, Duke, and Jay or sacrificing herself for the slightest possibility of catching the killer.

"Guys, why are you stopping me from leaving when I can help? Is your plan to make me choose? It would be so easy to just stay here, safe with you, making love to you, feeling protected by you, but at home my family is suffering, the public is outraged, your fellow agents are questioning Donald. There's so much chaos and I feel I can stop it all or at least try. Can't you understand that?" She looked at Sandman, Duke, then Jay, hoping that maybe one of them would agree.

"You can't do it, Grace. There's more to this than just being bait. You can't handle it," he told her straight out which made her feel weak and defeated but only for a moment as she allowed her will, her determination, and the hidden strength to emerge.

"I can handle it! Maybe you need to put your personal feelings aside and start focusing on the true objective here. We need to catch this killer and sitting here on our asses is not working. Whether you're with me or not, Sandman, I'm walking out that door and there's not one damn thing you can do about it." She stood there ready to defeat his challenge.

"Donald never showed up for questioning, Grace, and he's still nowhere to be found. Lancaster has pretty solid evidence against him and he's now the main suspect in this case," Big Jay told her and she knew he was trying to get her to stay. But she was still shocked. There was no way Donald was the killer. She felt it in her heart and she was still determined to leave.

"Well then if that's the case, then your agents know who they're after. I'm leaving, and that's final."

She headed up the stairs.

* * * *

"We have to do something. We won't be able to hold her here for much longer," Big Jay stated toward Sandman.

"She's stubborn and she's upset. Rightfully so, but heading home in the middle of this is not feasible at all," Duke stated.

"I'm going to call Frank. Maybe he'll be able to get through to her or figure out a plan," Sandman said.

"Why don't we make a few calls and see if we can find a safe house, closer to home just in case?" Duke added.

"Okay, let's do this. No matter what, we have to protect Grace," Sandman said then headed to his office while his brothers went downstairs.

* * * *

Grace grabbed her backpack, some money, and her cell phone then snuck out Sandman's bedroom window that he left opened. She knew the sensor on the alarm system only sounded when a door or window was opened. She prayed that she would figure out who the real killer was and that she made the right decision to sneak out and go alone.

Grace had planned on taking a bus back, but first she needed a disguise and some makeup to ensure she stayed undetected and unidentified.

As she headed across the field, she prayed that the men would forgive her. She knew that they loved her and wanted to protect her from this madman, but enough was enough. This guy had to be stopped before something happened to another member of her family. She hoped that she truly had the strength and capability to complete her plan successfully.

* * * *

Sandman got off the phone with Frank then received a phone call from Jim.

"Yes, Sandman, it looks like you might have caught something when you found the partial telephone number and short letter in the file. I've downloaded the information and have sent it through your secure e-mail," Jim said. He was good at his job as a detective but also had a knack for the high-tech stuff. Jim was a whiz at computers, satellite imaging, and every special tool the department had access to.

Sandman opened his e-mail and began reading the information.

"I figured out the telephone number by tracking down the victim's personal phone book which was included in one of many evidence boxes. I don't know why the detectives at the time hadn't checked there first. The number belonged to a Charlie Vasco," Jim said and Sandman listened as he wrote the name down on a notepad.

"So who is this guy?" he asked, wondering if he could be the killer.

"Well what struck me as strange, Sandman, is that it seems that this Charlie Vasco just fell off the face of the earth right after that first murder ten years ago. There are no records of him thus far, but I'm still looking over death certificates or any signs of name change."

"That's great work, Jim. Do you have fingerprints on this guy? Or maybe even a photograph?" Sandman asked.

"Yes, I do have fingerprints but no photograph yet. Hopefully I'll have his current name for you as well real soon," Jim stated and Sandman hoped he would as well.

"Okay, now onto something that Frank found out. It appears that those other three victims, the ones you felt may be connected to the Thompson murder, are linked by one main fact."

"That being?"

"They were all involved with a fundraising organization that applied for affordable housing in suburban developments."

"Shit, wasn't Donald involved with that?"

"Yes, but apparently Donald and these other victims were receiving threatening phone calls and e-mails from people for years. Those three men were heavily involved in the fundraising board. Once they were killed, the programs either were shut down or lost funding. Donald has been the only one able to help complete a development and right here in Houston."

"Are you thinking that this killer started killing these people so they wouldn't build affordable housing in the area?"

"Frank thinks that the killer was so used to killing for his pleasure, that perhaps he started killing to get his point across. Maybe some of the threats were from this same guy we're after."

"Jim, you have Frank there with you?"

"Yes. He's right here. He's trying to find copies of any threatening letters. His mom was involved with that board along with Donald. The affordable housing complex s just a mile or so from their house."

"See if you can find any of those letters. See if we can make a connection to the words in those letters and maybe the ones in the poems left with the bodies."

"Okay, we'll keep you updated."

He hung up the phone and explained to Duke and Big Jay what Jim and Frank found out.

"So Grace was onto something after all in finding that note and phone number in the file?" Big Jay asked then smiled.

"She sure was and maybe we can use this to get her to stay a little while longer. First I want to look at the files from the first few cases again. The first victim may have known the killer. Perhaps even had a relationship with him. We're looking at that particular case as his first killing but maybe something else triggered it. It may have been what led him to change his identity, fall off the face of the earth as Jim put it. Come on guys, grab a chair and start reading," Sandman said as he gathered up the files.

* * * *

"What do you mean she wants to come home? Today?" John asked all surprised.

"Yeah, that's what Sandman said and he wasn't very happy about it. We need to move fast, brother. Grace is stubborn and determined, and Sandman didn't sound too confident about changing her mind," added Frank as John leaned against the black unmarked police car.

"Well let's try to find Donald. I know Mom said that Eric had seen him at the town board meeting the other day. Maybe we can ask Eric if

Donald seemed preoccupied or maybe acting differently," said John.

"That's a good idea. We'll try to speak with Eric before he leaves for that small business trip to Dallas he mentioned. We'll head over there after we go talk to Mayor Donovan. Donald and him are good friends," added Frank. John walked around the unmarked police car to get in on the passenger side.

Ten minutes later they were at the municipal building and headed to the mayor's office.

"Hey what brings you two around here? I thought you hated this place," said Peter as he bumped into his brothers as they approached the mayor's office.

"Hey, Peter, what's going on?" asked Frank as he shook his brother's hand. Then John did the same.

"I'm running around between the courts and the office. What are you two doing here?"

They filled him in on the case as well as Grace wanting to come back home.

"Well Sandman and his brothers can't allow her to. She's in way too much danger and now the FBI is looking for Donald? They don't have a fucking clue," said Peter and both John and Frank laughed.

"Is that your professional opinion?" John asked with a smile.

"They don't have shit, guys. Every bit of so-called evidence they have against Donald is filled with holes. None of it would stand up in court," Peter added.

"Well hopefully it won't go that far. I don't believe Donald's the killer. I'm beginning to get worried about him. When we spoke last, he was actually looking forward to Agent Lancaster's questioning and even willing to take a lie detector test. Something's not right," said Frank

"Do you think he's in some kind of danger?" Peter asked.

"He may be in danger. That's why we're here. We wanted to see how Donald was acting at the meeting the other night. There's nowhere else for us to start looking," said Frank.

"Well Mayor Donovan is good friends with Donald and that's as good a start as any," said Peter as the men continued to talk.

* * * *

"Grace...Grace, Goddamn it, this isn't funny. Where are you? Answer me right now!" Big Jay yelled as he frantically searched the house.

"She's gone." Duke pointed toward Sandman's bedroom.

Sandman headed toward the door and saw that his bedroom window was opened. There was a note on his desk from Grace.

Sandman, Duke, and Jay,

Please understand why I snuck out and decided to do this on my own. My family is suffering. The community is suffering because of me. I don't want to put any of you or anyone else in danger. I'll contact the FBI as soon as I get to Houston. I know of a safe place to stay, and when I get there I'll contact you. I can't just sit around safe, happy, and out of control. I need to stop this guy and you're only willing to do this your way. I understand that you love me but I can't sit here in your house, miles away while innocent women are being killed. He nearly killed Jamie, and all he wants is me. You said you wouldn't help me or let the FBI use me as bait. Well that decision wasn't for you to make. I've made the decision and that's what I'll be...Bait...Anything to stop this madman. Please don't be angry. I love you all so much.

Love, Grace

"Goddamn her. What the hell is she thinking, guys?" Sandman yelled as he headed through the bedroom door and down the stairs.

"She couldn't have gotten far. We flew here by helicopter and there's no way she could get a plane ticket and pass through security without being identified. Everyone knows what she looks like," Big Jay stated.

"We don't know when she left. She came upstairs over two hours ago. She could take the train," Sandman said.

"Or she could play it real safe and take a bus, get there by tonight." Duke added.

"I better call her brothers and the agents and have some agents posted around the bus stations and train stations. We have to pack our bags. It looks like we're headed back to the Houston Police Department."

* * * *

Frank's cell phone rang just as Peter was about to walk away.

"Yeah, Thompson here," said Frank into the receiver.

"Frank, it's Sandman. Your sister pulled a Houdini on me. She's headed home and I don't even know how she's getting there."

"Oh shit. I was afraid this might happen. Damn it, what the hell is she thinking?" said Frank into the receiver as John and Peter stopped talking to listen to Frank.

"What are you going to do?" asked Frank.

"Well I'm going to call Jim and the guys, let him notify Lancaster, and have some men posted at the bus stations and train stations. I don't want this information leaking to the press. We have to find her before…"

"Before the killer does. I know, man. This is really, really bad news. I can't believe this. Did she leave a note?" asked Frank.

"Yeah she actually did and said something about a safe place she knew of. Do you know what she was talking about?"

"It doesn't ring a bell but I'll ask my brothers. They're right here," Frank said.

"Don't tell your mom yet. She'll be in a real panic when she finds out. When I get ahold of your sister, she's going to get it. I can't believe she did this."

"I hear you, man, and thanks for calling me right away," said Frank before hanging up the phone.

Frank stuck the cell phone back onto the clip attached to his navy-blue Dockers.

"What's the really bad news?" asked Peter as John waited to hear as well.

"Looks like our baby sister just ditched her men." Frank shook his head in fury.

Both John and Peter started talking at once. Frank settled them down and tried to keep in control.

"First of all we can't let Mom know. Sandman doesn't know when she snuck out, so he doesn't know how far she may have gotten. He's informing Agent Dickhead right now and he plans on stationing undercover agents at various bus stops and train stations," said Frank. Both John and Peter laughed a little at their brother's new name for Agent Lancaster.

"What does he want us to do?" asked John, wanting to get his sister to safety immediately.

"Stay put here. Maybe she'll contact one of us, and knowing her I'm sure she'll make it here without the agents even knowing it. She was always good at hiding and evading capture," said Frank as he thought about the strategic military games they would all play as children.

"What are you talking about, Frank? We were kids when we used to play ring-a-lario and manhunt," Peter said to his brother.

"Oh man, I remember that. She used to always win that game. Shit, did that piss me off and Clara, too," added John and the three men began reminiscing about old times.

"You used to get so mad at her, John. That was when you wanted to become a Marine," added Frank.

"Not just a Marine, he wanted to be a sniper or special forces," added Peter and they started laughing.

"This is a little bit different, guys. She never had a real killer after her. Never mind someone without a face or a name," John told them and once again they became serious. Frank's cell phone rang so he answered it.

"Yes, Captain. Okay, I appreciate it, sir. No, I haven't yet. Thank you again," said Frank. Then he hung up the phone.

"That was the captain. He wanted to give me the heads-up on Grace. Unfortunately the word's out about Grace and still there's no sign of Donald. The captain said Lancaster is about to release a statement to the press telling them that Donald is the serial killer," Frank told his brothers. They stood there in shock.

Frank called his mom to let her know about Grace, and John headed home to stay with her. Peter went along with Frank to talk to the judge. After their brief conversation they came up with nothing new.

"What are we going to do next?" asked Peter.

"Let's find Eric and ask him a few questions about Donald's behavior the other day. Then I'll start talking to his family and close friends. Maybe he had another place to go to. I'll get his mom's number in Pennsylvania. I'm sure Lancaster has already got her place swarming with agents," Frank added. Both men went their separate ways, hoping their baby sister would arrive safely.

* * * *

Donald was beginning to regain consciousness. His arms were tied tightly behind his back and his legs were tied together with masking tape. The pain in his shoulders and back was excruciating and his vision was blurred as he tried to regain his bearings. He wondered where he was and how he got there? The last thing he remembered was going outside to throw the garbage out, then the sharp pain in the back of his head, which radiated to his neck and shoulders. Then it hit him.

"The killer," he said out loud and wondered if anyone knew where he was. Who was the killer and what did he want with him? He asked himself numerous questions as his head throbbed with pain.

Now that he didn't show up for questioning, Lancaster would think that he was the serial killer. "Damn it," he said out loud again.

"If I were you, I wouldn't spend my last hours before committing suicide cursing and damning everything." The voice came out of nowhere. Then suddenly Donald focused on the silhouette image behind the sheer curtain. "Who are you? Why are you talking about suicide?" Donald demanded as he tried to break the restraints around his wrists.

"You couldn't take the fact that you have murdered so many innocent women, especially that female police officer. Then of course you tortured your own daughter-in-law. Your son would hate you forever for doing that. Finally you killed Grace and there was no reason to continue to live. It's all in the letter you wrote, Donald. Don't tell me you've forgotten already?" the voice asked sarcastically.

"Whoever you are you're not going to pin these murders on me. You don't even have Grace. She's safe and somewhere you will never find her."

"You've been resting, Donald, so you haven't heard the latest news. Grace has escaped the protection of one, Special Investigator Sandstone. She's traveling alone in disguise, I assume in order to avoid being captured by agents. She will find you, the serial killer, and I will be here waiting for her," the voice said.

"No way, asshole. You'll never get away with this. Grace will not come he…" Donald was about to say "here" when he realized where he was. Donald looked up toward the curtain where the real serial killer stood, and as he did, the figure appeared. Donald was shocked to see his face.

"No…it can't be…No!" Donald yelled and the killer laughed, as if excited and invigorated after revealing himself.

Chapter 17

Sandman, Duke, and Jay arrived at the precinct receiving police escorts as they pushed their way through the crowd of people and reporters. Grace's escape had made the news. Now everyone knew she was missing and began to assume the serial killer had her. Questions were being thrown at them about Donald and the rest of the Thompson family. It was a zoo outside, and finally Sandman and his brothers were inside. They immediately headed upstairs to the main conference room where Agent Lancaster, the captain, Frank, John, and other brass were gathered for updates and new information.

"You got through that mess huh?" asked Frank as he shook Sandman's hand and then his brothers' as Sandman introduced them.

"It's crazy out there. How long has this been going on?" Sandman asked.

"Since you let our only fucking clue escape your personal custody!" yelled Lancaster. The room became silent.

Sandman knew Lancaster well. One glance around the room showed it was obvious that the agent wasn't well liked.

"I didn't let her escape. She's one very stubborn, determined young lady who doesn't easily take no for an answer," Sandman said and hoped Lancaster would drop it.

"Yeah, well, if she dies, it's on your conscience, not mine," Lancaster snapped back then turned around, giving Sandman his back.

"Don't listen to him. We don't blame you one bit," said Frank. "We know our sister, and when she's determined to do something, she does it. There still hasn't been any sign of her. Whether she took a train or a bus, she would be here by now. I just know it."

"She has probably seen the news broadcasts and knows to stay clear of town and out of sight," added John.

"I hope you're both right about this. I know we'll all feel better once we hear from her," Sandman added.

"She's one tough cookie your sister. She's really smart and aware of the danger she's in. She only left because she didn't want anyone else to get hurt. She feels responsible," Duke told her brothers and they understood completely. A few hours later Sandman, Duke, Jay, Frank, and John sat in Donald's office hoping to hear from Grace. They'd heard about numerous false sightings of both Grace and Donald and knew time was running out.

John called his mother to see how she was holding up. Peter and the family were staying with her to keep her company.

"Eric still hasn't come home, Johnny. I'm beginning to worry now. Have you seen him or heard from him?" Sarah asked. Eric hadn't called her all day, and Richie, the teenage boy who helped run the hardware store, said Eric never came into work. Richie also said his girlfriend Michelle was missing. She hadn't shown up at her job either. Sarah told the story to John and he said he would check into it.

"Mom said Eric hasn't come home yet, and when she called the hardware store, Richie said Eric never came to work today," John told the others.

"Oh shit. This is not good," said Frank, thinking something bad could have happened to Eric as well.

"It gets worse. Richie said his girlfriend Michelle never arrived at work yesterday either," John added.

Frank opened his cell phone and dialed. "Captain, this is Frank. Has Michelle Maverick been found? We just heard that she was missing."

"Your timing is impeccable, Frank. Her body was just found about a half hour ago. Looks like our killer has struck again. The poor kid, she was only sixteen years old," the captain added.

"Oh no. Oh my God, that's horrible. Why didn't anyone call Sandstone?" Frank asked as Sandman listened.

"Because Lancaster's jealous, Frank. All I can say is that Lancaster has taken over. He's out of control and the word is he doesn't want anyone to inform Sandstone about anything. He's told the other agents that Sandstone has pretty much killed your sister," the captain added.

"Do they believe Lancaster?" Frank asked.

"As far as I can tell, Lancaster hasn't exactly made any new friends, and the other agents don't seem to be too happy with him right now."

"Thanks, Captain." Frank hung up the phone. He told Sandman and his brothers all about Lancaster just as Agent Lancaster entered the office.

"Why, look who it is. Just the person I wanted to talk to," Sandman said as he rose from the brown leather chair.

"I wanted to talk to you, too. What do you have Jim working on?" Lancaster asked.

"Just something Grace came up with."

"Grace? She came up with something else and you didn't inform me?" Lancaster asked as he moved closer to Sandman.

"Despite the fact that you don't feel there's a need for me to know everything that's going on, I haven't kept one bit of information from you."

"If I've kept any information from you, it's because of your lack of professionalism. While you're off playing house with Miss Fancy Pants, I've been working on finding the killer, Donald Friedman," Agent Lancaster said, raising his voice.

"There's no way Donald Friedman is our man," Sandman began to say before Lancaster cut him off.

"You don't believe that, Sandstone. The Thompson family doesn't want to believe it but it's a fact. I've got plenty of evidence and where the hell is he?" Lancaster was yelling now and everyone in the room was listening.

"You don't have shit, Lancaster, and you also better remember who's in charge of this investigation. From here on out you don't make a move without my approval, you got it? No one is to do anything without running it by me first," Sandman told Lancaster and now he was standing directly in front of him.

"This is bullshit. These people have you fooled. Frank and John are probably hiding Donald right now and you're too busy thinking with your dick instead of your—"

Sandman took the first and only swing, knocking Lancaster over a desk with one mighty punch to the jaw, sending his legs flying over his shoulders.

Lancaster hit the floor taking a few moments to pull himself together.

"Now I don't want to hear another peep out of you. Get up off your ass and start working with us instead of against us. We're a team, Lancaster, and don't you forget it. You got it!" Sandman yelled and Lancaster nodded yes before leaving the room. The other agents heard the fight and were glad Sandstone was back in charge.

"Damn, Sandman, you got yourself one wicked right hook," said John and the others agreed. Frank was glad Sandman got pissed off at Lancaster and put him in his place. It was something he was looking forward to doing himself. Right now they needed to figure out where Donald could be as well as Grace.

* * * *

Agent Lancaster headed down the hallway avoiding eye contact with his fellow agents. They were happy Sandstone was back and in charge. All the hard work he did while Sandstone was off screwing the brunette he was sure no longer meant shit. Who the hell did that fucking guy think he was, just because he served in the military, was a Marine in special commandos or some shit. He was fuming now as he closed the door to the small office he had taken over along with Justin Sullivan. Everyone had witnessed what happened and it was an embarrassment.

Justin walked into the room and neither man exchanged words. Suddenly Lancaster's phone rang.

"Hello," Lancaster answered.

"Agent Lancaster, this is Grace Thompson. Investigator Burbank gave me your number. I'm back in town as I'm sure you know, and I'm willing to use myself as bait to catch this killer. Investigator Burbank said to speak to you," Grace told him and Lancaster instantly felt that things were turning around. He would surely have the last laugh on Sandstone. He needed to be cautious and it was obvious he had to persuade Justin to keep his trap shut.

"Are you all right, Grace?" Lancaster asked and Justin turned to look. He definitely heard him.

"Yes, I'm fine and I'm safe. Is this line secure?" she asked.

"Yes, it is. Now tell me where you are and I'll come meet you." Lancaster was feeling the excitement of solving this very publicized case all on his own. He would do this without Sandstone or the others. This was his case. He worked the hardest. He deserved the full credit for solving it.

"I'm just about twenty minutes outside of town. There's an old abandoned farmhouse just past Coopers Way. Make a left turn onto Madison and follow the fields for about three miles. You'll see a large green house that looks abandoned. My family has owned it for years. No one uses it or has been there as far as I know. Pull your car around back just for precaution," she told him and Lancaster was impressed with Grace's calmness and professionalism. She may be more than just a pretty face after all.

"Okay, I'll wrap things up here then I'll meet you in a half hour," Lancaster said and Justin wrote down the directions just as Lancaster did.

"Agent Lancaster, is Sandman there?" Grace asked and she sounded hesitant. Maybe she was concerned that Sandstone might hurt her for sneaking away from him. Lancaster wondered if he could use that as his reasoning for not notifying anyone of this call. He smiled to himself.

The killer had to be stopped and she was willing to die trying.

"No, Grace, I'm sorry he's not here. I don't know where he is.

Supposedly he and his brothers are somewhere that they can't be reached. I'll try to locate him and inform him of our plan. You stay low and don't worry. We'll stop this killer together," Lancaster told her before he hung up the phone. He could feel his face turning red with excitement as well as the twinkle in his eyes and the somersaults in his belly, as he smiled, already celebrating prematurely.

Lancaster looked toward Justin "You didn't hear any of that, do you understand me?"

"But, sir, don't you think Sandstone and the others—"

"Fuck Sandstone, he's not thinking like an agent. He's thinking like a worried boyfriend. While he was hidden in a safe house having a fuck fest with her and his brothers, I was here busting my ass trying to find this killer. Grace's the only lure we have to catch this killer. I'll do everything I can to keep her alive and safe, but this is my case and I'll be damned if I'm going to listen to Sandstone anymore. Senior Investigator Burbank even gave her my number to contact and recommended me. He knows Sandstone can't handle this any further and he wants me to take over. You keep your mouth shut and your ears opened. Let me know what Sandstone comes up with. Meanwhile I'm going to try and get the killer to search out Grace," Lancaster said as he began to dial the telephone.

"How are you going to do that, sir?" Justin asked.

Lancaster didn't answer him. He just smiled as he asked for Debbie Clark, the lead newscaster for channel nine eyewitness news.

* * * *

Justin listened while Lancaster informed the reporter of Grace's decision to leave protective custody on her own and make her way back to Houston without the assistance of the FBI. He told Debbie Clark that Grace wanted to be with her family and that he was unable to locate her. They feared for her safety and she refused further protection.

Justin knew that Lancaster was asking for trouble but he made the call anonymously, only saying he was connected to the police department and this was inside information. Justin wondered if Senior Investigator Burbank really felt that Sandstone couldn't handle the case or if Lancaster was lying. He may just have to call the senior investigator as soon as Lancaster left the room.

Ten minutes later Lancaster was swearing Justin to secrecy and heading out the door to meet Grace.

* * * *

Grace made her way across the field and was merely a five-minute walk from the green-colored house. She could see a flickering light on in the basement downstairs and wondered if Lancaster was already there. She knew she was only seven minutes late. She had to take cover on her way to avoid being seen by a patrol car in the area.

Slowly she made her way around back and noticed the unmarked police car and that the door was unlocked. She cautiously entered the kitchen area and could see the dust and cobwebs that had built up over the years throughout the house. The place was abandoned and it was obvious no one had been there in years. Everything looked old and in need of major scrubbing, especially the brown, dirt-covered countertops that used to be bright, shiny, and white. As she walked toward the doorway that led to the living room, the dark brown, wide-planked hardwood floors creaked with each step she took. The living room furniture was covered with sheets that faded over time and now resembled a dull tan color. She heard someone move behind her and as she turned around toward them a sleeping bag was thrown over her head and she was tackled to the ground. She screamed for help, calling Agent Lancaster, but no one answered and no one came. She couldn't see anything. She tried to fight her attacker off but failed. He was way too strong for her and she instantly felt powerless.

* * * *

Her attacker brought her down a flight of stairs she assumed must have led to the basement. They definitely were still in the house. Suddenly she was being shoved across the room and as she lost her footing, she fell to the cement floor smacking her face and cheek to the concrete.

"Grace. Oh my God." She heard the voice and instantly she recognized Donald's voice. Was he the killer after all? Could Lancaster have been right?

Then she heard the other voice.

"Shut up. No talking!" the man yelled. She couldn't make out whom it could be. The killer must have taken Donald as well. If she could only see who was there. She wished the cover wasn't over her head. She felt the metal grab hold to her wrists then tighten and click. Handcuffs. She knew immediately they were handcuffs.

"Who's there? Tell me what you want?" she called into the darkness.

Out of nowhere she felt the boot make contact with her ribs and she screamed in agonizing pain. She had just been kicked somewhere from the left, no the right. She wasn't sure as she sensed the movement around her.

"Keep quiet," the voice said and she did so until she felt a large wooden pole against her spine then the handcuffs being removed. She instantly pushed forward into the large figure, her attacker. As he pulled the pillowcase off her head, she saw a fist headed straight toward her face. She couldn't move quickly enough as it made contact with her mouth and sent her flying into the wooden pole. She slammed back against the pole, then hit the floor. Severe pain shot through her system. But she wanted to know who the killer was. She wanted to see his face and put an end to the madness.

As she turned her head to look up, she saw the face of the serial killer and her heart dropped into her stomach. She suddenly couldn't breathe, couldn't move. It was as if she lost her life in a split second and time stood still. She felt the deep hollow feeling, then the absolute shock to her soul.

"Oh my God, no," she screamed.

* * * *

The phone rang just as Sandman began opening his e-mail messages on his laptop. He was receiving a message from Jim and hoped it was a picture of Charlie Vasco. He could be the real serial killer.

"Yeah, Jim, I was just downloading your message. I'm assuming it's a picture of Charlie Vasco."

"Yeah, Sandman, it sure as shit is and you better brace yourself. I found out who he is and what his current name is as well."

Just as Sandman was about to ask who it was, the computer screen blinked and showed the full download. A picture of Sarah's husband, Eric, stared into Sandman's eyes. He grabbed the arm of the chair then looked up toward Frank, John, Duke, and Big Jay and the others who were in the office. He couldn't believe it as he spoke into the phone.

"Jim, I got it. Are you one hundred percent sure?" he asked him calmly.

"Yeah, buddy, I am and I also sent you the information I recovered about his past. He was never married and his parents are both deceased. He had a sister Cynthia who died at age twenty. I took the liberty of finding out how and that's where things get a little fishy. He apparently found his sister's body and there was no evidence to show that he was a suspect in the case. It was definitely murder."

"Did they ever find out who killed her?" Sandman asked which got everyone's attention in the office. They all stopped what they were doing and listened.

"No, sir, they didn't. It gets worse, Sandman. I pulled up a picture of his sister Cynthia. I've e-mailed that to you as well."

Sandman scrolled down with the mouse pad to search out the picture. His eyes widened at the sight. Cynthia had long brown hair, hazel eyes, and was a knockout. All the victims had the same characteristics.

"Oh shit, Jim, this is crazy. What was found at the crime scene? How was she killed?" Sandman asked and Jim told him all about the sexual torture and multiple stab wounds. Once again a very long thin, sharp object was used just like in the other murder cases. Sandman continued to speak to Jim, pulling together further information. Then he looked over the e-mails before breaking the news to the others.

"Sandman, what is it? What's going on?" Frank asked and the others could tell something was up.

Sandman took a deep breath and knew this wasn't going to be easy. How was he going to break the news? How would they react? He rose from the desk where he was sitting and asked Frank and John to have a seat. Of course they both declined and knew it was going to be bad.

"That was Jim, with some new information. Donald is definitely not the killer. Your sister came across some evidence while we were at my place looking over the case files. She found something interesting left behind by the killer at the first crime scene. Anyhow we came up with the name Charlie Vasco along with some fingerprints but no picture. Jim identified who Charlie Vasco is and confirmed the information. He e-mailed me a picture." Sandman told them as he turned his laptop toward the others. Frank and John gasped for air. He would never forget the look of shock that came over their faces.

* * * *

Grace looked toward the corner of the room where she saw Donald leaning against the wall. Both of his legs were bleeding and she couldn't tell what kind of wounds they were.

"Grace, I wanted to surprise you a bit differently than this. I had it all planned out for us," Eric told her as he held an extremely sharp ice pick in his hands.

"I don't understand." She shook her head in confusion. "Why?" she asked as she slowly backed up.

"Because I love you. You're the one I have been waiting for, yearning for all my life. I was devastated when you went away. Killing your sister was supposed to bring us closer." He took a small step toward her.

"You? It was you who killed Clara? Maggie and the others?" Grace asked, raising her voice. She was beginning to get over her shock, as fear and anger began to take control.

"They were substitutes for you, my love, but they just wouldn't do," he told her, still standing there confident and ready to attack. Grace held her ground.

Just keep him talking, she told herself.

"What about Donald? What are you going to do to him?" Grace asked.

"He's the serial killer everyone's been looking for. He found you, brought you here, performed his sadistic rituals on you, then killed you. Afterward he was so disgusted with himself and what he had done, all of those women he killed over the years. He was ashamed now and he committed suicide." Eric looked toward Donald and laughed.

Grace knew he could get away with it just like he'd planted the evidence in Stew Parker's house. He'd planted evidence in Donald's house as well. They would be dead and he would be a free man living two separate lives with her mother Sarah. *Oh my God, Mom.* What would she do when she found out?

"I'm not going to let you get away with this, Eric," Grace said as she stepped back a little further. Soon there would be nowhere else to move.

"I don't think so, beautiful. We have a date." He lunged forward with the ice pick attempting to stab her. She tried to move but she wasn't quick enough as the ice pick pierced through the skin on her upper arm. She stepped back trying not to fall but she tripped over something. What the hell was that? She asked herself and there was something very large on the ground. In an instant she was on her back scrambling to get to her feet. She was slipping, sliding and she couldn't grip the floor with her feet or her hands. She looked down and all she could see was red. She screamed. She was horrified as she looked into the eyes of a dead Agent

Lancaster. It had to be him. She saw a picture once that Sandman showed her. *Oh, Sandman, Jay, and Duke. You'll never know who the killer is. Not unless I stop him.*

Eric was laughing as he took Grace by the injured arm and she cried with pain. He threw her against the wooden beam in anger then grabbed her by the throat.

"I'm in charge now so listen up. You will speak only when told to. You will do what I say or be punished. I have waited too long for this moment and it will be perfect," he said to her strongly then kissed her hard on the mouth as his arms wrapped around her and pulled her snugly against him.

Grace bit his lip. He pulled back appearing angry and she spat at him then grabbed his forearms. He didn't budge as she dug her manicured nails into his flesh, pushing down as hard as she could until her nails bent and broke. He was squeezing her throat now so that she couldn't swallow or breathe. She didn't want to die like this. She had accomplished so much on her own. She had abandoned safety with her men to help capture a killer and that was what she was going to do. With all her will and her might she lunged her body forward as she thrust her forehead forward against his chin, surprising him. He loosened his grip on her neck and then she stomped on Eric's ankle and foot as hard as she could. He let go of her neck and she kneed him in the groin, and then she clocked him in the jaw with a right hook.

She frantically looked around for a weapon. The ice pick lay on the floor and she grabbed it then went running toward the stairs. She didn't turn back. She could hear him gasping for air. She made it to the kitchen then heard the pounding of footsteps running up the basement stairs behind her. She headed toward the back door running toward the fields. She stopped a moment and thought about getting into Lancaster's car when she heard the screen door slam open. Eric was coming. He was chasing her. She ran around the side of the house then toward the high grasses. She could lose him in the woods. She knew those woods well. They would lead to the main road then the highway. Maybe she could stop a car for help? Maybe the police were looking for her? She did see that patrol car earlier. They must be in the area. She hoped as she continued to run for her life.

* * * *

Frank and John were trying to get over their initial shock. They were searching for answers, and possible locations Eric could hide. The other agents were informed of the situation and the manhunt was on. They were making the connections to other cases, coming up with timelines of when Eric left on business trips and murders taking place. The evidence was piling up and the other detectives working on Michelle's murder had a witness who saw her enter Eric's car. The coroner's reports were back and indicating that the possible weapon used for the killings was an ice pick. The oil used to blind Jamie was also found on the tape used to cover his other victims' eyes. Frank explained everything to Peter and he decided he would be the one to tell Sarah. Other agents were sent to Sarah's house as precaution in case Eric decided to go after his wife as well.

"Where the hell is Lancaster?" Sandman yelled through the chaos in the office. "Hey, Justin, we've been looking for you and Lancaster. Where is he?"

"There's been a break in the case. Sandstone figured out who the killer is," one of the agents told him, and he practically dropped his ceramic cup of hot coffee.

"It's Donald, right?" Justin asked.

"No, man, it's not him. It's Eric, Grace's stepfather. We're trying to find out where he could be hiding. Where's Agent Lancaster?"

Justin ran to Sandstone and told him about the phone call from Grace.

"Everybody shut up right now!" Sandman yelled out to the chaos of loud voices and people panicking. Everyone in the office stopped talking. Agents held their hands over telephone receivers. Others hung up their phones entirely. Frank and John joined Sandman by Justin and Big Jay and Duke stood at attention.

"Grace called over an hour ago. Lancaster said that Senior Investigator Burbank gave her Lancaster's number to set up a trap for the killer. She was in a safe place somewhere outside of town," explained Justin as he filled everyone in on the details.

"That fucking asshole could get our sister killed while he's trying to play hero agent. What if they're dead already?" Frank said.

"Let's stay positive. You said you had an address. Where is it?" Sandstone asked and Justin ran to his office.

"Calm down, Frank. Just because Lancaster and Grace are together it doesn't mean that Eric knows where they are. John, get together your SWAT team. I want as much manpower as possible to assist if needed," Sandstone stated.

"Here it is, sir, I wrote it down as Lancaster received it from Grace," Justin said, handing the piece of paper to Sandstone.

"Where is this place?" Sandman asked Frank and his eyes widened as he looked at the directions.

"It's a place our family owns. No one's been there in years. It's abandoned," said Frank

"Okay, everyone, this is how it's going down. I want ten agents to stay here and handle any information that comes through as well as updating me on new information. Call me if you hear from Grace, Donald, Eric, or anyone." Sandman directed the crowd of people as he gave the orders to the first group of agents.

"You guys get the gear and meet us downstairs in five minutes. We're going to the house. When we get there, let's come up on the house slowly. We don't know if this is a hostage situation or what. John will have his SWAT team go inside first along with some of my agents. No sirens, no info over the radios until we've entered the house. Got it?" Sandman asked then headed toward the stairs with Frank, Duke, Big Jay, and the others.

* * * *

Within twenty minutes the SWAT team and FBI agents had the house surrounded. With their guns drawn, Sandman, Frank, and the others followed the SWAT team into the house. They made their way toward the basement where they found Lancaster and Donald.

"He's dead, Sandman," said John as he checked Lancaster for a pulse. Now they feared for their sister's life. Where was she? What happened?

"He's alive, man!" yelled Frank as he helped Donald sit up against the wall.

"Grace," Donald whispered. He was having difficulty talking.

"Where is she, Donald?" Frank asked as Sandman and Big Jay kneeled down next to him.

"She ran. The stairs. Eric's the killer," he told them.

"We know, Donald. Where would Grace run to?" Duke asked, practically yelling. He was afraid they might be too late.

"Go help her. Eric is chasing her. The fields, the swamp," said Donald as he began to pass out.

Sandman got to his feet along with Frank.

"You know this area. I don't. We don't know how long ago she escaped so we're going to have to move quickly. Frank and John, you come with me. I want to organize groups to try and cover as much area as quickly as possible. Duke, Big Jay, you get the groups started. Grab whoever knows these woods and we'll meet up as we case the area, and Frank, John, and I will head out now. Let's go."

Everyone ran up the stairs.

* * * *

Grace felt the exhaustion, but she forced herself to continue running. *God, I'm out of shape. I can't believe Eric is the killer. Fucking Eric killed my sister.*

She could hear the rustling of branches and high grasses behind her. Eric was getting closer. He was gaining on her. Grace's T-shirt was drenched with sweat. Her hands and knees were dirty from numerous falls she took. She wondered if she could escape. As she ran through the muddy terrain, she came upon a small creek about twenty feet wide. She thought if she could get across it, get down the hill, and across the next open area, she would reach the road. If she ran to the right, it would lead to the same location where she found her sister's body. The thought frightened her, but she couldn't stop her mind from the crazy, erratic thoughts that were now consuming her brain. The heavy feeling in her chest grew with every breath she took. Had she asked for this? By leaving Sandman, Jay, and Duke, had she asked to become another one of Eric's victims? The police would know it was him. Sandman and his brothers would track Eric down and kill him. She felt the urge to give in. Give up and die out here, too. Would Eric kill her like he killed Clara? *My mom. My mom would never survive all of this. Clara's murder, Eric as the killer, and me dead, too.*

No one was coming. This was all her fault and she blamed herself for everything. She should have stayed with her men, in their cozy private cabin, lost in their embraces and lovemaking, and now she may never see them again. They would be too late if they even found out the truth. Her brothers would lose another sister and her mom would lose another daughter. The thoughts kept repeating in her mind, pounding away at her will, her determination. She was losing the battle physically and mentally.

Just then she heard her name.

"Grace!"

Someone was calling her and it wasn't Eric. She ran through the creek, tripping over branches and rocks beneath the water's surface. Then she fell in the water slamming her knees against the jagged edges of a cluster of rocks. She grabbed the ground through the water, pulling herself up and pushing herself to continue to run. She made it to the hill. It was in front of her now as she dove at it grabbing fistfuls of dirt, scratching, clawing, using all her might to climb it and make it to the road just yards ahead.

She screamed with terror as Eric grabbed ahold of her ankles pulling her back down the hill. Her belly scraped across the dirt. She struggled to hold on, grabbing more dirt, ripping her nails and fingers, feeling the stinging caused by each attempt.

He jumped on top of her tackling her as he rolled her onto her back. He backhanded her once, twice across the mouth, then again with his forearm. This was it. She couldn't take it anymore. She had dropped the ice pick that now laid only inches away from her.

"Grace!" She heard the voices screaming her name. Frank, John, Sandman, Duke? They were coming. They found her. She scraped together what little strength, momentum, and hatred she had left and threw her body to the side and attempted to grab the ice pick. She would not die, not without a fight. Eric would not be the one to survive.

"Help!" she screamed as loud as she could, feeling the strain, the ache in her throat and voice as she grabbed hold of the pick, striking Eric in the shoulder with it. She let go of the handle as she backed up the hill on her elbows, crying as she watched the hatred fill Eric's eyes. He pulled the pick from his shoulder yelling like some wild beast and raised it over his head aiming it toward Grace's heart.

"Time to die," he said and Grace heard the shots. One, two, three, large bangs rang out as she covered her head and pulled herself into the fetal position for protection as Eric fell to the ground beside her then rolled down the hill.

She was crying now with her hands over her face, lying in the dirt, weak and exhausted.

"Grace, thank God you're alive." She heard Sandman's voice, Frank's, then John's. They were at her side as she opened her eyes. All three men were still holding their guns in their hands as Sandman pulled her into their arms. Each of them had saved her life by firing at Eric.

"Jesus, is she okay?"

She heard Duke's voice and saw him and then Big Jay through

blurry eyes. Her three ginormous men had come to her rescue. Her brothers were there, too.

"You're bleeding, baby, are you all right?" Sandman asked as he gently checked the wound on her arm.

"I'm okay and I'm so glad to see you guys. I love you."

* * * *

Sarah slowly opened the door to the hospital room where Donald was resting. She had spent the last two days trying to recover from the shock that Eric was a killer. Eric had killed Clara and all those other innocent people. The thrill of killing consumed him. Then there was his involvement in the housing projects in Colton. He didn't want Donald or the other contributors to succeed. Eric had received election endorsements from some business tycoon that wanted to buy the land and use it for vacation home development. They didn't want low-income families living on the same property. They wanted it all to remain high class. It was disturbing. Those involved had a lot of questions to answer for the district attorney.

Then she thought about Donald.

He had risked his life for Grace, for all of them and she nearly lost him, too. She wondered if he would even want anything to do with her now. After Eric tried to frame Donald for the murders. Why would he? She just wanted to stop by to see him. He meant so much to her and it was the right thing to do.

The tears welled up in her eyes as she walked closer to the bed.

He opened his eyes and she was grateful that he appeared surprised not angry.

"Sarah?" he whispered, his voice a little rough and groggy.

She moved beside the bed and placed her hand over his and used the other hand to clutch her purse to her chest for support.

"I'll leave if you don't want to see me."

"What? No, stay. Why would you think that?" he asked then clasped his hand over hers and brought it closer to his chest.

She loved the feel of him touching her. His strength, his charismatic way.

"I thought you would hate me for what Eric did to you."

"Baby, no way. No freaking way would I blame you for that sick bastard. God Sarah, all I thought about, all I ever think about is you. I care about you."

She smiled softly then swallowed hard as she held his gaze.

"I care about you, too."

They held one another's gaze and then he whispered to her, "I've always cared for you, Sarah. Before Eric, during the years as the kids grew up around us. I should have told you then how I felt." She shook her head as a tear rolled down her cheek.

"I had no idea. I felt it, too. I cared for you, too, but thought, oh, I don't know what I thought. I was stupid. So stupid."

He pulled her hand up toward his lips as he shook his head.

"Not stupid. You're a good woman. You see things through. Forget about the past. Forget about Eric." He kissed her knuckles and she felt her heart leap with joy and perhaps hope that there was still something between the two of them they could save.

"I wish."

"Shh," he told her then pulled her closer.

"Come here, sweet Sarah."

She slowly leaned toward him and his firm lips, his bruised face and felt his hand caress up her arm, to her shoulder then neck.

"I've always loved you, Sarah. It's our time now. Our time."

The tear rolled down her cheek as he pulled her closer and kissed her softly.

I love you, too, Donald.

Epilogue

The house was filled with family and friends. It was just what everyone needed. Grace watched as Donald sat on the rocking chair sipping some ice tea enjoying a friendly argument with Sarah about the better way to season steaks before cooking them on the grill. Frank was adding his comments, contributing fuel to the fire. Aunt Betsy was talking to Jamie and Tod about an old family heirloom she wanted them to have for their new home. They had sold their old place and moved to a newer, larger house a few blocks away. Jamie didn't feel she could live in the same house where she was almost killed.

Grace couldn't believe six months had passed. She held off on her photography career to help Sarah with her political campaign. Sarah was running for town mayor and had a really good shot at the position. The whole town agreed she would be perfect for the job.

She looked out across the open land and thought about her weekly visits to Clara's gravesite. The first time was the most difficult, but as she made each trip there, it became easier. She was finally at peace knowing that Clara's killer was not just identified, but dead. She had closure now, and felt that life could only get better from here on out.

Then she felt the twinge of regret and sadness in her heart.

Grace hadn't heard from Sandman, Duke, or Big Jay in weeks. She knew that Sandman had been busy going over the aspects of the case as well as receiving another job. They spoke on the phone a few times and Sandman expressed his upset with her for leaving the way she did. He told her if a relationship was going to continue between them, then she needed to be less independent. He wanted to take care of her, share the responsibilities with her, or a relationship just wouldn't work.

He explained that a ménage relationship was complicated enough and that he and his brothers wanted her to trust them equally and fully. By taking off the way she did and scaring the crap out of them, she betrayed that trust and the fear of losing her was too much. She knew he was angry, but then Duke and Big Jay called. They forgave her, but expressed similar concerns and wanted to give her time to think about how serious she was about a ménage relationship with the three of them. Duke explained that Sandman was stubborn and had really closed up his heart after experiencing some awful things in his life. She had made a difference and they felt that she completed them.

She knew they were right and she loved them for their honesty and for confronting her, challenging her to change, wanting her to need them. They were military men. They were strong-willed leaders, dominant and experienced men who wanted to protect their woman. She knew that was all they wanted. For her to need them to trust them and allow them to take care of her.

Everyone was laughing, enjoying one another's company at the house, and her brother Frank walked by, giving her a kiss on the cheek and a huge smile. John, Sarah, Peter, the whole family acted the same around her, around each other, taking every opportunity to say "I love you" or just show some kind of affection. They would never take one another for granted. They knew that life was precious and time went by too quickly to have regrets.

She smiled as she enjoyed watching her family looking so happy as more relatives arrived. It was a Thompson celebration and the backyard was filling up with family. The children were playing tag and Frank was trying to gather them together for a picture. Grace walked around to the side of the house. She leaned against the porch railing absorbing all the wonderful sounds of laughter, joy, and happiness from her family. They were all smiling, celebrating, and enjoying the party. Grace reached up and touched the flowering pink-and-purple potted planter that hung from one of the high porch beams. Sarah had the wraparound porch decorated with the hanging planters. It was so country, so pretty to look at.

Suddenly she felt someone behind her, a strong arm instantly around her waist then a bouquet of wild flowers appear in front of her. She knew instantly it was Duke, as she absorbed his cologne. She inhaled deeply as she leaned back against his chest. Once again one of her men snuck up on her without her knowing.

"How do you do that?" she asked, sounding a little annoyed yet smiling.

"It involves special training. If you're good maybe I'll teach you," he teased her as he turned her toward him.

Duke touched her cheek then took her face between his hands. She spotted Big Jay standing next to him, arms crossed and appearing angry.

"I've missed you." Duke whispered to her as he stared into her beautiful hazel-green eyes.

"I missed you, too," she replied and he kissed her softly on the lips. She heard Big Jay clear his throat and Duke released her lips then touched foreheads with her. "I love you, baby, and I want you back."

She smiled at him then hugged him tight. When Duke released her, Big Jay pulled her into his arms and lifted her up so that she straddled his hips. He pressed her against the side of the house and held her tight. She could hardly catch her breath. One look into the intense blue eyes and she smiled at him.

"I take it you missed me as much as I missed you."

"More," he replied then kissed her. It was a long, sexual kiss, filled with promises of more to come. She was aroused, felt needy and as he pulled away, she moved forward trying to get more of his delicious kisses.

"We have things to discuss and confirm," he stated seriously.

"Like what?" she replied.

"Like, what we expect in a wife and what our wife can expect from us."

She gasped as she turned toward the voice and saw Sandman approaching. He looked so good and his facial expression mimicked his brothers' when they first approached.

"What did you say?" she asked. Her heart was pounding inside of her chest.

In a flash he placed his hands against her cheeks then stared down into her eyes.

"We can't live without you, Grace. I can't live without you. But this stubborn, 'I can take care of myself' attitude has to stop. We're your protectors. We're the ones who will protect you and take care of you and if you can't accept that and trust us—"

Grace grabbed his hands that were against her cheeks and kissed him hard on the mouth. She made love to his mouth, absorbing his counter kisses until they were breathless. When she pulled back she smiled at him. "Okay," she whispered.

"Okay?" Duke and Big Jay replied in sync.

She nodded her head and Big Jay lowered her feet to the wooden plank flooring.

"We love you," Sandman said.

"I love the three of you, too."

All three men smiled then each got down on one knee. They all held her one hand and she gasped in shock.

"Grace Thompson, will you marry us?"

"Yes," she replied immediately as Sandman pulled out a gorgeous three-karat ring and placed it onto her finger. They kissed her fingers and she was filled with joy.

"What in the world?"

All four of them turned to see Frank standing there in shock.

"Did they just propose to you?" She nodded her head and Frank hooted and hollered then ran to tell the family.

"You three better hurry up and kiss me. You have no idea how bombarded with relatives we are going to be in about five seconds."

All three men stood up. Sandman kissed her first, then Big Jay and then Duke just as loads of relatives came piling around both sides of the house.

The cheers and congratulations exploded around them and Grace was filled with more joy and happiness than she could ever imagine experiencing.

She smiled at her men as relatives they hadn't even met hugged them, welcomed them to the family and instantly accepted them as part of the Thompson family.

She loved her family and she loved her Sandman, Duke and Big Jay with all her heart.

Aunt Betsy grabbed her arm and asked rather loudly, "How the heck did you snag three sexy, good-looking soldiers like these three?"

Duke came up behind them and kissed first Aunt Betsy on the cheek and then Grace.

"Because she's amazing," he whispered.

"That she is," Sandman said.

"Our amazing Grace." Big Jay added and Grace smiled with joy. Her men loved her and she loved them. What more could a woman ask for?

THE END

WWW.DIXIELYNNDWYER.COM

ABOUT THE AUTHOR

People seem to be more interested in my name than where I get my ideas for my stories from. So I might as well share the story behind my name with all my readers.

My momma was born and raised in New Orleans. At the age of twenty, she met and fell in love with an Irishman named Patrick Riley Dwyer. Needless to say, the family was a bit taken aback by this as they hoped she would marry a family friend. It was a modern day arranged marriage kind of thing and my momma downright refused.

Being that my momma's families were descendents of the original English speaking Southerners, they wanted the family blood line to stay pure. They were wealthy and my father's family was poor.

Despite attempts by my grandpapa to make Patrick leave and destroy the love between them, my parents married. They recently celebrated their sixtieth wedding anniversary.

I am one of six children born to Patrick and Lynn Dwyer. I am a combination of both Irish and a true Southern belle. With a name like Dixie Lynn Dwyer it's no wonder why people are curious about my name.

Just as my parents had a love story of their own, I grew up intrigued by the lifestyles of others. My imagination as well as my need to stray from the straight and narrow made me into the woman I am today.

For all titles by Dixie Lynn Dwyer, please visit
www.bookstrand.com/dixie-lynn-dwyer

Siren Publishing, Inc.
www.SirenPublishing.com

Lightning Source UK Ltd.
Milton Keynes UK
UKOW06f1908030817
306652UK00011B/569/P